CAT & MOUSE

CAT & MOUSE

A Parker City Mystery

Justin M. Kiska

First published by Level Best Books 2026

This novel is entirely a work of fiction. The names, characters, and incidents portrayed in it are the work of the author's imagination. Any resemblance to actual persons, living or dead, events, or localities is entirely coincidental.

Justin M. Kiska asserts the moral right to be identified as the author of this work.

First edition

ISBN: 979-8-89820-211-8

Cover art by Level Best Designs

This book was professionally typeset on Reedsy.
Find out more at reedsy.com

To my in-laws who welcomed me into the family without a background check, never asked too many questions about my research habits, and continue to treat me so well despite knowing exactly how my mind works. Your unwavering confidence that I'll only ever use this knowledge for fictional purposes means more than you know.

Praise for Cat & Mouse

"*Cat & Mouse* is an entertaining detective drama about duality—twin timelines, a Jekyll and Hyde theme, and two nicely contrasted cops determined to track down a stalker whose threat becomes increasingly deadly."—**Martin Edwards**, CWA Diamond Dagger Award-winner

Prologue

December 1965...

The first letter arrived the day before Thanksgiving.

It was typewritten, folded with precision, and sealed inside a simple white envelope. The address, also typed, was not accompanied by the name of the sender or from where it came. The message inside was brief, impersonal, but unmistakably threatening. It promised that someone was watching. That someone knew where she lived, what time she left for work, and how often she walked alone at night. It ended with a warning: *Be careful.*

The second letter arrived two days later, the day after Thanksgiving. Almost identical, but in the mailbox of a second woman.

Neither of the two took them very seriously, dismissing them as a bad joke. A prank meant to scare them, perhaps a cruel trick from a jealous co-worker or a jilted lover. They were immediately thrown in the trash and forgotten.

Two days later, two more women received similarly menacing letters in their mailboxes.

For the first time, one of the recipients had the sense to go to the police. She turned the letter over to an officer who said it was probably just a practical joker trying to get a rise out of her, but suggested, all the same, she make sure to lock her door at night. The officer's dismissive attitude did little to ease any fear.

But as the days passed and letters continued arriving, more women turned to the Parker City Police Department. After a dozen letters were turned over to the PCPD, Lieutenant Wallace Kerns, the chief's deputy, finally opened an investigation. And once the police took serious notice and became involved, it was only a matter of time before the newspapers picked up the story. When they did, it was all anyone could talk about. The *Blue Ridge Herald* ran its first article under the headline: Anonymous Stalker Targets Local Women—Who Will Be Next? The *Chronicle Dispatch*, never one to be outdone, took a more dramatic approach: Is Parker City's Police Force Failing to Protect Women?

The stories fanned the flames of paranoia, and soon, reports of a dark figure lurking in neighborhoods at night flooded the police station. No two sightings were identical, however. Some claimed the figure was tall and broad-shouldered; others said he was slim and moved like a shadow. But they all agreed on one thing: he was watching. And he was waiting.

The letters were no longer just an eerie nuisance; they had become something else entirely. A warning of what was to come. Though there was not a single person who knew what that was. Except the person sending the letters, leaving the city in a near panic.

Real crime was a rarity in Parker City. It had its share of bar fights, a few domestic disturbances, the occasional armed robbery, but this, this was something else entirely.

Chapter One

Elizabeth Blakely didn't think much about the letters at first. Like everyone else in Parker, she was aware of what was going on, reading the news every morning over breakfast. The headlines were difficult to ignore. And as more letters began showing up, as a single woman, she found herself just as unnerved as all the others in town. So far, the police had made no connection between any of the recipients, which meant anyone could be next.

But it was a thought Elizabeth tried to put out of her mind as much as possible. During the day, the hum of the office filling the air—telephones ringing, papers shuffling, murmured conversations behind closed doors—allowed her to forget about what was going on outside and the anxiety spreading across the city. Unfortunately, her days at the office brought with them a different type of unease.

Elizabeth knew that all of the men she worked with couldn't keep their eyes off her. Whenever she was in the breakroom, making herself a cup of coffee or standing over the Xerox machine running off the latest department reports, she could feel their eyes roaming up and down her body. It was something she'd grown used to because it'd been the case ever since she was a teenager. But it wasn't her fault that she'd been blessed—or cursed, depending on who you asked—with an incredible physique.

Tall and slender, with the right curves in exactly the right places, coupled with the face of an angel and piercing crystal blue eyes, she drove the men wild. While she couldn't deny she enjoyed the attention, she realized deep down it was more a sense of lust than anything else that had the heavy-breathing, testosterone-jacked-up men circling. On the rare occasion a man would actually take the time to get to know her, he'd discover Elizabeth was one of the sweetest people one could ever meet. She'd give you the shirt off her back if you asked, which is what most of the lecherous men were hoping for.

But she was also smart and full of life. She loved reading and dreamed of traveling to far-off destinations, learning about the cultures and peoples around the world. Even though it was a time when women were beginning to stand up and demand to be seen as more than simply pretty faces meant to cook and pop out babies, she was desperate to find a kind, intelligent man to settle down with. The kind of man who would hold her in his arms and make her feel safe yet never smothered, and who would honestly listen to her and never treat her as an object.

What Elizabeth wanted was the perfect life.

"A pie-in-the-sky dream!" her best friend Joyce would yell at her, trying to get her to see some sense. "You can't have it all, sweetie. No fuckin' way. No fuckin' how."

Granted, this was usually after Joyce would come home blitzed following a night of partying, riding high on a wave of feminine self-determination, and still aglow following a meaningless one-night stand. But liquor made Joyce strong…and mouthy. After a few drinks, she wasn't afraid to tell you what she really thought. Not that she didn't do that when she was sober. The only difference was she didn't use as much profane language when she wasn't half in the bag.

At the end of the day, though, Elizabeth just wanted to be happy. She'd grown up seeing her parents madly in love with one another. Her father always doting on her mother and his two little girls. Her father was a "businessman"—which was all her mother ever said he was—who seemed to do well for himself, judging by the fact she and her sister grew up wanting for nothing.

They lived in a big house with a pool, went on a family vacation every year, and always had money for new clothes to start school. For good or bad, her parents also encouraged their girls to follow their dreams. When

Elizabeth said she was interested in business and wanted to go to college and earn a degree that would land her a good job, her parents didn't try to dissuade her. Her father did sit her down and explain how she might find the going difficult at times, but he said he was more than willing to support her.

Her mother never said it to her, but Elizabeth knew she was worried that pursuing a career would hamper any chance she had of finding a husband and having a family. *Career women* weren't something her mother grew up with, so she couldn't understand any woman's desire to work in an office all day and not find the joy in making a home for her family. She'd raised two wonderful girls and loved every minute of it. She felt being a good wife and mother was enough of a job. There was no need for any other type of satisfaction. Most importantly, though, Elizabeth's mother desperately wanted grandchildren. And with Elizabeth having just turned thirty and still not being married and seeing no prospects on the horizon, all hope now fell on Patricia.

Elizabeth's younger sister seemed to have found exactly what their parents had. Kenneth, her husband of less than two days, was almost too good to be true. A handsome and loving former high school football star turned banker. Patty was in her glory and transformed into a glowing bride as she walked down the long aisle of Saint Joseph's Episcopal Church with all their family and friends gathered for the occasion.

While all eyes had been on Patty, Elizabeth could still hear the whispers of those wondering why it was the younger sister getting married first. But for the most part, she was able to put the remarks out of her mind and celebrate the love her little sister had found.

As she sat at her desk in the Accounting and Business Office of Upton's Department Store the Monday following the wedding, she did admit there was something about seeing Patty in the long, flowing, white chiffon dress that was nagging at her. It wasn't jealousy. That wasn't it. But there was a surprising yearning in the pit of her stomach that she'd never experienced before.

Elizabeth always knew she wanted to be married and have a family, but she'd never felt envious after attending someone's wedding. But she was getting older. A fact her mother had taken to pointing out to her more and more recently in the subtlest of fashions.

She shook the thought away and returned her focus to the stack of papers in front of her. Numbers didn't lie, and they didn't demand introspection.

Brushing a lock of chestnut hair from in front of her eyes, she turned back to her typewriter and the report that was only half complete. She'd been so wrapped up in her thoughts, she hadn't noticed the young man in a dark gray mohair suit quietly approach her desk. But suddenly, he was standing there, hovering over her with a smile on his face that would put a shark to shame.

"Where was that pretty head of yours, sweetheart?"

The voice made her skin crawl.

"Dick! You scared me," she said, instinctively placing a hand on her chest.

"I didn't mean to scare you, honey," Richard Calhoun offered, not even trying to conceal his eyes lingering on her perfectly shaped breasts beneath the green cardigan she was wearing. The way he looked at her, like she was something to be devoured, set her teeth on edge.

"A little daydreaming on the job? No harm in that, kitten."

"No, just thinking about my sister's wedding," she said, forcing a smile.

"Hey, that's right," he said, snapping his fingers and perching himself intrusively on the edge of her desk. "Penny got married this weekend, right?"

"Patty," Elizabeth gently corrected, desperately trying not to roll her eyes. "Yes. She did. This past Saturday."

"Patty, right. Sorry. Hey, I bet you were a real fox in your bridesmaid dress." The smirk on his face made her fingers curl into a fist beneath the desk. Leaning in just enough that all she could smell was the overpowering scent of his after shave, he said, "We should grab a bite after work. You can tell me all about it."

She felt the familiar tightness in her chest. The uncomfortable balance of politeness and self-preservation. Saying no outright would only make him more persistent.

"Not tonight, Dick. I'm still pretty tired from the weekend. And I might have to work late to finish these reports."

His smile remained, but the light in his eyes dimmed. Just slightly. There was a shift in the air, subtle but unmistakable.

Calhoun was the guy in the office that none of the girls wanted to be left alone with. He was always on the hunt, just ready to pounce. With his Brylcreemed hair and the cloud of Aqua Velva aftershave that continuously lingered around him, Dick Calhoun fancied himself a true ladies' man. And he'd had luck with a number of the salesgirls in the store, but the few women who worked in the executive offices on the third floor found the young associate business manager to be an obnoxious skirt chaser. Not that any of them could say anything about his behavior to any of their bosses, because he was also Old Man Upton's nephew.

"Maybe another time," she added quickly, hoping to smooth over the rejection.

"One of these days, you're going to take me up on my offer," he said, his voice lower now, his gaze fixed on hers. "And when you do, you'll realize how lucky you are."

Elizabeth forced a tight-lipped smile, her pulse quickening. Calhoun held her gaze for a moment longer before sliding off the desk and sauntering back toward his office. But just before he disappeared behind the door, she swore she saw him lick his lips.

A shiver ran down her spine.

"Everything alright, Miss Blakely?" she heard a deep voice ask from behind her.

That was the second time someone managed to sneak up on her without her noticing. At least in this instance, it was someone she didn't mind seeing standing next to her desk. Alfred Marsh was the opposite of Dick Calhoun. Where Calhoun was all slicked-back bravado and leering stares, Marsh was effortlessly charming with a quiet confidence, wrapped in a shy demeanor. He wasn't just handsome—he was dreamy, the kind of guy who, without even trying, made a girl's heart skip a beat.

Tall and handsome, with a strong jawline and a pair of deep-set hazel eyes that always seemed to be thinking a step ahead, he had the kind of looks that made women whisper behind their hands and giggle like schoolgirls. And he didn't even know it. That made him all the more attractive.

Unlike the other men in the office who made it their mission to gawk at her whenever she walked by, Alfred Marsh actually looked at her—like she was a person, not just a set of curves poured into a pencil skirt. It was unnerving in a way Elizabeth hadn't expected. A man like him could make a girl forget herself.

Joyce, ever the blunt one, had taken one look at him and whistled. "Now that's a fox," she'd declared, loud enough for half the department store to hear. "And if you don't make a move, sweetheart, I will."

Elizabeth had rolled her eyes at the time, but now, with him standing there, hands tucked casually in the pockets of his well-tailored suit, she had to admit Joyce wasn't wrong.

"Is everything alright, Elizabeth?" he asked again.

"Yeah," she said quickly, too quickly. His hazel eyes flicked toward Calhoun's door, and though his expression remained calm, there was a sharpness behind it. He knew. Of course, he knew.

"Good," he said, but there was something else in his tone. A quiet understanding.

She felt herself exhale, only now realizing she had been holding her breath.

Alfred hesitated, then nodded toward the papers on her desk. "I came by to grab the updated sales figures. I thought I'd save you the trip."

She blinked, then laughed, relieved for the subject change. "Your office is right there," she pointed out. "Wouldn't have been much of a trek."

He grinned, that easy smile that could knock a girl sideways if she wasn't careful. "I owe you one."

She grinned. "I'll add it to the running tally, but it's kind of my job."

He chuckled, the sound rich and warm, and for the first time that day, the tightness in her chest eased. He turned to leave, then hesitated. "By the way, heard about your sister's wedding. How was it?"

Elizabeth raised a brow. "Word travels fast."

He shrugged. "I might have overheard something."

She shook her head, smiling despite herself. "It was nice. You know how weddings are. Too many flowers, too much crying, and way too much cake."

"Sounds about right." He considered her for a moment, then gave her a small nod. "Well, I have some calls to make. Thanks again for these."

Removing the files, he uncovered a copy of the day's *Dispatch* with its headline staring directly at him, declaring the city was gripped with fear by the mysterious letter writer. A concerned look crossed his face. He looked as though he was about to say something but caught himself. Giving Elizabeth a little nod of the head, he walked to his office, leaving behind only the faintest trace of cologne—subtle, clean, nothing like the overpowering scent Calhoun left in his wake.

Elizabeth let out a breath. She glanced toward the office door where Calhoun had disappeared and then back to the stack of papers in front of her.

By five-thirty, most of the office had emptied, except for a few stragglers finishing up their work. One of whom was Dick Calhoun. Elizabeth had no idea what he'd been up to in his office behind closed doors all afternoon, but when he emerged ready to leave for the day, he appeared agitated.

Passing by Elizabeth's desk on his way out, he looked down at her and said, "Be careful out there."

Elizabeth's heart stopped, quickly casting her eyes down to the newspaper lying on her desk. Wasn't that the way all the mysterious letters ended? *Be careful.*

No, Elizabeth told herself. She was just being paranoid. All he meant was to be careful getting home because it had started snowing a little earlier, which would make getting around more difficult. That had to be it. She shouldn't let her mind play tricks on her.

When she'd finished her work, she gathered her things and slipped on her coat, shivering slightly as she stepped out into the brisk December air. A light layer of snow lay on the ground as the city streets were lit by the golden glow of shop windows, adorned with festive garlands and twinkling lights. Christmas was just around the corner, but the usual excitement that came with the holiday season was dampened by the underlying tension that gripped the city. There were many who hoped the festive season would help people forget about the recent headlines. But so far, as everyone continued with their annual traditions of decorating and preparing for the holidays, the women of Parker City still found themselves looking over their shoulders, wondering if someone was watching them from the shadows.

Even with the sidewalks filled with people on their way home from work or heading to a restaurant for dinner, Elizabeth felt uneasy. She couldn't stop thinking about Dick Calhoun's last words to her as he walked out the door. And the way his dark eyes looked at her from under the brim of his hat. It set her nerves on end. And now, even as she told herself she was being ridiculous, she felt as though someone was watching her.

Picking up her pace, her heels clicking against the pavement, as she turned the corner onto her street, she felt her pulse quicken ever so slightly. She was letting her imagination get the best of her. She forced herself to relax, seeing her apartment building just down the block, its brick façade glowing in the streetlamps. She and Joyce shared the apartment on the first floor of the converted townhouse, only a few blocks from Upton's Department Store. They'd turned the place into a comfortable and inviting home where they'd often have girlfriends over for dinner and game nights.

Fishing her keys from her purse and unlocking the building's main door, then the door to her apartment, Elizabeth breathed a sigh of relief to be home. Turning on the light in the tiny entry hallway, she noticed that Joyce's coat was missing from the closet, meaning she wasn't home yet. Not having spoken with her yet today, she also didn't know what her plans were for the night or if she'd even be coming home. So, Elizabeth figured she was on her own. Not an uncommon occurrence.

Turning on the lights of the small Christmas tree the roommates had set up in the corner of the living room, she took a moment to enjoy the decorations, rearranging a few of the ornaments that still didn't look like they were in the perfect place. Standing back to see if the changes helped to balance the tree better, she smiled at her work.

Heading into the bedroom, she dropped her purse on the bed and kicked off her shoes, rubbing her aching feet before walking into the kitchen at the rear of the apartment. It was small, just big enough for two people to move around comfortably, but not without brushing against a chair or grazing the counter's edge. The walls were a pale yellow, faded from cooking and the occasional cigarette smoke curling toward the ceiling. A Formica table with chrome legs stood in the center of the kitchen, its surface clear except for a set of salt and pepper shakers and a stack of mail. Apparently, Joyce had come and gone already, collecting the day's post and depositing it on the table for Elizabeth to see.

The linoleum floor, patterned in a checkered design of dull green and cream, let out a soft creak as Elizabeth walked to the compact refrigerator humming in the corner, pondering what to make for dinner. Eyeing the ceramic cookie jar in the shape of a rooster sitting on top of the refrigerator, Elizabeth begrudgingly admitted a plate of cookies would not be a good dinner. Letting a sigh of disappointment escape her lips, she opened the refrigerator and began examining its contents. But as she had her head in the refrigerator, deciding what she wanted to eat while watching *To Tell the Truth* that night, behind her, outside in the building's backyard, a shadow quietly passed by the kitchen window.

Chapter Two

June 1985...

"All I'm saying," Detective Tommy Mason said to his partner as they walked down the sidewalk, "is that this was the craziest thing I've ever seen. And I've seen crazy. You know I've seen crazy. But this...this was *crazy*."

"I don't see why a trip to the vet has gotten you so worked up," Ben Winters, Tommy's partner, friend, and commanding officer of the Parker City Police Department's Detective Squad said, shaking his head.

"I'm getting to it. I'm trying to set the mood. Let me tell it, will you?"

Ben rolled his eyes and chuckled but let him continue. He should have known. This was just how Tommy was. The two men had known each other since they were kids. They'd grown up together, gone to school together, joined the academy together, and put on the uniform together. They weren't just friends; they were more like brothers. Which is why Ben was well aware of Tommy's penchant for storytelling. The trick was to only believe about half of what he said. Tommy had a flair for the dramatic.

"Just hear me out," Tommy pleaded, stopping under an awning to get out of the warm sun for a moment. "So, I'm spending the day with Christine, right? And she tells me her cat has a vet appointment. Okay, I mean, I'm not a fan of her cat. Truth is, I hate the thing. It's pure evil wrapped in fur. But, as the good boyfriend that I am, I said I'd tag along. You know, trying to be sensitive and show an interest in things she cares about blah, blah, blah."

"You're terrible," Ben interrupted.

"Hey! That cat cornered me one morning and tried to kill me."

"Is this the time you hid in the bathroom like a five-year-old?"

"Really? You're going to take the cat's side when I've saved your life how many times now?"

"You're a trained police officer. You shouldn't be afraid of a little cat. And don't even try to say you've saved my life more than I've saved yours."

Anyone who spent any amount of time around the two detectives, whether on duty or off, knew this is how they talked to one another. They were like an old married couple. Constantly taking shots at each other and making wisecracks. It was their friendly jibes that helped to keep them grounded. Especially when they were working a particularly difficult case. And after only four years as detectives, they'd already seen more than their fair share of tough cases.

"*Anyway*," Tommy said. "We take Satan's pussy cat to this little townhouse out there on 9th. I swear, the sign in the window was written on cardboard, which made me start to question this vet's credentials. Turns out, she's some sort of all natural astrological pet healer. I didn't even know that was a thing. But this vet—and I use that term loosely because she looked more like a gypsy fortune teller—comes out and takes the demon cat—"

"Satan's pussy cat," Ben reminded with a smirk.

"Satan's pussy cat—and puts it on this card table to examine it."

"Is the cat male or female?"

"I don't know."

"What's its name?"

"Hellraiser…it doesn't matter."

"I'm just trying to get all the facts," Ben said, knowing he was getting under Tommy's skin. "It's kind of what we do."

Ignoring him, Tommy continued. "So, *Lucifur* is on the table, doing everything possible to get away and this voodoo priestess pulls out a tuning fork. She puts her hand on the cat's back, then she whacks the back of her own hand with the tuning fork and listens. She does it a second time and turns to Christine and says the cat hasn't been eating because it's unhappy with where she moved the food bowl."

Ben stared at him. "You're kidding me."

"I shit-you-not. And the worst part is, Christine then paid this hippie. *Paid her!*"

"I'm really not sure what to say. But I do have a question. Did Christine move the bowl back to wherever it was before?"

"Yes."

"And?" Ben found himself surprisingly eager to hear the answer.

Tommy looked away, clearly annoyed. "Damn cat ate the whole bowl of food."

Ben burst out laughing. He couldn't help it. The whole story was so ridiculous. Absolutely absurd yet fitting somehow. Leave it to Tommy to find himself in a situation like that. But he was happy to see his friend getting so serious with someone. He and Christine weren't just going out on wild dates anymore. They were doing the more mundane things couples did together. This was the longest relationship Ben could remember Tommy ever being in. Long enough that Christine was going to be Tommy's date at his and Natalie's wedding. Nat was thrilled. Not just because she liked Chistine, but she didn't have to worry about Tommy sleeping with one of the bridesmaids now. And with the wedding only a matter of weeks away, it was nice to have one less thing to fret about.

Taking a final sip of the soda he was carrying, Ben tossed the empty cup in the trashcan next to the curb as the two continued walking down Commerce Street.

Today was a special day in Parker City. Six blocks of downtown had been shut down for the Summer in the Streets festival. Shops and restaurants had set up booths, offering local goods, special menus, and giveaways. The sidewalks were packed with residents and visitors as music from local bands and church choirs echoed through the air.

An event like this would have been unthinkable just a few years ago. In 1978, Parker was devastated by a terrible flood that destroyed the city's business district, leaving the once thriving commercial corridor in ruins. The damage had been so extensive, most business owners simply boarded up the windows and walked away, leaving empty, derelict buildings sitting for years. Right in the heart of the city.

The economics of the '70s had already taken its toll on Parker City to begin with, so the flood was the final nail in the coffin. A once bustling city practically turned into a ghost town in the span of three days as the rain fell and the murky waters surged through the streets. Once it was all over, the destruction was so severe, no one could see a clear path to restore the area. No one except the city's young, energetic mayor. He made it his mission to return the downtown to its former glory. And though it had been slow going, the fruits of his labor were beginning to show. The abandoned buildings were being cleaned up, renovated, and leased, welcoming new shops and restaurants, and even a small art gallery. There was still a long way to go, but this outdoor market was a chance to show that the city was coming back to life.

As Ben looked around at the crowded festival, he figured at least half the city had shown up, not to mention the out-of-town visitors. Ben wasn't sure who'd be happier with the turnout, the president of the Chamber of Commerce or the mayor. Regardless, it looked like the first Summer in the Streets was a huge success.

As members of the Parker City Police Department's Detective Squad—albeit the *only* members of the Parker City Police Department's Detective Squad—Ben and Tommy would not usually be on the street like this. But with an event of this nature, they'd been asked to lend a helping hand. Both were happy to do so, though Tommy made it very clear he would not be putting on his old uniform. Not on a hot June day in Maryland. Instead, the detectives were comfortably patrolling while wearing simple white polo shirts with the word POLICE emblazoned on the back and their badges hanging around their necks on silver chains.

If it were up to Tommy, that's how they'd dress every day. But Ben insisted that they wear full suits and that only the police detectives on television and in the movies wore T-shirts, leather jackets, and jeans. Though he grumbled about it every chance he got, Tommy begrudgingly listened to his supervisor, Detective Sergeant Winters, and put on a suit in the mornings.

As they reached the corner of Commerce and 1ˢᵗ, Tommy glanced up the block. With wooden barricades set up at every intersection, there was no vehicular traffic, leaving cross streets virtually empty. Halfway up that particular block, next to a sandwich shop Tommy frequented, was a Maryland United Bank branch. Looking at his watch, seeing that it was one o'clock, he was just about to suggest they grab a bite to eat when something caught his eye.

A flash of red.

Doing a double take to make sure his eyes weren't playing tricks on him, he turned to Ben and asked, "It's still June, right?"

Ben gave him a puzzled look. "Yeah. Still June. Why?"

"And it's pretty warm out here today? About eighty-five degrees or so?"

"Right…" Ben nodded.

"Then seeing a guy dressed as Santa Claus would be considered suspicious," Tommy said pointing up the street toward the bank.

Following his finger, sure enough, Ben saw a man in full Santa gear pacing around outside the bank, shifting his weight nervously, swinging a sack from shoulder to shoulder.

Unhooking the walkie-talkie from his belt, Ben keyed the button on the side and said, "Dispatch, this is PC-12. Come in."

"Hey, Ben. How's it goin' out there, sugar," the voice crackled over the radio.

"It's a beautiful day and there's a big crowd," Ben answered. "So, Shirley, Tommy and I are looking at a suspicious person outside the Maryland United Bank on 1ˢᵗ. We're going to check him out."

There was a momentary pause before she came back with, "I show Spurrier on patrol in that area. I'll send him your way. Do you have a description for me?"

Ben hesitated. "Um…yeah. It's Santa Claus."

"Come again?" she asked, her surprise coming over the radio loud and clear. "I don't think I heard you right, puddin.'"

"No. You heard me. The guy's dressed as Santa Claus. Full suit. Sack and all."

"Well, ho, ho, ho," Shirley said before sighing off.

Tommy looked at Ben. "So…think we're looking at a robbery, or just a nutjob?"

Ben shrugged. "Either way, it's going to be interesting."

Chapter Three

Moving quickly in the direction of the bank, Ben watched Santa Claus disappear into the building. Just being dressed like Santa wasn't a crime—even if it was the middle of the summer. Standing around outside of a bank looking suspicious also wasn't a crime. Running out of the bank carrying bundles of cash that didn't belong to you was a crime though. They needed to see exactly what the man in red did next.

"I swear. This better not be some guy promoting a Christmas in July sale or something," Tommy grumbled as they slowed to a stop in front of the sandwich shop next to the bank.

From their vantage point, Ben couldn't see into the bank next door. There was too much glare on the windows and he didn't want to take a chance and move any closer. Even though they weren't wearing uniforms, they still wore shirts that read POLICE on the back. He didn't want to spook the guy. Not knowing if Saint Nick had a gun, he would rather err on the side of caution to protect anyone in the bank.

The detectives stood anxiously for several minutes, waiting to see if Santa came strolling casually out of the bank or, as they were afraid, running out with a bag full of loot.

After five minutes, Ben motioned for Tommy to cross to the other side of the bank's entrance so there would be one of them on either side as Santa emerged. Covering his badge as he passed the bank, he stole a quick look inside. What he saw was exactly what he expected. The bank tellers and several customers all stood with their hands held in the air.

Santa was robbing the bank.

As he took up his position opposite Ben on the other side of the bank, Tommy pulled his service revolver. He gave a quick shake of his head to let Ben know it was the real deal.

Ben cursed under his breath and grabbed the radio. "Dispatch, this is PC-12. We've got a robbery in progress at Maryland United on 1st. Suspect is the Santa we mentioned."

Shirley's voice crackled back. "Spurrier is three blocks over en route. I'll send a couple more cars your way. Be careful."

Ben drew his own weapon. The street in front of them was still blessedly empty. The noise and crowd of the street festival were down the block, and it looked like no one had wandered this far up. For now, it was just them…and a bank being robbed by Kris Kringle.

Then the doors burst open.

Santa bolted. He charged out of the bank with the massive red sack over one shoulder, beard askew, wearing a pair of sunglasses. Turning, he came face-to-face with the barrel of Tommy's Smith & Wesson.

"Ho, ho, hold it," Tommy said with a grin.

Ben shouted, "Stop! Police! Drop the bag…Santa."

For a jolly fat man, Santa was extremely agile. In one fluid, unexpected motion, he swung the sack around taking Tommy by surprise and knocking him off balance. As the detective staggered sideways, trying to stay upright and not lose the grip on his gun, Santa took off down the street.

"You've got to be kidding me," Ben muttered as he watched the man in the red velvet suit hustle down the sidewalk.

Looking from Ben to their bank robber then back to Ben, Tommy said, "We really have to chase Santa Claus?"

Santa was surprisingly fast. The oversized coat flapped as he ran, and the sack bounced wildly behind him.

Ben and Tommy tore down 1st Street after him, shoes slapping the pavement. A few startled pedestrians shouted and ducked out of the way as Santa blew by them. Most being left with a look of confusion plastered on their face. After all, it wasn't every day one saw Santa Claus being chased by two police officers.

Ahead of them, at the end of the block, a PCPD patrol car squealed to a halt blocking the route forward.

Seeing the obstacle, Santa took a hard right into the alley between a hardware store and shoe repair shop, disappearing out of sight.

A few steps behind, when Ben rounded the corner, he found Tommy peering around the edge of a dumpster.

"What's he doing?" Ben whispered.

"Trying to climb," Tommy said. "There's a fire escape at the end of the alley. He's trying to get up the ladder."

Ben took a breath. "Does he have a gun?"

"Doesn't look like it. He's struggling to keep both hands on the ladder and not drop the bag. How do you want to play this?"

Ben thought for a moment. "Well, we already tried yelling, 'Stop! Police!'"

"Yeah. Didn't work too well," Tommy agreed. "So let's try this."

Reaching into the dumpster, Tommy pulled a five foot length of 2x4 out of the trash. Stepping out from their concealed position, he launched the piece of wood as if he was throwing a javelin in the Olympics. The two watched as the projectile sailed through the air and struck the fleeing Santa square in the shoulder. Already off-balance trying to climb the rickety fire escape while holding onto his sack, the impact caused him to lose his grip. As his gloved hand slipped from the rung of the ladder, he began flailing. It was only a second more before he lost his footing.

Ben and Tommy watched as the robber fell backwards, tumbling toward the pavement. If it hadn't been for the fact he'd released the bag and it landed on the ground before him, Santa would have crashed hard. As it was, he landed on the sack with a loud thud, followed by a long, low grown.

"Didn't stick the landing," Tommy said as he carefully approached, gun trained on the bright red heap in front of him. "Stay down, Santa."

Ben had his cuffs in hand as he rolled Santa over and pulled the robber's arms behind his back. "Do you think this guy's going to end up on the naughty list," he asked Tommy over his shoulder.

From his position on the pavement, the man moaned, "My back..."

Sirens in the distance were getting closer. Back-up was arriving. They'd get the guy to the hospital to be checked out, but he didn't look too worse for wear. Besides the bag filled with cash breaking his fall, the padding of the costume also helped.

The detectives were lifting Santa to his feet when Officer Spurrier came running down the alley. He skidded to a stop, eyes wide as he took in the sight of Ben and Tommy hauling a dazed Santa Claus to his feet amid a scattering of loose bills fluttering on the ground.

"You guys just arrested Santa Claus," Spurrier said shaking his head, a smile playing at his lips. "Looks like we know who's gonna be getting coal in their stocking this Christmas."

Chapter Four

After a visit to Tasker Memorial Hospital, where a doctor gave Santa a once-over, he was cleared to be taken to the police station to be booked. They'd make it simple and start with robbery. If the Parker County State's Attorney wanted to include any additional charges, Ben and Tommy were more than happy to let them handle the paperwork on that. As it was, their report was already going to be one for the record books. It was the first time a holiday character had ever been arrested in Parker City.

Ben was just thankful that the whole situation had been wrapped up without much fanfare. If there'd been a standoff at the bank or the robber had run into the crowd on Commerce Street, there would have been a good chance a photograph of Ben and Tommy leading Santa Claus away in handcuffs would end up on the front page of the *Herald-Dispatch* in the morning. Not that they would have had any choice in the matter—the guy having robbed a bank—but it wouldn't *look* good. And as much as Ben and Tommy hated the political side of law enforcement, they were forced to acknowledge its existence.

By the time they arrived back at the station, word of their afternoon takedown had already spread. As they expected. Police officers were notorious gossips and loved to share a story. Needless to say, there were more than a few jokes thrown their way as Santa was fingerprinted and tossed in a holding cell. But they took it all in stride. In fact, it was more than welcome because just a few years ago, when they'd been tapped to form the department's new Detective Squad, Ben and Tommy had been the closest thing to pariahs the PCPD had ever had.

The old-timers fell into one of two categories. In one, they felt Officers Winters and Mason were too young and green to take on such a prestigious assignment, or they didn't see the need for a Detective Squad because they liked doing things the way they always had and didn't care much for change. In the other were the few younger officers who'd joined the force around the same time as Ben and Tommy. Their dislike of the two was out of pure jealousy.

For the first couple of years, Ben and Tommy had not been the most popular. Gradually, though, they'd proven themselves and shown they weren't just a pair of hotshots playing at solving crimes. They'd been confronted with cases some twenty-year veteran detectives at large departments would never come across. They'd never let the snide remarks get to them, and in the end, their hard work and dedication paid off, earning them a great deal of respect.

Tommy offered to walk Santa through the booking process, not out of the kindness of his heart, but rather because he was more than happy to let Ben write up the report on the incident.

"You know how much you love writing reports," he'd said to Ben as the booking officer instructed Santa to turn to his right and the camera flashed, capturing the non-festive mugshot.

"Fine," Ben said, giving in.

He knew if it were up to this partner, it would take the rest of the day to write the report. Tommy hated using the computer in their office. Not that he'd have complained any less if he were using one of the old typewriters to fill out the report. But Tommy acted as though the big IBM was his mortal enemy. Ben still hadn't been able to convince him how much easier it was going to make things for them in the long run.

As Ben made his way from the basement of the station up to the second floor, he noticed how quiet the place was. But it made sense. Not only was it a Saturday afternoon, but nearly everyone on duty was either out on patrol or assigned to the Summer in the Streets event. Only the minimum number of personnel required to keep the station running were in the building.

The Detective Squad's office was a converted storage closet in the middle of the second floor. It had no windows, an air vent that rattled constantly, and just enough room for two desks, a couple of file cabinets, and a single trash can. Be it ever so humble, Ben thought as he sat down and turned on the computer.

The chief had recently put forward a plan to reorganize the entire department. And one of its main pillars was expanding the Detective Squad, possibly even rolling the Drug Task Force into the unit. If that were the case, Ben knew they were going to need a new workspace. He just couldn't imagine where it would be. The station house was ancient and in much need of repair. Chipped paint on the walls, terribly worn linoleum floors, and a leaking roof were just a few of the issues the members of the department saw on a daily basis. He couldn't foresee a full renovation giving them a decent-sized office in the cards. But then again, Mayor Oland had told the chief he was one hundred percent behind the plan. And a final vote by the City Council on funding was coming up at the end of the month. So, for the moment, they were all waiting to see what ended up happening.

In the middle of filling out the arrest report, Ben looked up when there was a knock at the open office door. Nick Brent's large, barrel-chested frame filled the opening. Still wearing his customary aviator sunglasses, the chief smiled when he said, "So…I hear Christmas is cancelled this year."

"You too, Chief?" Ben asked, returning the smile.

"It's not every day one of my men locks up one of the most beloved figures in the world."

"Well, you don't have to worry about that. Our jolly friend's real name is Peter Gilmartin. A mall Santa—hence the costume—and a part-time security guard. He has an arrest for drunken disorderly from a few years ago, but other than that, a clean record."

"So, he just woke up, saw it was a nice day, and decided to hit a bank? He say why he did it? Other than for the money?"

"He's not saying anything," Ben answered. "After giving us his name, he asked for a lawyer."

"How much money did he walk out with?" Brent asked, removing the sunglasses and tucking them into the front pocket of his shirt.

Ben looked down at the notes he'd made. "Quick count was about five thousand. He was in and out real fast. One of the tellers I spoke with said he didn't even wait for them to empty all the drawers."

"Finish up the paperwork and kick it over to the state's attorney. Let them deal with it."

Nodding, Ben turned back to the computer just as Tommy joined them. He held a cold can of Coca-Cola against his shoulder.

"You alright there?" Brent asked, raising an eyebrow.

"I tweaked my shoulder," Tommy said.

"Oh, please," Ben sighed from behind the computer screen.

"I threw that piece of wood pretty hard," Tommy protested. "I have delicate ligaments."

Ben rolled his eyes.

"I heard that," Tommy said.

Chief Brent chuckled. "Delicate ligaments, huh? Maybe next time, try not to audition for the track and field team with lumber."

"All I'm saying is, if there's a city competition for 'Most Creative Use of Construction Waste in a Felony Arrest,' I want a trophy. Or at least a commemorative patch."

"I'll talk to the mayor," Brent said dryly, then turned and left the room.

As the chief's footsteps disappeared down the hall, Ben reached for his coffee mug, only to find it empty. He sighed and stood up, stretching his legs.

"Where you going?" Tommy asked.

"Coffee. If I'm going to write up this fairy tale, I need caffeine."

Tommy leaned back with a grin. "Get me one too. I've got a long recovery ahead of me."

Ben gave him a look. "It was a ten-foot toss at best."

"Ben, my ligaments!"

Ben disappeared out the door with a muttered, "Unbelievable."

Tommy threw his feet up on the desk and settled in, the thousand-watt smile for which he was known, on his face. "Best job in the world."

Chapter Five

1965...

After heating up a TV dinner—meatloaf and mashed potatoes—Elizabeth collapsed onto the sofa, the flickering glow of the Christmas tree throwing shifting patches of color across the dim living room. The exhaustion hit her all at once. The last few nights had been a battle—too much tossing and turning, too little rest. Maybe tonight would be different.

By the time the local CBS station signed off at midnight, Elizabeth had been asleep for hours, curled beneath the quilt her grandmother had made when she was a girl. The television screen bathed the room in a soft, ghostly static, but she didn't stir. For once, sleep firmly held her in its grip.

At five a.m., the rumble of a garbage truck outside the front window jolted her awake. For the briefest of moments, she wasn't sure where she was, a mental fog having settled over her sometime in the night. Blinking against the early-morning darkness, she rubbed the back of her neck, her body stiff from the awkward position she'd slept in. Still in yesterday's clothes, she pushed herself upright, listening. No sounds of movement. No sign of Joyce.

No surprise there.

If her roommate had come home at all last night, she would have made it known—crashing through the door, filling the apartment with drunken giggles and the scent of someone's cologne. But the place was silent.

Elizabeth had no doubt she'd get the full play-by-play later. Along with the details of whoever had been keeping Joyce entertained.

She stretched, padded into the bathroom, and turned on the shower, watching as steam curled up from the water. Stripping down, she flung her dress and sweater across the hall into her bedroom, the apartment's chill against her bare skin sending a shiver down her spine.

The hot water shocked her awake, the steady pulse of it shaking off the last remnants of sleep. By the time she stepped out, toweling off in the fogged-up mirror, she felt like she could face the day. Maybe.

Wrapped in the lingering warmth of the shower, she crossed into her bedroom, the cold morning air nipping at her skin. She dressed quickly, then made her way to the kitchen, setting the coffee pot on the stove. The quiet surrounded her.

Another morning alone.

The rich scent of coffee filled the kitchen as Elizabeth poured herself a cup, the heat feeling good against her fingers as she wrapped them around the mug. That first cup of coffee in the morning was always her favorite. She pulled a chair out from the table in the center of the room and settled in with a plate of eggs and toast in front of her. The apartment was still silent, except for the occasional drip from the faucet and the faint hum of the refrigerator. It was too quiet. She needed some noise.

Reaching over to the counter, she flipped on the radio. The kitchen quickly filled with the sound of the Supremes singing their latest holiday tune, "Children's Christmas Song." Elizabeth had heard the song a few times since it came out the previous month and thought it was pretty catchy.

Finishing her breakfast, she pushed the plate aside and reached for yesterday's mail, still piled on the table where Joyce had dumped it. A few bills, a Christmas card from her cousin in Florida, and a plain white envelope with no return address, just her name written in bright red ink.

Just the sight of the envelope made her blood run cold.

As she slowly slid a nail under the flap and tore it open, the music on the radio took a decidedly different—yet far more appropriate—turn as Dean Martin began singing "Ain't That a Kick in the Head?"

Chapter Six

Elizabeth hesitated outside the Parker City Police Department, gripping the folded letter in her coat pocket. The December wind howled down Rockwell Avenue, sharp and relentless, cutting through her layers of clothing. The sky was a dull gray, threatening snow, the sidewalks dusted with a thin layer of frost this early in the morning.

Set against the ominous winter sky, the police station rising in front of her looked like what it was meant to—a police station. A solid brick building with bars on the windows of the lower floor, it looked like a much, much smaller, much less ornate version of City Hall just around the corner.

Elizabeth had never set foot in the building, nor did she think she ever would. She'd debated coming here at all, pacing back and forth in the living room of her apartment, hoping Joyce would come home so she could talk to her.

For all she knew, this was just a prank. Joyce's idea of a bad joke, maybe. But she knew it wasn't Joyce's style. It wasn't funny. She'd never do something like this. Not to her.

Maybe she was overreacting. Her first instinct would be to laugh it off…if it weren't for the fact letters like this had been showing up for the last several weeks and it was all anyone could talk about.

But this letter was different. She'd read the news articles about the previous ones. They'd all been typed. The one she now held was *handwritten*. Just a single sheet of paper, folded neatly, slipped inside an envelope with her name on it. The dark red ink had bled slightly into the paper, as if the writer had pressed too hard, carving the words into the page with anger. It was the handwriting that chilled her most. The strokes appeared sharp and impatient.

The knot in her stomach only tightened the closer to the police station she got.

Taking a deep breath, she slowly walked up the front steps and pulled open the heavy wooden door. Stepping inside, Elizabeth was thankful to be out of the cold. Until she was assaulted by the smell of the station. A combination of old paper, stale coffee, and cigarettes tickled her nose.

At the front counter, a couple of officers in uniform stood there, talking in low voices. One of them—tall, broad-shouldered, with a tired expression—glanced up at her.

"Help you, miss?"

Her voice steady despite the flutter in her stomach, she said, "I need to speak with someone about a letter I received."

The officer—his name badge read J. STULL—tilted his head slightly. "What kind of letter?"

Elizabeth pulled the envelope from her pocket and handed it over. Stull unfolded it, his eyes scanning the words. His expression didn't change, but his jaw tightened just a fraction.

"Did this come in the mail?" he asked.

"No return address. No stamp," she answered. "I guess someone must have put it in my mailbox."

He nodded, pressing his lips together, then motioned for her to follow him past the front desk and into an interview room. It was small and windowless, lit by a flickering fluorescent light hung from the ceiling. It was nothing like what she'd seen on television.

"If you'll have a seat in here, miss," Stull said, pulling a chair out for her, "someone will be with you shortly."

Elizabeth slowly sat down and watched as the officer left the room, pulling the door shut behind him. Tapping her fingers nervously on the metal table in front of her, she bit her lower lip as she waited.

It was ten minutes before the door to the interview room opened again. This time, a different officer entered, carrying several file folders and a notepad. He was older than Stull, Elizabeth noted, and seemed to carry himself with more authority. In fact, he reminded her a great deal of her father. Not necessarily in looks, but his demeanor. In his mid-fifties, she guessed, he was average height, but through his glasses she could see the weary eyes of a man who had seen it all and was surprised by very little.

Taking the seat across from her, in a stern but not unkind voice, he introduced himself. "I'm Lieutenant Kerns, miss. And you are?"

"Elizabeth. Elizabeth Blakely."

The lieutenant began taking notes immediately. After asking the perfunctory questions about where she lived and worked, if she was married or lived with any roommates, he then wanted to know how and when she'd found the letter. Elizabeth felt as though he was taking down every word she said verbatim, which made her anxious that she might say something wrong.

Finished with the first round of questions, Kerns removed his glasses and rubbed his eyes. Then, from one of the folders he'd carried in with him, he carefully withdrew the letter Elizabeth had received along with its envelope. Laying them in the center of the table, he replaced his glasses and took a moment to reread what was written.

Elizabeth,
    I'm watching you.
    Be careful.

Seeing it again in such a stark manner, laying on the surface of the bare metal table caused Elizabeth's breath to catch. The words swam for a moment before settling into sharp focus.

She read it again. As did Lieutenant Kerns.

Gently turning the envelope over, he searched for a postmark or anything that could indicate where it had come from, but there was nothing. Meaning whoever wrote it had slipped this into the mailbox themself.

As if speaking to himself, Kerns said, "This *is* different."

"I'm sorry?" Elizabeth asked. Unsure of what else to say.

Kerns tapped his fingers against the top of the table before responding. "You've heard about the letters women have been receiving?"

"Of course."

"This letter is very different from those."

"What does that mean?"

"Well, first," Kerns began, pointing at the letter, "all of the others were typed. This one was handwritten. Clearly. Second, it's addressed to you by name. None of the others mentioned the recipient's name. This one's personal." He met her gaze. "And third…the others were officially postmarked. They went through the mail. There's no address or stamp on this one. It was hand-delivered, it seems."

A chill ran through her. "Do you think it's the same person? The one sending the other letters?"

Kerns didn't answer right away. Instead, he reached for the pack of cigarettes in his pocket. Tapping one out, then offering one to Elizabeth— which she declined, he took a slow drag before exhaling. This letter didn't fit with the others. Except for the fact it was a threat…of sorts. Other than that, the lieutenant wasn't ready to say whether it was from the same person or not. He'd been around long enough to know it was never good to jump to conclusions.

Tapping his pen on the table, he asked, "Anyone you can think of who'd want to send you something like this?"

Elizabeth pressed her hands flat against her thighs. "No one that comes to mind."

He slid the letter back into the folder. "We can dust the letter for prints, but you, me, and Officer Stull have all handled it. And if the sender was careful, there may not be much to find." He leaned back in his chair, studying her. "Have you noticed anything else unusual lately? Any strange men watching you? Unusual phone calls?"

Elizabeth hesitated. There had been that feeling lately, that nagging sense of unease. But was that just paranoia? Everyone was on edge. The holidays were coming up. She'd just gotten through her sister's wedding. The women in the city were being terrorized by an unknown person sending threatening letters. Of course, she was feeling anxious.

"I don't think so," she said finally.

He nodded again, though he didn't look convinced. "I'll file a report and include this with the rest for now as part of the larger investigation. In the meantime, be careful. Make sure you lock your door, stay aware of your surroundings. If you notice anything or get another letter, call us right away."

Elizabeth swallowed hard. "Do you think it's serious?"

Lieutenant Kerns glanced down at his notepad, then met her gaze. "Someone took the time to write this and hand-deliver it to your home," he said. "That means he wanted you to read it. And he wanted you to be afraid."

Elizabeth bit her lower lip, trying to prevent the tears she felt welling up in her eyes from cascading uncontrollably down her face.

A father himself, Kerns had seen the look before. He knew how scared Elizabeth was, even if she was trying to put on a brave face. He hated what these letters were doing to the town. This was the time of year people were supposed to be celebrating the holidays. Instead, they were afraid to go to their mailbox for fear of what they might find waiting for them.

The sad truth was that these letters had been arriving for weeks, and they still had no idea who was behind it. Worse yet, the letter he now had from Elizabeth Blakely seemed like it was something completely different. Could they have a copycat to deal with? Or had the person behind all of the original letters evolved somehow? Or had he finally found the specific target he was looking for?

Looking at his watch, Kerns asked, "Miss Blakely, do you need to go to work today? I can have one of the officers drive you."

"That would be very nice, Lieutenant," Elizabeth said, taking a deep breath. "Thank you."

Chapter Seven

Elizabeth sat stiffly in the passenger seat of the patrol car as Officer Stull drove her to work. The city outside the window passed in a blur of grays and whites—the early morning traffic, the Christmas decorations swaying in the cold wind, pedestrians bundled in their coats as they hurried to wherever they were going. It should have been a normal winter morning. It didn't feel like one.

Her fingers traced the edge of her coat pocket where the letter had been, as if she could still feel it. Someone had taken the time to write her *name*. To deliver it by hand. To make sure she knew she was being watched.

But why her?

Stull kept his eyes on the road, one hand on the wheel, the other draped lazily over the gearshift. He hadn't said much since they left the station, but she caught him glancing over at her every now and then.

"You okay?" he finally asked.

Elizabeth sighed. "I don't know."

"Yeah." Stull nodded. "I get that."

The cruiser slowed as they reached Upton's on the corner of Commerce and 3rd Street. It was the largest department store in town, tracing its roots back to the original Upton's General Goods store of the 1800s. What began as a humble general store was now a three-story building taking up an entire block, offering everything from clothing to home furnishings to tools to cosmetics and jewelry.

Looking up at the third-floor windows where her office was, Elizabeth knew once word got out about the latest letter—and the fact that she had received it—everyone would be talking.

As the car rolled to a stop, Stull shifted into park and turned in his seat. "You want me to walk you in?"

Elizabeth shook her head. "No, I'll be fine. Thank you, though."

He hesitated. "Look, I know Lieutenant Kerns already said it, but just… keep your eyes open, okay? We're taking these letters seriously. If anything else happens, call us right away."

"I will," she promised, though the words felt forced.

She stepped out onto the sidewalk, adjusting the strap of her purse over her shoulder as she made her way toward the front doors. She could feel Stull watching her, waiting to make sure she got inside safely. When she turned back to glance at the patrol car, he gave her a nod before pulling away from the curb.

Inside the store, the holiday displays sparkled with tinsel and golden ribbon, eager to remind shoppers of the Christmas bargains. The warm air was thick with the scent of pine, perfume, and polished wood. Festive music played softly from the overhead speakers as customers browsed the merchandise. Elizabeth moved past the busy perfume counter, where one of the salesgirls was charming a well-dressed woman with a spritz of the latest fragrance from Chanel. The store hummed with early morning activity, but Elizabeth barely noticed it. Her mind was elsewhere.

Quickening her pace, she ducked through a service door for employees, which led to the elevator those working in the executive offices on the third floor rode if they didn't want to climb the stairs. She was thankful no one else was in the elevator with her, allowing her a moment to compose herself before stepping into the office and being confronted by her co-workers. It wasn't that she didn't like them; she just wasn't in the mood to talk to anyone today. As the door slid open, she wondered if she should take the day off—tell Alfred she was sick, and go home. Not that she would feel all that safe there by herself, come to think of it.

Opening the door to the Accounting and Business Office, the buzz of telephone conversations and clacking of typewriters pushed all thoughts from her head, drowning out everything else. Maybe it was best for her to throw herself into work and forget about the letter. She always felt better when she kept busy.

Flashing a weak smile to Donna, the secretary whose desk sat behind her own, Elizabeth hadn't even been able to remove her coat before she heard Dick Calhoun's smarmy voice, as if he'd been waiting for her. "Getting a late start this morning, sweetheart? That's not like you. You're usually here long before me."

She gritted her teeth for fear of saying something she might regret.

"You okay?" he asked, registering the expression on her face.

Elizabeth frowned. "Why wouldn't I be?"

Calhoun wasn't expecting the sharp response. "You just seem a little…not yourself this morning. That's all. I don't like seeing a frown on that pretty face of yours. Anything I can do to help cheer you up?"

Elizabeth wanted to rip the cocked eyebrow right off his forehead, but instead said, "I'll be fine. And I'll apologize to Alfred for being late." Dropping into her chair, she picked up a stack of files and slammed them down on the other side of the desk.

The oily smirk she was so used to seeing on his face never changed. "Cool out. Alright? I was just asking."

With that, he disappeared back into his office, closing the door just short of slamming it shut.

Moving the same files back to where they'd originally been, she saw she'd dropped them on a copy of the morning's paper that someone had left sitting on her desk. Unfolding and reading the headline, her stomach dropped.

MYSTERIOUS LETTERS CONTINUE TO TERRORIZE CITY

Beneath the bold type was a grainy black-and-white photograph of the latest letter that had been sent to an unnamed woman. How the paper had been able to get a photo of it, she couldn't fathom, but it was clearly different from the one she'd received—typed with a vague warning not addressing anyone specifically. Seeing it printed in stark black ink sent a fresh wave of unbearable dread through her.

Elizabeth's throat tightened as she skimmed the article. There were no new leads. No suspects. Just more speculation and fear.

Her eyes were filled with tears when Alfred Marsh walked in wearing his coat and hat and carrying his well-worn briefcase. She hadn't even noticed that the door to his office was still closed and the lights were off. He stopped dead in his tracks when he saw her.

"Elizabeth…what's wrong?"

The genuine kindness and concern in his voice released the floodgates. All the emotions Elizabeth had been holding back all morning came pouring out.

"Elizabeth?" he said, stepping over to her, setting his briefcase down, and tossing his hat on the desk. "Are you alright?"

She swallowed hard, quickly wiping away the tears. The last thing she needed was for the entire office to know she was rattled. But Alfred had already seen.

"I'm fine," she said, clearing her throat. "Just…a long morning."

Alfred glanced at the newspaper still unfolded on her desk. The bold headline about the letters was impossible to miss. His jaw tightened ever so slightly.

"I take it you've seen the latest news. It's getting ridiculous. The police really need to do something. Ladies like you shouldn't need to be worrying about something like this."

His words sounded so comforting, but Elizabeth still hesitated. She wasn't sure why she suddenly felt uneasy. Alfred had always been professional and fair, running the department with precision, and though he was one of the only men at Upton's who hadn't tried putting the moves on her, she felt a real connection with him. He'd never given her a reason to feel uncomfortable. If she had to admit it, she usually felt safe when he was around. But now, with everything that happened this morning, her stomach was tied in knots.

"It's all anyone can talk about," she said, just above a whisper.

Alfred exhaled, reaching up and running a hand through his blonde hair. "It's terrible."

Shifting in her chair, Elizabeth finally admitted, "I actually went to the police this morning."

Alfred raised his eyebrows. "You did? Why? Did you…?"

She nodded, glancing around the office, making sure no one else was listening. Donna was chatting with a colleague near the filing cabinets, and Dick Calhoun's door remained shut. She lowered her voice. "I got a letter."

His face went white. But before he could say anything, a frantic redhead, wearing a quilt patch coat, ran into the office, practically knocking him to the ground.

"Joyce!" Elizabeth exclaimed, surprised to see her, but relieved at the same time.

"Liz! I got the note you left at home. I went to the police station, and they said you'd already gone. Oh, my God! Are you okay? Oh, my God!"

Joyce's sudden appearance began to draw stares from others in the office. *Subtle* was not a word anyone used to describe Joyce Osbourne. Noticing how people were beginning to look at them, Alfred suggested they move into his office so they could all speak privately. A small gesture, but Elizabeth was grateful. She didn't want to be the subject of conversation over the water cooler.

In his office, Alfred pulled one of the guest chairs over for Elizabeth to sit, then removed his coat, tossing it on his own chair without much concern. Gesturing for Joyce to take the other guest chair, he perched on the edge of his desk.

"You got a letter?" he asked.

Elizabeth nodded as she struggled to hold back tears. "But it was different from the others."

"What do you mean?" Joyce asked, holding her friend's hand tightly in her own.

Taking a deep breath to collect herself, when she continued, Elizabeth said, "It was handwritten. And it was addressed to *me* personally."

Alfred's expression hardened before asking, "What did the police have to say?"

"They're looking into it. But they don't know if it's the same person."

Not able to contain himself any longer, Alfred stood and began pacing behind his desk. "It was actually addressed to you, not just an anonymous—" he stopped before the word *threat* left his lips.

"No. The letter was written to me. Saying that he was watching me."

"Dammit!" Joyce exploded. "The police have to do something!"

"They haven't been able to crack the case yet, so who the hell knows what…" Alfred trailed off again. Elizabeth had never seen him in such a state before. It made her feel good to think he cared and was so concerned about her well-being. "If you want to take the rest of the day off, I won't hold it against you."

Talking to both Joyce and Alfred and seeing their worry for her made Elizabeth feel less alone.

"That's exactly what we're doing!" Joyce said, standing and pulling Elizabeth to her feet. "We're getting out of here, and we're going to…I don't know what we're going to do. But we're going to go do it."

"Elizabeth, if you need anything…" Alfred said as they headed for the door.

"Thank you," she said with a smile.

As she closed the door behind her, the last words she heard Alfred say were, "And be careful."

Be careful.

The same words from the letter.

Chapter Eight

Elizabeth hardly heard the daily sounds that she'd become so accustomed to as she and Joyce stepped out of Alfred's office. Her mind replayed his words on a loop.

Be careful.

Maybe it was just a coincidence. People said that sort of thing all the time, didn't they? But after everything that had happened, coincidence didn't feel like an option anymore.

Joyce kept a tight grip on her wrist as she steered her toward the elevator. "You need a drink," she declared without concern for who might hear.

Elizabeth almost laughed. "It's not even ten in the morning."

Joyce pressed the elevator button with an exaggerated roll of her eyes. "Fine, then coffee. And a donut or something. Anything that doesn't involve you sitting at your desk all day, pretending like everything is normal. I know you. You'll try and force yourself to forget about all of it, but won't be able to. Then it'll just eat at you all day until you finally have a nervous breakdown. Tell me I'm wrong. Go ahead."

Elizabeth hesitated. As much as she wanted to drown herself in work, part of her was relieved Joyce was being so tough. Maybe she did need a break.

The elevator doors slid open, and as they stepped inside, Elizabeth caught a glimpse of Dick Calhoun watching them from down the hall. His arms were folded, a sneer twisting his lips.

"Who's that jackoff? What's his problem?" Joyce muttered as the doors closed.

Elizabeth exhaled. "That's Dick Calhoun."

"*That's Dick Calhoun*! You're right. He does look like a total creep."

Out the main doors and across the street, Joyce—her arm linked through Elizabeth's—led the way to a coffee shop the two would meet up at some days for lunch. Halfway across the street, they could already smell the fresh coffee and pastries.

"Sit," Joyce instructed once they found a booth toward the back. "I'll get the coffee."

Elizabeth sank into the vinyl seat, trying to ignore the sick feeling in her stomach. Joyce returned moments later, setting a steaming cup in front of her before sliding into the seat across from her.

"You need to tell me everything," she said, dumping almost half the shaker of sugar into her cup. "And don't even think about saying 'it's nothing' because I'll throw this coffee right in your face. You know I will."

Elizabeth managed a small smile. "I believe you." She took a breath to steady herself. "It was with yesterday's mail."

"Shit...I never even looked at it when I brought it in. I just threw it on the kitchen table."

Elizabeth shrugged and took a sip of her coffee.

"What did it say?" Joyce continued stirring her coffee absentmindedly.

Fighting back tears, Elizabeth said, "Elizabeth, I'm watching you. Be careful."

Joyce's expression darkened. "And the police? What did they say?"

"That they're investigating. But they don't know if it's the same person who sent the other letters."

Joyce scoffed. "Right. Because that makes it better."

Elizabeth wrapped her hands around the coffee cup, staring at the swirling steam. "Who would do this?" she whispered.

Joyce was quiet for a moment. "You think it's someone you know?"

Elizabeth didn't answer right away. "Lieutenant Kerns thinks it's a possibility. He asked me if I knew anyone who would do something like this."

"Like it was some sort of joke?" Joyce asked, her tone a cross between disgust and disbelief. Then, after thinking for a moment, she said, "Okay. Let's think about this. Who knows where we live?"

"It isn't exactly a secret. It's on my work forms. The landlord has it. The electric company—"

"I mean someone who *shouldn't* have it."

Elizabeth's fingers tensed around the cup.

Alfred.

She quickly dismissed the notion. No. Not Alfred.

What about Dick Calhoun? Her mind drifted back to him watching them leave and she started thinking about how he was always trying to put the moves on her. What if she'd rejected him one too many times and he'd finally had enough and wanted to teach her a lesson?

Or it could be someone she didn't even know who just picked her name out of the phone book! Anyone could have sent the letter.

Then she heard Alfred's voice again saying, *"Be careful."*

Elizabeth's stomach turned. She wanted to trust Alfred. But how well did she really know him? He was her boss. He was professional, even though she thought maybe he always wanted to say more. As charming as he was, she'd always thought he was a bit awkward because of how he behaved around her. Had she been blind to the fact that he might have feelings for her and couldn't show them?

Her head was beginning to hurt. Desperate to change the subject, she asked, "Where were you last night?"

"After work, I ran home to change, then went out with Ted."

"Mustache and glasses?" Elizabeth asked, trying to picture his face.

"No. That's Tony. Ted's the artist with the curly blonde hair."

"That's Ted? I thought the artist was Ron."

"He's an artist too. I met Ted through Ron," Joyce said, shaking her head as if she understood the confusion.

"They're both artists and you...both of them?"

"Yeah."

Joyce said it so innocently. Elizabeth would never truly understand her friend. She just shook her head.

"I'm sure they have an artist friend for you, if you're interested. Hell, you can have Ron if you want. Or Ted. I don't care. Maybe that's what you need to take your mind off all this?"

"A one-night stand?!"

"Well, no one said anything about a *one-night stand*. Maybe you and Ted would hit it off. I don't know. I'm just trying to help."

Even though she and Joyce were very…very different people, she loved her. Not entirely certain if she was being serious with the whole Ted-Ron thing, she was still grateful for someone who cared enough to try to make her feel better.

Just then, another thought struck her. How was she going to tell her parents about what happened? Her mother would not handle it well, not that her father would be any better, but he wouldn't become hysterical. They'd both insist that she come home to stay with them until the cops found whoever was behind the threatening letters.

But what if they never found him? Or what if he wasn't the same person who delivered the letter right to her front door?

Seeing that her friend's mind had wandered into a dark place, Joyce tapped a fingernail against her mug to get Elizabeth's attention. "Why don't we go to the movies? You said you wanted to see *That Darn Cat!* And since I'm being a good friend, helping to take your mind off things, I'll go with you."

Elizabeth smiled. She knew Joyce didn't like those kinds of films, but she really did want to see the new Disney comedy. She needed to laugh. And maybe Joyce would like it. Stranger things had been known to happen.

"I'll go. But you're buying the popcorn," Joyce said, standing up and pulling her multi-colored coat on over the outfit she was still wearing from the night before.

"Don't you want to go home and change first?" Elizabeth asked, pointing at the evening dress. "It's still a little early for the movies anyway."

As they stepped back out onto the sidewalk, a gust of cold air tore down the avenue, causing both women to shiver. Elizabeth was wearing a dress, sweater, and coat, and she was chilled to the bone. She couldn't imagine how cold Joyce was in the tiny outfit she had on. It was definitely not something to be worn on a cold winter day.

As they started down the sidewalk in the direction of their apartment, Elizabeth couldn't shake the feeling that someone was watching them.

She turned, scanning the faces of the others along the street. People rushed past, heads down against the wind.

But just for a second, she could have sworn she saw a man in a dark coat, lingering just across the street with his hat pulled down so she couldn't see his face.

She blinked as another blast of frigid air hit her in the face. When she looked again, he was gone.

Chapter Nine

A steady snow had begun coming down by the time Elizabeth and Joyce reached their apartment building. With the wind whipping the white flakes across their faces, it was becoming difficult to see more than a few feet in front of them. But the conditions didn't stop Elizabeth from continuing to watch everyone on the street around them. She was looking for anything, or anyone, out of place.

She hadn't mentioned the man she thought she saw earlier when they left the coffee shop. It might have been nothing. It might have just been a trick of the light, a stranger passing by at the wrong moment. But she couldn't shake the feeling that something was off, and he'd been looking directly at her.

Joyce gently elbowed her in the ribs. "You're thinking too much again."

Elizabeth offered a weak smile. "Sorry. I'm still trying to… I don't know what."

"You have to put it out of your mind for a little while. We're going to the movies, and for the next few hours, your only thoughts should be about… What exactly is this movie about again? A cat robbing a bank? Seriously, is that what the movie is going to be about?"

"No!" Elizabeth said with a laugh. It felt good to let it out. Whether Joyce seriously thought that was what the movie was about or not, she appreciated her friend trying to take her mind off what had happened that morning.

Unlocking the front door to the building, Elizabeth stepped into the entry, still laughing at Joyce. The familiar hallway, with its orange carpeting and soft lighting, was a welcome sight. It was home. It was safe.

Or at least, it was supposed to be.

Elizabeth unlocked the door to their first-floor apartment and pushed it open with a slight tremor in her hand. She didn't know what she was expecting to see, but when she walked in, everything was exactly as she'd left it.

Joyce kicked off her heels and started toward her bedroom, saying over her shoulder as she went, "Let me change real quick, then we can head back out. See if you can find the movie listings in the paper and find out what time it starts."

Elizabeth set her purse down on the sofa, exhaling for what felt like the first time all day, and looked at the little Christmas tree in the corner. She always loved Christmas. It was her favorite time of the year. Thinking back over past holidays, with Patty and her parents, and all the happy memories, for a moment, things felt normal again.

Then Joyce screamed.

Elizabeth's heart lurched as she spun and saw Joyce standing in the hallway. "What? What is it?"

Joyce stood frozen in the doorway, one hand gripping the frame, the other clamped over her mouth. Her wide eyes were locked on something in Elizabeth's bedroom.

Rushing to her side, Elizabeth looked over her shoulder.

The door was open, but Elizabeth couldn't see anything that would have elicited such a reaction from her friend.

"What is it?" Elizabeth asked.

"Over there," Joyce answered. "I went into your room to borrow that brown sweater I like, and I saw it."

"Saw what?" Elizabeth asked as she walked into her room, crossing around to the other side of the bed.

When her eyes moved to the floor, a jolt surged through her entire body.

Strewn across the hardwood floor in a heap of pale blue fabric was the bridesmaid dress she'd worn at her sister's wedding. Or rather, what was left of it.

The fabric had been slashed, jagged tears running through the bodice and skirt as if someone had taken a knife to it. The sleeves were ripped clean off, the delicate embroidery shredded. It looked like something a wild animal had gotten its teeth into and savagely torn to pieces.

Elizabeth took a step back, her mind struggling to catch up with what she was seeing. She'd just worn the dress that past weekend, standing beside Patty as she said her vows. It had been one of the happiest days of her life.

And now, someone had destroyed it.

Joyce was the first to speak. "Liz…someone was in here."

Elizabeth swallowed hard, forcing herself to stay calm. "The door was locked when I left this morning. I locked it. Was it locked when you came in?"

"Yes! But when I got in, I saw your note pinned to the board by the front door. I turned around and went to the police station right away to find you. But I know I locked the door behind me. I always do. You know I do."

"What about the windows?"

They quickly ran around to each of the windows in the apartment, a total of five. All were shut tight and latched.

A fresh wave of fear gripped Elizabeth so tightly, for a moment, she couldn't breathe. How did they get in?

Suddenly, Joyce grabbed her by the wrist. "We need to call the police!"

Elizabeth hesitated. "And tell them what? That someone ripped up a dress?"

"Liz!" Joyce gestured wildly at the ruined fabric. "This isn't just a dress. This is a message."

She knew Joyce was right. This wasn't random. This wasn't a prank. This wasn't some practical joke.

First, the letter. Now this.

Whoever was behind this didn't just want to scare her. They wanted her to know she wasn't safe.

Elizabeth's fingers clenched into fists. No. She wasn't going to fall apart. Not here. Not now.

She took a shaky breath. "Okay. We'll call the police."

Joyce nodded, already heading toward the telephone in the kitchen.

Chapter Ten

1985...

As magnificent as the weather had been for the Summer in the Streets event on Saturday, the very next day was a complete washout. While the last of the festival-goers strolled along Commerce Street and the booths were being packed up, gray clouds began rolling in, erasing the crystal clear blue sky. By breakfast the next morning, rain had soaked the city, with showers continuing throughout the day. It had turned into a wet, summer Sunday that most people spent at home watching television or doing household chores they'd been putting off.

By Monday, though the rain had come to an end, the gray clouds lingered, causing the June sky to hang low over Parker City. The overcast gloom added to the somber mood at Hillcrest Cemetery, where Elizabeth Marsh stood beneath a black umbrella, her gloved hand gently resting on her husband's arm as the last of the mourners drifted away from the graveside.

The funeral of Kenneth Sharpe had been simple but dignified—exactly the kind of farewell the quiet, dependable man would have wanted. A modest crowd had gathered at the cemetery on the edge of town, many of them from the same neighborhoods and church pews they'd shared with Kenneth and Patty for decades. Now they were leaving, climbing back into their cars and returning to their lives.

"She held up better than I expected," Alfred said softly, guiding Elizabeth along the gravel path toward their Lincoln parked behind the limousine from the funeral home.

"She's always been good at putting on a brave face," Elizabeth murmured, brushing a lock of hair from in front of her eyes.

They reached the car, and Alfred opened the passenger door for her. He moved a little slower than he used to—his hair now much thinner and more silver, his stomach slightly rounder—but he still carried himself with that gentle determination that had first drawn her in all those years ago. The two had shared almost twenty years of marriage now—most of them spent far from Parker City.

They had left in 1966, less than a year after all the unsettling events of that unforgettable winter. They'd wanted to put as much distance between themselves and the city as they could afford, while still being close enough to see their family and loved ones, unwilling to completely sever ties with their earlier lives.

After enough time had passed—time for the shadows to fade—the couple moved back to Parker. Alfred, along with a business acquaintance, opened an accounting firm that had quickly grown in size and reputation. As the firm's managing partner, it was Alfred's experience and old-school integrity that attracted clients. And instead of moving into one of the city's wealthier neighborhoods, they bought a modest home in a quiet part of town. Elizabeth never expected to be that close to her sister again, but Alfred saw how happy she was from the moment they moved the first boxes into the house. Elizabeth, the love of his life, was home.

As she settled into the passenger seat, Elizabeth pulled off her gloves as Alfred slid behind the wheel and started the car. She stared out the window as they left the cemetery, watching the rows of gravestones roll past. Her sister's black-clad silhouette lingered in the corner of her eye, still standing beside the casket.

"Do you think she'll be alright?" she asked after a long moment.

Alfred nodded, eyes on the road. "She's got the boys. And her friends. And us."

Elizabeth smiled faintly but said nothing.

Her brother-in-law's death had been sudden and unexpected. Everyone who knew Kenneth thought of him as healthy and energetic. He'd been a wonderful husband and father, and a hardworking man. No matter how stressful the situation, he always took it in stride, making him a person everyone turned to. So, when Elizabeth got the call from Patty saying Kenneth had suffered a massive heart attack while out golfing with some of his fellow bank executives, it was earth-shattering news.

At the funeral home, Elizabeth stood by her sister's side and heard it over and over again—how Kenneth was too young to have been taken, how hard it would be to imagine him not showing up for work anymore, how much he would be missed at all of the civic organizations with which he was affiliated. Elizabeth had always liked her brother-in-law, but she never realized how involved in the community he was. Even the mayor showed up at the funeral home to pay his respects.

Patty appeared composed on the outside, but Elizabeth could see the pain in her sister's eyes. Still, there was comfort in the kind words shared by Kenneth's friends and associates.

Alfred kept stealing glances over at Elizabeth as they drove through town. Both had been surprised to see how much Parker had changed in their absence.

"Still think this was the right move?" he asked as they waited at a stoplight.

She looked at him. The wrinkles around his eyes could not distract from the warmth she saw when looking into them.

"I do," she said. "It feels good to be home."

She smiled and laid her hand over his.

They arrived home just before the rain started again, soft and steady against the roof as they stepped inside. The house smelled like lemon polish and the faint lavender perfume Elizabeth liked to spray in the air. She kicked off her shoes in the front hall, glad to be out of the black heels and away from the weight of the funeral. She'd been at Patty's side since learning of Kenneth's death, so was eager for an evening alone with just Alfred.

"Want some tea?" she asked.

"Sure," Alfred said, loosening his tie.

She headed into the kitchen, flipping on the electric kettle. While it warmed, she glanced at the mail on the table from that morning. Mostly junk. A water bill. A grocery flyer. Nothing pressing, which was good because she felt a headache coming on and didn't want to have to think about anything for the rest of the evening. She just wanted to spend a quiet evening at home curled up next to Alfred—the place where she always felt the safest. Even if, every so often, her mind flashed back to the troubling events of twenty years ago.

Chapter Eleven

The headache was already booming behind Elizabeth's eyes before she opened them. A low, throbbing pulse—like someone tapping the inside of her skull with a rubber mallet.

She lay still in bed for a few moments, trying to will it away. The ceiling fan spun lazily overhead, pushing around the early summer air, but it did little to ease the heaviness pressing on her chest.

Her dreams had been scattered and strange. Not dreams exactly—more like fragments. Shapes. Glimpses. Most of all, color. That awful, vivid red.

She sat up slowly, pressing her palm against her forehead, then reached for the glass of water on the nightstand. Alfred had already left for the office; the other side of the bed was neatly made. He was always so tidy.

She padded across the room, tying her robe at the waist, and went into the bathroom in search of a couple of aspirin. She just wanted the headache to go away.

The house was quiet. She liked it that way, usually. Today, the silence felt a little *too* quiet, though.

In the kitchen, she poured a cup of coffee from the pot Alfred had brewed before leaving. She stood by the sink, watching the neighbor's cat slink across their backyard, tail flicking as it disappeared through a gap in the hedge. The first few sips of coffee had thankfully begun to clear the cobwebs from her head.

Maybe it was just the funeral. The emotions. The memories it stirred.

But the images from her dream kept flashing before her eyes—red handwriting scrawled across torn envelopes, tattered chiffon material.

She shook it off and went to shower and dress. By ten o'clock, she was pulling out of the driveway to run her errands—determined to feel normal.

The grocery store was busier than usual. A shipment had come in late, and the produce section was just being restocked. She guided the shopping cart through the narrow aisles with her list in hand, grateful for the mundane task. But the feeling didn't last.

Somewhere near the frozen foods, she felt it—a sensation so sudden her chest constricted, taking her breath away. Steadying herself, she gripped the handle of the shopping cart so tightly her knuckles turned white.

Someone was watching her.

She paused beside the glass door of the freezer case, pretending to study the selection of peas and green beans. Her eyes scanned the reflection. Nothing out of the ordinary. Just a few shoppers, mostly older women.

She moved on, trying to shake the feeling, but it trailed her through the store. Her headache pulsed with renewed vigor.

At the checkout, the cashier—young and friendly—made a comment about the gloomy weather. Elizabeth forced a smile, paid, and hurried out of the store.

Outside, she glanced around the parking lot before pushing her cart to the car. Again—no one. Just a mother wrangling a toddler into a minivan and an old man smoking next to his station wagon as he watched his wife struggle to put the grocery bags in the trunk.

Still, the feeling persisted.

She made two more stops—making a quick deposit at the bank and picking up a prescription at the pharmacy. Each time, the sensation returned. Fleeting but unmistakable.

It wasn't paranoia. It was *instinct.* And she hadn't felt it in twenty years.

By early afternoon, she was home again, groceries put away, curtains drawn just enough to dim the light. She made a sandwich but only managed two bites before setting it aside.

The ringing phone startled her.

She reached for it while removing her earring, pressing the receiver to her ear. "Hello?"

"Hi, honey. It's me," Alfred's voice came through, warm and reassuring. "Just checking in."

She sank into one of the kitchen chairs.

"That's sweet of you," she said, rubbing her temple. "I'm alright. Just had a rough night."

"Sorry. Do you need anything?"

"No. I just didn't sleep well. Headache. Strange dreams."

"Still about…?" He didn't have to finish the question.

"Yes," she said. "But I'll be fine. Just need some rest."

There was a pause.

"Do you want me to come home early?"

"No," she said quickly, forcing a steadier tone. "No, really. I'm okay. I've got a few things to catch up on here. And I have to start dinner."

He hesitated for a moment, then said, "Alright. But call me if you need anything."

"I will."

She hung up, staring at the receiver for a long moment before placing it back on the hook.

The kettle on the stove whistled softly—she hadn't even remembered turning it on. Taking her cup of tea back to the kitchen table, she reached for the mail she'd brought in with the groceries. Again, mostly junk mail and bills.

Then she froze.

Her name, scrawled in bright red ink, stared her in the face.

Chapter Twelve

The kitchen began to tilt, the white cabinets turning a shade of gray as Elizabeth's world began to constrict right before her eyes. For a moment, she thought she was going to be sick.

Realizing what she was holding, she dropped the letter and jumped up so fast she knocked the chair over. The metal frame hitting the floor seemed to echo throughout the house louder than it should.

Her hands were trembling as she pressed her back against the refrigerator, trying to catch her breath.

The whole time, the letter stared back at her from the tabletop.

This couldn't be happening, she thought to herself. Not again.

She wanted to reach for the phone and call Alfred back, but she couldn't move. She was frozen in place. Her body and mind were locked in an unmoving state of terror.

It was the red ink. That unmistakable, sharp, angry red.

It looked exactly the same.

She squeezed her eyes shut and tried to slow her breathing, but it was no use. All she could think about was *the letter*.

Was it possible? Could someone really have waited twenty years?

She forced herself to move, inching forward like a skittish kitten. Her fingers hovered above the envelope before finally snatching it up. It was standard white—ordinary in every way but one. Her name was written across the front in a stark, slanted script.

ELIZABETH MARSH

The last time she had seen handwriting like that was in 1965. Only then, she wasn't Elizabeth Marsh. She was Elizabeth Blakely.

Her knees buckled as she lowered herself back into the chair, now upright again but as unsteady as she felt.

She stared at the envelope. No return address. No postmark.

Had it been hand-delivered?

Just like the first ones!

She stood again and ran to the front door, pulling it open and stepping out onto the porch. The neighborhood was quiet. There was no one on the sidewalk, no cars passing by. Just a steady drizzle that had begun falling.

Stepping back inside, she slammed the door and threw the deadbolt. Hands quivering, she made sure the door was securely locked before returning to the kitchen.

Part of her wanted to rip the letter open and see what it said. Part of her never wanted to read another word from whomever had tormented her all those years ago.

But she had to know.

She slid her finger under the flap and unfolded the single sheet of paper inside. The message was short.

WELCOME HOME.

It was simple…and terrifying.

How could this be happening? Could someone be playing a trick on her?

She tried to think logically. Maybe someone from town remembered. Maybe the story still floated around in whispers and old newspaper clippings. Maybe someone thought it would be funny, or cruel, to reawaken the nightmare.

But she knew better. She knew that handwriting. There was no way she would ever be able to forget it. It was seared into her mind's eye.

This was no copycat. This was *him!*

She took a deep breath and sat down. Her fingers were ice-cold against the warm ceramic of her tea mug. The headache she thought had faded now roared back to life.

She picked up the letter again and turned it over, scanning for any clue— any mark, any impression from a pen or fingerprint. But there was nothing.

Everything had changed so much since 1965. She had changed. Grown older, stronger, more guarded. She'd built a life with Alfred. She'd survived the worst of it. She'd buried the past deep enough she no longer thought about it every day.

But now?

Now it felt as fresh and raw as the first time she'd received one of the damn letters.

Her stomach clenched.

She slowly went to her bedroom and opened the closet. From the top shelf, tucked under a set of old sheets, she removed a small wooden box and carried it to the bed. Inside were the old newspaper clippings, the grainy photo the police had once circulated of a "man of interest," and a copy of one of the letters she'd kept.

She pulled it out and laid it next to the new one.

The handwriting matched.

She felt dizzy again, her vision blurring for a moment.

Whoever he was, he knew she'd returned to Parker City!

But how?

They hadn't told many people. The move had been quiet. There had been no formal announcement. No big welcome home party.

And yet he knew.

Elizabeth paced in front of the bed, wringing her hands. She needed to do something. Call someone. But who? Alfred? The police?

Would they even believe her?

She knew how it would sound. A woman in her fifties receiving a suspicious letter with no clear threat. The town had changed. She was sure the police department would have as well. She didn't know if anyone there would even remember what had happened.

But *she* remembered. And that was enough.

This wasn't just a prank or a coincidence.

He was back.

Chapter Thirteen

1965…

Lieutenant Wallace Kerns arrived at the apartment less than twenty minutes after Joyce's frantic call to the police station. The only reason it took that long was because he'd taken an early lunch, and the officer who'd initially answered the phone needed to run across the street to the little coffee shop most of the department ate at to find him. With him, he brought the two officers assigned to investigate the recent rash of threatening letters, George Wallenbeck and Nick Caruso. Not that they'd uncovered much over the last several weeks, but they were doing what they could.

Elizabeth was ashamed when she realized she was slightly disappointed Officer Stull wasn't with them. She'd taken an instant liking to him, unlike the two officers who were now in her home. Though their presence did alleviate some of her immediate anxiety, Stull had just seemed to be so pleasant and personable. These two were all business. But then again, wasn't that what she wanted? Policemen who were going to take her seriously?

Sitting as motionless as a statue on the sofa, Elizabeth held her hands clenched in her lap as she listened to the three men talk in low voices near the door. Joyce paced by the window, arms crossed tightly over her chest, shooting glances at her roommate every few seconds.

Kerns was the first to step away from the others, rubbing his jaw as he walked over to Elizabeth. Taking a seat in the armchair next to the sofa, he looked at her with tired eyes. The lines on his face appeared deeper than they were earlier that morning, she noticed.

"Miss Blakely, walk me through your day again. Every detail."

Elizabeth took a breath and began from when she woke up in a bit of a haze from her night sleeping on the sofa, recounting everything—from the moment she found the letter while having breakfast to her visit to the police station, then her short time at work, and finally, returning home to find her dress in ruins. Unlike the first time she spoke to the lieutenant, he wasn't taking any notes. It was Officer Caruso taking down what she said. At the same time, his partner was walking through the apartment, examining all the windows and front door.

When she'd finished, Kerns let out a deep sigh and, turning to look at Caruso, who was standing next to him, then asked, "Well?"

A short, round man with very little hair sticking out from under his patrol cap that Elizabeth could see, Caruso didn't appear to be the most fit officer on the force, but his eyes were sharp and alert. She'd watched him as he scanned every inch of the apartment since arriving.

Looking over the notes he'd just taken, he finally said, "With this," then paused to motion toward the bedroom, "and what you told me about the letter itself on the way over here…this doesn't fit the pattern."

"Yeah. This seems a hell of a lot more personal, Lieu," Wallenbeck added, joining the conversation after returning from the kitchen. Unlike his partner, he was rail-thin with curly hair and a thin mustache that barely looked like it had grown in.

Elizabeth swallowed hard. "You think it's a different person?"

Kerns ran a hand over his chin before saying, "Could be. Or could be the same guy…just escalating."

"Escalating!" Joyce repeated, her voice filled with a combination of anger and fear.

Wallenbeck shrugged. "Wouldn't be the first time. Some guy gets a taste of stirring up trouble. Seeing how everyone is reacting to the random letters, but that ain't enough anymore. So, he decides to go a little further this time."

Elizabeth shivered. The thought of someone going from making an anonymous threat to breaking into her home was almost too much to bear.

The lieutenant stood and walked over to the front door, examining the lock and handle. "Windows and door?"

"No signs of forced entry anywhere in the apartment," Wallenbeck answered. "Windows are locked tight and can't be opened from the outside. Only way in could have been the front door. Lock's not broken either."

"So," Kerns picked up the thought, "that means the door was left unlocked, he picked the lock, or…he had a key."

Joyce let out a horrified gasp. "Oh, my God."

"Are you sure you both locked the door when you left this morning?" Caruso asked, looking from one roommate to the other.

"Yes!" they both said in unison.

Realizing what that meant, Elizabeth's stomach dropped. "But only Joyce and I have keys." It came out as barely a whisper.

"What about the landlord?"

Joyce shook her head. "My aunt owns the building. She'd never do this."

As the room fell silent, Kerns turned and walked into Elizabeth's bedroom, careful not to step on the shredded dress as he scanned the room. "What about friends or co-workers? Anyone you've given a spare key to?"

"No," Elizabeth said quickly, but then hesitated. She was always so careful with her keys. Was it possible someone had managed to get them away from her and make a copy without her noticing? Impossible. But then there was Joyce. She *wasn't* so careful with her keys.

Elizabeth's head spun. The idea that someone had planned this—had gotten access to her apartment, waited for the right moment—was worse than the letter itself.

Joyce gritted her teeth. "So what do we do now? Just sit here and wait for the guy to waltz in again?"

Kerns adjusted his jacket, which only served to make the badge on his chest crooked. "The boys are gonna take some pictures and dust the door for prints. And we still need to talk to the landlord. Just to see who might have had access to any spare keys. You haven't noticed any maintenance men hanging around or doing any work lately?"

Both women looked at each other and shook their heads.

"In the meantime," Kerns continued, "I'd suggest finding somewhere else to stay for a while. Will you be able to do that?"

"We'll be fine," Joyce said defiantly, grabbing Elizabeth's arm and pulling her close.

"That's the spirit, sweetheart," Officer Wallenbeck said.

Joyce shot him a glare that could melt glass.

Kerns ignored the exchange. "Miss Blakely," he said, squaring his shoulders and looking directly into her eyes with a combination of compassion and somberness, "you got any idea who might be doing this? Anyone at all?"

Elizabeth hesitated. Faces flashed through her mind like she was watching a film. Could someone she knew really be behind this? Dick Calhoun was always trying to put the moves on her. And hadn't he said something to her as he was leaving work last night? *Be careful...* Just like in the letter. But then again, Alfred said the same thing just that morning. She didn't want to accuse anyone without having good reason. She was sure it was a coincidence both of them had said that to her. People said it all the time. Still...

"I don't know, Lieutenant Kerns. I'm sorry."

He studied her for a long moment. "Alright then. The boys are gonna do their thing. And we'll let you know if we come up with anything."

"We won't hold our breath," Joyce said under her own, yet still loud enough to be heard.

Ignoring the remark, he finished by saying, "If anything else happens, you call right away."

"I will, Lieutenant. I promise."

"And if you think of anyone who might be trying to scare you, you let me know. We're gonna get this guy," he said, the words echoing in Elizabeth's head.

Chapter Fourteen

Back at the station, Lieutenant Kerns dropped into his chair, tossed his glasses on the desk, and started rubbing his eyes with the palms of his hands. The Christmas decorations his well-meaning secretary had strung up around the office felt out of place under the harsh fluorescent lights. He exhaled, watching Wallenbeck and Caruso settle into the chairs on the other side of his desk. They'd spent a good part of the afternoon at Elizabeth Blakely's apartment speaking with the landlord and the neighbors.

"This case is a damn mess," Caruso muttered, flipping open his notepad. "We got nothing solid."

Wallenbeck leaned forward, resting his elbows on his knees. "Doesn't make any sense. The first letters seemed random. No names, no real threats. Just trying to scare people. But this last one? The break-in? It feels personal if you ask me."

"Which is exactly what I was gonna ask you." Kerns nodded, chewing on the end of a pencil. "So...what does it mean? Either we're dealing with two different people, or the bastard's getting more confident and decided to fixate on one person."

"I'm not sure which is worse," Caruso said, stretching his meaty legs out in front of him. Tapping his notebook on his thigh, he continued, "Let's break it down piece by piece. The first letters—typed, sent through the mail with vague threats to multiple recipients. Now Elizabeth Blakely gets a handwritten one, hand-delivered specifically to her, and next thing we know, someone's tearing through her apartment."

"With no sign of forced entry," Wallenbeck added.

Kerns exhaled sharply. "That's what bothers me. Means whoever did this either had a key or knew how to get in without drawing too much attention."

"We talked to the landlord," Caruso said. "Sweet little old lady. Offered us cookies and milk. Said she hasn't replaced the locks in years and never misplaced her keys. Says she only keeps one spare locked up."

"And it was still there?" Kerns asked.

"Yeah. Untouched." Caruso sighed, shutting his notepad. "Either this guy's a professional, or he got a copy some other way."

"Coworkers, friends, anyone with access to her things," Wallenbeck suggested. "We need to start looking into the people around her."

Kerns leaned back in his chair, deep in thought. Like Caruso, he didn't know which was worse. Two separate cases or one guy behind all of it. He didn't want to even mention the idea of two possible miscreants.

Edgar Stanley, the longtime head of the department, had been hounding his men to find whoever was behind the letters—always using choice words when referring to the culprit. Stanley was known for his vulgar language. While he'd been putting the pressure on his officers, he hadn't offered them any suggestions on how to go about catching the perpetrator. It had not been his abilities as a law enforcement officer that landed him the top job. It was his ability to keep from rubbing any of the powers-that-be the wrong way and always kissing the right ass that propelled him through the ranks. He was an old-school copper who thought the best way to get a confession out of a suspect was with a phonebook to the temple.

Unfortunately, they didn't have any suspects. And the chief would no doubt lose his mind if Kern now told him the case was going in a new direction, and they could be looking for two guys instead of just one.

At one point, Kerns had suggested bringing in the Parker County Sheriff's Department for some extra bodies to work the case, but the chief wouldn't hear of it. He didn't want anyone thinking the PCPD couldn't handle things themselves.

"How long's it been since the last anonymous letter showed up?" Kerns asked.

"'Bout a week," Caruso answered.

Sighing, Kerns said, "I need to tell the chief."

Wallenbeck shook his head. "I wouldn't want to be in your shoes."

The lieutenant raised a stern eyebrow. "We need to make sure this Blakely business stays out of the paper. It could send the city over the edge. Any idea yet on how the *Dispatch* got a photo of one of the letters? I thought they were all locked up for evidence?"

The two officers looked at each other sheepishly.

"We haven't really had time to look into it yet, Lieu," Wallenbeck said. "It was just in the paper this morning, and we got called right over to Blakely's apartment. We were already trying to follow up with some of the first women who got letters to see if anything else had happened."

Caruso nodded in agreement. "We're spread a little thin, just the two of us."

"I get it. But..." Kerns trailed off, turning and looking out the window.

He was about to speak again when the door to his office flew open, shaking the frosted-glass pane. Chief Edgar Stanley stalked in like a bull in a China shop, his perpetual cigar clenched tight between his teeth. The scent of cheap tobacco trailed him like a storm cloud, and the three men inside instinctively straightened in their seats.

Stanley's bulldog face was red, his beady eyes locking onto Kerns. "Jesus H. Christ, Kerns, you planning on solving this case before the goddamn New Year, or do I need to start handing out pink slips?"

Kerns sighed, already exhausted. "We're working on it, Chief."

"Workin' on it," Stanley mimicked with a sneer, shifting the cigar from one side of his mouth to the other. "You mean sittin' on your asses while some sick bastard plays peekaboo with half the dames in this city?" He shook his head, muttering something under his breath. "The mayor's breathing down my neck, and I don't have a damn thing to tell him except that my guys are 'working on it.'"

Caruso exchanged a glance with Wallenbeck but kept his mouth shut.

Kerns leaned forward, trying to remain as calm and in control as possible. "We don't have much to go on. And...there's been a development this morning."

"What's that supposed to mean? A *good* development?"

"No," Kerns admitted, then quickly filled him in on what had happened with Elizabeth Blakely since he'd first spoken with her that morning.

Stanley snorted. "Sonofabitch." Pacing back and forth for a minute, he turned to the officers and jabbed a thick finger in their direction. "So you don't got squat and now this nut job has actually broken into one of the women's apartments!"

"Or it could be a different guy," Wallenbeck said, then shrank into his seat as all eyes turned to him.

Kerns exhaled sharply. "Chief, we're working the case as best we can."

Stanley grumbled something indecipherable as he stopped pacing and looked out the window. "Alright, fine. What's next?"

"Until another letter shows up…if one does…we focus on Blakely," Kerns said.

Stanley grunted, chewing on his cigar. "What about the paper this morning? How the hell'd that happen? Who gave them access to the letter?"

Kerns shook his head. "It's another part of the investigation, Chief. Maybe it's time to bring in some help from the Sheriff's Department? At least to look into the newspap—"

"No!" Stanley snapped. Then, brushing ash from his shirt, said, "I want this sonofabitch caught before I have to stand in front of the mayor and tell him my department can't stop a lunatic from writing love notes."

He turned toward the door, then stopped and glanced back. "Get it done, boys. I don't care how."

And with that, he stormed out, leaving the office thick with the smell of tobacco and frustration.

Caruso let out a low whistle. "Guy sure has a way with words."

Kerns ignored him, running a hand through his thinning hair. "Alright. Let's get moving. Wallenbeck, you start asking questions around here about who might have let a reporter get a picture of that letter."

"I don't think people are gonna like me asking questions like that, Lieu."

"Then tell them to come see me if they got a problem."

Wallenbeck shrugged.

"Caruso," Kerns went on flipping open his own notepad, "without ruffling too many feathers, go talk to Blakely's boss over at Upton's. His name's Alfred Marsh. See if he knows of any problems or anybody who's been making trouble for the lady. If this is the same guy sending all the letters, she's the key to all of this."

The men stood, the only sound in the room the ticking of the clock on the lieutenant's wall. The weight of the situation was pressing down on all of them, while outside the building, the city moved about its day as if a woman's life hadn't just been turned upside down.

Chapter Fifteen

Looking at his watch, Officer Nick Caruso pulled the collar of his coat up around his neck to shield it from the wind as he ducked out of the squad car and crossed the sidewalk toward the doors to Upton's. Like almost everyone in Parker City, he'd shopped at the department store most of his life. He'd just never paid the place an official visit in uniform before. He suddenly felt odd and out of place stepping through the grand entrance.

The scent of all the perfumes mixed together tickled his nose as he cast his eyes around the busy shop floor. Christmas decorations hung from the ceiling, red and gold banners draped across display cases, and the sound of "Silver Bells" played softly over the speakers.

The festive atmosphere didn't match his mood.

He wasn't thrilled about spending his afternoon talking to a department store executive, but Kerns wanted them checking every angle. And if someone at Upton's had a problem with Elizabeth Blakely, it was worth looking into.

Caruso approached the nearest associate, a young woman arranging a display of silk scarves. Standing there in his PCPD uniform, there really wasn't much need to introduce himself. Instead he said, "I'm looking for Alfred Marsh. Business Office."

The girl's eyes widened, but she nodded quickly. "Uh…third floor. Elevator's that way. If you take it all the way up, there will be a door to your right for the offices."

Caruso gave her a quick thanks before making his way to the elevator. As he rode up, he took in the polished brass fixtures, the velvet-trimmed walls. Upton's was a class act, but that didn't mean everyone working there was.

When the doors opened, he saw the Home Furnishings Department laid out in front of him. Turning as he'd been instructed, he saw a glass door with the words EXECUTIVE OFFICES etched on it. Stepping through it, he found himself in a hallway with several doors running down one side and another elevator all the way at the end of the corridor. Examining each door as he passed, he found the one marked ACCOUNTING & BUSINESS at the very end of the hall. Inside, desks lined the space, typewriters clacking away as employees worked, only briefly glancing up at the uniformed officer in their midst.

"Can I help you?" a woman at one of the first desks asked, eyeing him curiously.

"Officer Nick Caruso, Parker City PD. I need to speak with Alfred Marsh."

The woman—Donna, according to the nameplate on the desk—nodded. "One moment." She stood and crossed the office, knocking on a door before pushing it open. A few seconds later, a tall, neatly dressed man with combed-back blond hair stepped out.

"Officer Caruso, is it?" Alfred Marsh extended a hand. "Come in."

Caruso shook his hand and followed him inside, shutting the door behind him. The office was tidy, everything in its place—no clutter, no mess. Marsh was obviously a man who liked things orderly.

"What can I do for you, Officer?" Marsh asked, settling into his chair.

Caruso took the seat across from him, studying him for a beat before answering. "We're looking into the letters that have been sent to women across the city—including Elizabeth Blakely. I understand she works under you."

Marsh frowned. "She does. She told me about the letter she received. It's awful. I can't imagine how frightening this must be for her. I told her to take the day off. I wish there was something more I could do."

Caruso nodded slowly. "You're familiar with everyone who works in this office, correct?"

"I am."

"Anyone here who's ever given Elizabeth trouble? A co-worker, a manager, anyone who might have had an issue with her?"

Marsh considered the question. "Elizabeth is well-liked. She keeps to herself mostly, does her job, and does it well. I wish I had more girls like her."

Caruso studied him. The concern in his voice seemed genuine. But he'd been around the block enough times to know that sincerity could be faked.

"That doesn't mean someone doesn't have a problem with her," Caruso prodded. "Anyone in the company who's been bothering her?"

Marsh's lips pressed into a thin line. "Well...Dick Calhoun can be...he pays some of the girls a lot of attention."

Caruso arched a brow. "How's that exactly?"

Marsh hesitated. "He flirts, makes suggestive comments, but as far as I know, he's never done anything beyond that. Still, I've seen Elizabeth brush him off more than once."

Caruso made a mental note. "Anyone else?"

"No one comes to mind." Marsh leaned forward, clasping his hands together. "Look, Officer, if I thought anyone here was capable of sending threatening letters, I'd tell you. I want this person caught as much as you do. I really do like Elizabeth."

Caruso nodded but didn't say whether he believed him. He pulled out a small notepad. "Well, Mr. Marsh, things have progressed a little beyond just sending threatening letters. At some point this morning—after Miss Blakely left her apartment—someone got in and made a bit of a mess."

Alfred's eyes widened. "Is Elizabeth alright? Someone broke into her apartment? I thought this was just some guy sending letters, scaring people."

"He may be getting bolder, and the letters alone aren't doing it for him anymore. That's one possibility we're looking at."

"*One* possibility?" Alfred asked curiously, the surprise registering on his face.

"This could also be a completely separate thing," Caruso admitted. "Have nothing to do with the other letters."

He was watching Alfred's reaction carefully. At the moment, the man looked ashen, like he was taking it all very seriously and it was weighing on him. Caruso couldn't help but wonder if he cared this much about everyone who worked for him or if Marsh had a special place in his heart for Elizabeth Blakely. Which could be something to look at.

"This Dick Calhoun fella," Caruso began to ask, "was he here all morning?"

"Um…I really couldn't say. I got in a little late myself this morning. I believe he was here when I arrived, but I can't say how long he'd been here. I'm sure someone saw him come in. He tends to make a bit of an entrance."

Caruso wrote something down in his notebook. "You say you were late this morning? What time did you get in?"

"Me? Um…about nine-thirty, or so. I don't remember exactly. You can ask Elizabeth. I saw her first thing when—" Alfred stopped abruptly. "Sorry. It's just that Elizabeth tends to keep me on time and knows when I'm coming and going. Sometimes I think she could run this whole department."

"Hmm. That so? Why is it you were running late today, Mr. Marsh?"

"Car trouble. My car tends to act up when it gets cold."

Caruso jotted down another note, then stood. "Thanks for your time, Mr. Marsh. If you think of anything that could be helpful, please call the station."

Marsh stood as well. "Of course. And if Elizabeth needs anything, I want her to know she can count on me."

Caruso didn't respond. He wasn't ready to decide whether Marsh was a man concerned for a colleague, or a man covering his own tracks.

Standing in the doorway to Alfred's office, Caruso turned and asked, "Could you point me in the direction of Dick Calhoun?"

"Yes. Of course. I think he's still here," Alfred said, coming out from behind his desk. "Unless he left early. He does that sometimes."

Walking out with Caruso, he spotted Calhoun at the far end of the office. He was leaning against the wall, practically pinning a young brunette in a pencil skirt into the corner. She looked uncomfortable, shifting her weight from one foot to the other as she forced a polite smile.

"That's him," Alfred Marsh said, motioning with his chin.

Calhoun's grin made Caruso clench his own jaw. He'd seen this act plenty of times. Guys like Calhoun thought they were charming, but they were just pests in cheap suits.

Caruso sighed, rubbing a hand over his face. "I'm gonna need to talk to him."

Chapter Sixteen

There were two main roads that people could take to get between Parker City and Wakeville to the north. Neither took longer than ten minutes. In fact, along one particular stretch of land, the two municipalities' boundaries nearly touched, they were so close. So, after Elizabeth left home, she hadn't really gone all that far. But while the distance between Parker and Wakeville wasn't great, the two could not be more different.

Compared to Parker City's bustling streets and what seemed like constant building and expansion, Wakeville felt frozen in time. A small town where people still waved from their front porches and the biggest event of the season was the annual Christmas pageant at Saint Luke's.

As dusk began to descend, Elizabeth and Joyce drove through what could only be considered Wakeville's "downtown" in Joyce's old turquoise Ford Fairlane. Christmas lights twinkled from the eaves of houses, and the glow of shop windows cast warm light onto empty sidewalks. Unlike Parker City, Wakeville felt untouched by fear, a world away from the threatening letters and torn dresses.

Joyce pulled up in front of Elizabeth's childhood home—a two-story house with dark green shutters and a wreath on the front door. In the yard, a Nativity scene sat under a layer of newly fallen snow from earlier in the day.

"I can't believe I'm back here," Elizabeth muttered, folding her arms.

Joyce shot her a look. "You say that like it's a bad thing."

Elizabeth didn't respond. She loved her parents. And still living so close, she spent a lot of time with them. But coming home like this—under these circumstances—made her feel like a child again, running back to the safety of her childhood bedroom because the outside world was too much to handle. She hated it.

Before she could even get out of the car, the front door swung open.

"Elizabeth!" Her mother, Marian Blakely, called from the house before scurrying out and down the driveway to meet her.

"Hi, Mom," Elizabeth said, stepping out of the car.

Throwing her arms around her daughter and pulling her in tight, Marian said, "We've been so worried since you called us. Are you okay?"

Forcing a smile, Elizabeth answered, "I am now."

Clifford Blakely hadn't run out of the house as quickly as his wife, but was now standing beside her, looking down at his daughter with concern written all over his face. It broke Elizabeth's heart to see her parents so worried, and it all being her fault. Causing such a fuss.

"Let's get your bags and get inside before everyone freezes out here," Cliff said, heading around to the back of the car. "Dinner's on. Your mother made enough food to feed an army. I hope you're hungry, Joyce."

"What are we having, Mr. Blakely?" she asked, opening the trunk.

"Everything!" he answered. "Marian cleaned out the refrigerator when she heard you two were coming."

Once inside, the warmth of the house surrounded her. The smell of dinner filled the air, a fire crackling in the hearth in the den. For a brief moment, Elizabeth allowed herself to believe she was safe.

But as she set her bags down in her old bedroom, a chill ran through her. In the back of her mind, a terrible thought lingered.

If the person behind the letters really was watching her…would leaving Parker City be enough to make them stop?

Or would they follow her here?

Chapter Seventeen

As her father promised, Marian made more food than any of them could possibly have eaten that night. It's what she did when she was nervous—went into the kitchen and tore through her cookbooks and recipe cards, cooking and baking up a storm. Sometimes Clifford Blakely wondered how he'd managed to stay so trim with as much worrying as his wife did. But he was used to it after all these years.

"I'm fine, Mom," Elizabeth said unconvincingly from across the table as her mother looked at her with concern in her eyes.

Her father sat at the head of the table, arms crossed, studying his daughter the way he had when she was a child and had something to confess. When he'd asked her exactly what happened, she'd hesitated at first. But there was no use avoiding it. She told them about the letters, the torn dress, the police. Everything. She didn't want to worry her mother any more than she already was, but if she didn't tell her the truth, her imagination would only run wild.

When she finished, Marian looked horrified. "My God, Elizabeth. Who would do such a thing?"

"I don't know," Elizabeth admitted. "The police don't know either."

Her father exhaled sharply. "Sounds like they don't know much of anything. It's been weeks, and they don't have *any* clues?"

"They're trying," she said.

"Not hard enough."

"And it might not even have anything to do with all those other letters."

Tapping his fingers on the table, he shook his head and said, "Well, if someone wanted to scare you, they've done a damn good job of it."

"I don't want to be scared," she said, barely above a whisper.

They sat in silence for a moment until Joyce clapped her hands together. "Well! Now that we've had our serious talk, I think we need something to take the edge off. Mrs. B., do you still have a bottle of sherry in the cabinet?"

Marian chuckled. "You're terrible."

"I try." Joyce winked.

For the first time that day, Elizabeth almost laughed.

But as the night wore on, as the house grew quiet and the snow fell steadily outside, she couldn't shake the feeling that no matter how far she ran, she wasn't safe. It was a sensation she still felt later while she was curled up in the corner of the couch with a blanket wrapped around her shoulders. The fire in the hearth lit the room, sending shadows dancing across the walls, the Christmas tree glowed softly, and a Nat King Cole record played on the stereo. Joyce had long since stretched out in the armchair with a half-empty glass of sherry, her head tilted back, eyes closed but still listening. Marian had gone upstairs an hour ago, offering one last worried glance before heading to bed.

The clock on the mantel chimed ten. The warmth of the house should have been comforting, but Elizabeth still felt a chill.

She stared out the window at the snow-covered street. Wakeville was quiet at this hour. Most of the houses were dark, except for the Christmas lights. The stillness should have felt peaceful. Instead, it felt suffocating.

"Do you think he's still out there?" she asked suddenly.

Joyce blinked her eyes open. "Who?"

"*Him*. Whoever's doing this. Do you think he knows I came here?"

Joyce sat up, rubbing her hands down her arms. "No. I mean…how would he? It's not like you told anyone, right?"

Elizabeth hesitated. "Just Lieutenant Kerns, in case he needed to reach me."

Joyce made a face. "I still don't know how much I trust the police to solve this. No offense to the fuzz or anything, but the Parker City PD doesn't exactly scream 'top of their game.'"

Elizabeth let out a breath, rubbing at her temples. "I don't know who I can trust. And when I go back to work tomorrow, do I tell Alfred?"

Before Joyce could respond, they heard heavy footsteps coming down the hall. Sticking his head into the den, Clifford said, "I'm heading up to bed, girls. If you need anything, just holler." His eyes softened as he looked at Elizabeth. "You stay here as long as it takes. Both of you."

"I can't just hide forever," Elizabeth said, though the idea of staying put in Wakeville, surrounded by people who cared about her, was tempting.

"You're not hiding," he said firmly. "You're being smart. You stay here, and you don't go anywhere alone."

"I have to go to work, Dad."

Clifford sighed and was about to protest when Joyce said, "You don't have to worry, Mr. B. I'll drive us to and from work every day. I'm gonna keep an eye on our girl, here. No one's gonna get through me."

He smiled, knowing how protective the girls were of each other. "Don't stay up too late."

As Clifford Blakely headed for the stairs, the wind howled outside, rattling the windows. Elizabeth pulled the blanket around her tighter as somewhere out in the darkness a shadow silently glided across the snow.

Chapter Eighteen

Elizabeth hadn't slept much.

Even after returning to Wakeville, after the comfort of her mother's cooking and Joyce's attempts to lighten the mood, she was still a bundle of nerves. She lay in bed, staring at the ceiling, flinching at every creak in the old house.

Her mind was spinning out of control. She couldn't stop thinking about everything that had happened.

Every time she closed her eyes, she could see a dark figure taunting her. She was being watched.

But she couldn't stay locked away forever.

The morning air was cold, but the sun was bright, with no signs of any more snow for a few days. Stepping out of Joyce's car in front of Upton's, her friend told her she'd be back to pick her up after work, and she was only a telephone call away if she needed anything. Pulling her coat tighter around her as Joyce drove off, Elizabeth looked up and down the street to see if it looked like anyone was watching her.

Wakeville was quiet, and she had felt some sense of safety. Even if she was only fooling herself. But being back in Parker City, she was in the middle of it all—cars honking, people rushing down the sidewalks with their collars turned up against the wind. The world hadn't stopped just because she'd been terrified out of her apartment.

Steadying herself, Elizabeth pushed through the store's heavy doors. The warmth inside was immediate and welcome. The Christmas decorations still sparkled under the chandeliers, festive and bright, a stark contrast to the dread she was feeling inside. The store hummed with early shoppers. Women in wool coats lingered in front of the jewelry counters, while others sampled perfume in the Cosmetics Department. Here on the first floor, the men would congregate toward the back of the store near the tobacco section, picking out expensive cigars. Everything looked normal.

Elizabeth felt anything but.

She kept her head down as she weaved past the customers and slipped through the employee entrance. The familiar clang of the elevator doors closing around her was a relief. A moment of quiet.

She had to keep moving.

The ride up to the third floor felt endless, but as soon as the doors slid open, she knew avoiding attention would be impossible. She barely made it two steps toward the door to the Accounting and Business Office when Alfred Marsh spotted her from down the hallway.

"Elizabeth!"

His voice was filled with surprise, and before she could react, he was already moving toward her. Alfred was always professional, but now he was looking at her like she might break into a million little pieces right there in the middle of the office.

"What are you doing here?"

Elizabeth forced a smile. "I work here, remember?"

Alfred didn't return the smile. "I didn't expect you back so soon. After what happened…" He lowered his voice, glancing around. "You could've taken more time. I figured you'd need to—"

"I need to not be afraid and get out of the house," she said, cutting him off. "If I sat around all day, I'd go crazy. Work will keep me busy."

"You're not staying at your apartment, are you? If you need somewhere to stay, you can come stay with me." Realizing what he'd just said, Alfred turned bright red. "I don't mean it like that. I moved into the Worthington Arms over near the Harlequin Theatre, and I have a spare bedroom."

Elizabeth couldn't help but notice how cute Alfred was, embarrassed by what he'd said and afraid she'd misinterpret his intention. He really was a sweet man, she thought.

"Thank you. That's really very nice," she said, trying to put him out of his misery. "But my parents are putting Joyce and me up for a while." Biting her lip, she instantly regretted telling him where she was staying. "Please. Don't tell anyone."

"Of course. I just want you to be safe. My lips are sealed. I promise. I just wish you'd take a little more time."

"I can't hide away for the rest of my life."

"Not for the rest of your life. Just until the police catch whoever's doing this."

"Who knows how long that will be?"

Alfred studied her for a long moment before nodding. "Alright. But if you need anything, you let me know. And don't think I won't send you home if I think you're pushing yourself too hard."

"Yes, sir," she said, giving him a mock salute.

It was the closest thing to a joke she could muster, but it seemed to relax him just enough.

"And," he continued, "lunch today. If you feel comfortable, I'd be happy to go across the street with you for sandwiches…if you don't go out with the girls for lunch, of course. I just don't think you should be going anywhere alone right now. That's what I mean."

Gently putting her hand on his arm, Elizabeth said, "Thank you, Alfred. You're really very sweet."

The flush returned to his cheeks. "I, um, have a meeting in a few minutes," he said, looking awkwardly at his watch. "I should get the files from my office that I'll need for that."

As he led the way into the office area, Elizabeth could feel eyes on her as she made her way to her desk. Was she imagining it, or did they all know what happened? The morning paper ran another story about the letters, but she hadn't had the nerve to read it.

Lieutenant Kerns telephoned early that morning to warn her that the *Blue Ridge Herald* had learned about the letter she received and that her apartment had been broken into. They were going to publish a piece saying the anonymous letter writer appeared to be becoming violent. But he'd made them promise not to use her name for fear of what he threatened to do if they exposed her identity and jeopardized the investigation.

"Didn't expect to see you today, sweetheart."

Elizabeth tensed.

Dick Calhoun was leaning against the doorway to his office, arms crossed, that insufferable smirk firmly in place. He was always like that—too familiar, too pleased with himself. But this time, something in his expression made her stomach tighten.

"Thought you'd still be off recovering from that nasty little incident yesterday," he went on, stepping toward her.

Elizabeth frowned. "How did you—" She stopped herself. Of course, he knew.

"I was questioned by a police officer yesterday. Wanted to know where I was at the time of your break-in. As if I was a suspect or something. Can you believe that? Me?" He stopped to shake his head as if he couldn't figure out why anyone would think he was behind what had happened. "I think everyone around here has put it together—you leaving early yesterday, all upset, a cop coming around asking questions. Then the article in the paper this morning. People talk." He shrugged his shoulders.

Elizabeth swallowed back her irritation. She had no patience for his games today. "I have work to do, Dick."

"So do I," he said dryly. "But you know me. Always got time for a pretty face."

The comment, usually nothing more than an annoyance, settled in her stomach like a rock. The way he was looking at her was different. Cruel. Calculating.

Before she could respond, Alfred's voice cut through the tension.

"Dick!"

He turned, raising his hands innocently. "Relax, Alfred. Just welcoming Elizabeth back. Didn't know that was against company policy."

Alfred's expression was unreadable. "It's not. But wasting time on idle chit-chat is."

Calhoun let out a low chuckle, giving Elizabeth one last lingering look before sauntering back into his office. She let out a breath she hadn't realized she was holding.

Alfred caught her eye, his concern evident. "I'm sorry. He's just…Dick."

Elizabeth nodded, but she was still a little shaken.

Something about Calhoun's behavior felt… off. Even for him. He enjoyed getting under her skin, but this time it wasn't just teasing. It was something more.

As Elizabeth slid down into her chair, Donna came up beside her and put a hand on her shoulder. "Are you alright? No one knows what's going on. But Dick's been saying the police told him you got one of those letters. And Rosella down in Housewares said she heard you'd been attacked in your apartment."

Elizabeth sighed. The rumor mill at Upton's Department Store was in full swing. After telling Donna what actually happened and setting the record straight, she said she really didn't want to talk about it anymore and just wanted to focus on her work for the rest of the day.

"I understand," Donna said, a look of apprehension in her eyes. "But if you need anything, you know you can count on me and Stan. He may be a first-class yutz sometimes when he's around the guys, but he'd do anything for you."

"Thanks, Donna. I think I'll be okay. I'm staying out—" Elizabeth stopped midsentence. "Lieutenant Kerns said I shouldn't tell anyone where I'm staying right now. But if I need anything, I'll let you know. I promise."

As the two settled into their desks, the office fell into its usual daily routine. Elizabeth was thankful for the moments when she'd be able to forget how truly terrified she was. She'd been putting on a brave face, but deep down, she was scared. She just prayed the police would be able to find whoever was behind all of this before she received another letter or worse. Not that she even wanted to think about what that could be.

Chapter Nineteen

The thin layer of snow remained on the ground, covering Wakeville in a soft, white blanket. From her parents' front porch with a steaming cup of hot chocolate, Elizabeth watched as the neighborhood children ran around, bundled up in scarves and mittens, their laughter ringing through the crisp December air. It was peaceful here. There was no question about that.

Yet, she still found herself looking over her shoulder.

It had been a little over a week since she and Joyce left Parker City and came to stay with her parents. A little over a week since she'd last set foot in her apartment. A little over a week without another letter.

That should have been reassuring.

But instead of relief, Elizabeth felt trapped in limbo, waiting for the other shoe to drop. Had the threats stopped? Or was the sender merely biding their time? She didn't know, and that uncertainty gnawed at her.

And then there was the other unsettling news.

Though she hadn't received another letter, two other women in Parker City had. Both of them worked downtown, both of them had no obvious connection to Elizabeth, and both letters contained the same anonymous, typewritten messages as the first ones. Hers was still the only letter that had been handwritten, leaving the police to lean further into the theory that they needed to be looking for two separate suspects. But they were still investigating.

To avoid dwelling on it, she tried to keep busy. She still went to work every day, and though Joyce would turn around and go out again in the evening with friends, Elizabeth preferred to stay in and watch television with her father or help her mother with housework.

She'd ventured out by herself once, the Sunday after getting to Wakeville, when she ran to the grocery store down the street to pick up something her mother needed for dinner. It had been less than a twenty-minute outing, and she'd been on pins and needles the entire time.

At work, it seemed that the girls in the secretarial pool had all banded together to make sure she was never left alone. One of them would ask her to join them for lunch, while another would stay a little later if Joyce wasn't going to be able to pick Elizabeth up on time.

There'd even been a couple of times when Elizabeth had taken Alfred up on his offer to accompany her to lunch. Which Joyce, of course, found endlessly amusing.

"That's three lunches now, Liz."

Elizabeth rolled her eyes as she dried the last of the dishes, handing the plate to Joyce to put away. "It's only been twice. And so what?"

Joyce grinned. "So, you're telling me that the boss, the very proper Alfred Marsh, is just being nice?"

Elizabeth sighed, setting the dish towel down. "I don't know. Maybe. Maybe he just feels bad about everything that's happened."

"Or maybe he's sweet on you."

Elizabeth gave her a look, but Joyce only cocked her head and raised an eyebrow. "Oh, come on. The way he looks at you? That's not just concern, sweetheart. That's interest."

"Joyce," Elizabeth warned.

"I'm just saying, under different circumstances, it wouldn't be the worst thing. He's handsome, successful—"

Elizabeth threw the dish towel at her. "You're impossible."

Joyce caught it, laughing. "And you're avoiding the question."

"What question?" Clifford Blakely asked as he walked into the kitchen looking for the sports section from the afternoon paper.

"Whether she's gonna marry Alfred Marsh or not?"

"Joyce!" Elizabeth's eyes were the size of golf balls, but she couldn't help but smile. The truth was, she enjoyed her time with Alfred. He was kind, easy to talk to, and his quiet strength made her feel...safe. But she wasn't ready to entertain anything beyond that, not with everything else hanging over her.

Thankfully, she was saved from Joyce's teasing—and the questions it looked like her father was about to throw at her—by the sound of a car pulling into the driveway.

"Patty's home," Marian Blakely squawked as she ran through the kitchen toward the front door.

Peering through the window, Joyce said, "And she looks...rested. Must've been some honeymoon."

Elizabeth dried her hands quickly and went to join her mother and father on the front porch. Climbing out of the car, Patty looked as radiant as ever, her cheeks flushed from the cold, her natural wavy hair bouncing as she greeted everyone. She was bundled up in a stylish new coat, and Elizabeth noticed the way her gloveless hand flashed—her new wedding ring catching the late afternoon light.

"Liz!" Patty hurried up the steps, wrapping her in a tight hug. "I missed you! I didn't know you'd be at Mom and Dad's."

Elizabeth hugged her back. "I missed you, too."

Patty pulled away, giving her a once-over. "You look...well, you look tired, actually. What's wrong?"

Elizabeth hesitated, but Joyce, never one for subtlety, cut in. "Oh, just a little stalking, breaking and entering, and a threatening letter. You know, the usual."

Patty's smile faltered. "What?"

Elizabeth shot Joyce a glare before turning back to her sister. "It's... complicated."

"Well, start explaining." Patty's tone had shifted. "What the hell happened while I was gone?"

Elizabeth sighed.

Their mother said, "Let's go inside. I'll put on a fresh pot of coffee, and I have some carrot cake and cinnamon rolls. There may still be some brownies if your father didn't eat all of them. Inside everyone."

As they settled into the den, Elizabeth recounted everything. The letter. The dress. The feeling of being watched. Patty's face darkened with every detail.

When Elizabeth finally finished, Patty exhaled sharply. "And you didn't tell me?"

"You were on your honeymoon. What was I supposed to do? Call you at the lodge and ruin your trip?"

"Yes!" Patty snapped. "Liz. This is serious."

"I know that."

Patty shook her head. "And the police? What are they doing?"

Elizabeth hesitated. "They're investigating."

Patty didn't look convinced. "And in the meantime, you're just—what? Hiding out here at Mom and Dad's?"

Elizabeth stiffened. "I'm not hiding. I'm going to work every day."

Patty gave her a look. "Liz."

"She's also got a new boyfriend," Joyce chimed in with a devilish grin.

"What?!" Patty sat forward in her chair.

"Ignore her," Elizabeth said. "I'm not hiding. I just don't know what else to do. I haven't gotten another letter, but that doesn't mean it's over. Women are still getting letters. Two more this week. It's all over the papers. And a Baltimore TV station did a news story on it last night."

Patty's mouth pressed into a thin line. "And you're telling me you're *not* hiding?"

Elizabeth glanced away, unsure how to respond.

Patty was quiet for a long moment. Then she reached for Elizabeth's hand, squeezing it. "If you want, you can come stay with me and Kenneth. You don't have to stay here at Mom and Dad's."

Elizabeth blinked. "What?"

"What about me?" Joyce asked.

"You can both come if you want. We have plenty of room."

"So do we," their mother protested, giving her youngest daughter a stern look.

Elizabeth hesitated. "You just got married. The last thing you want is Joyce and me to…be a burden."

Patty scoffed. "You're my sister. You're never a burden."

"And I'm a delight to have around," Joyce added.

"But can any of you cook a pot roast?" Marian asked, looking at the girls.

"I'm learning," Patty admitted sheepishly. "But Kenneth knew I wasn't the best cook before he asked me to marry him."

Taking it all in, Joyce said, "I think you have a point, Mrs. B. It's probably best for Liz and me to stay here."

Elizabeth laughed, shaking her head. For the first time, she felt like she wasn't facing this alone.

Chapter Twenty

The house on Sycamore Street was still. Outside, a light December breeze rustled the bare tree branches, tapping them softly against the windows. The town of Wakeville had long since gone to sleep, its streets empty, its homes dark. The only glow in the Blakely house came from the television in the den, flickering ghostly images across the walls.

That evening, after they'd stopped Patty peppering Elizabeth with questions, the conversation turned to a much more cheerful topic—Patty and Kenneth's honeymoon. The stories of the newlyweds' week in the mountains filled the house with laughs and a momentary relief from the strain under which everyone had been living.

After finally saying goodbye to the loving couple, Elizabeth and her parents turned in for the night, leaving Joyce to entertain herself. Too tired to go out but not tired enough to go to bed, she decided to pop some popcorn and watch television.

As the clock ticked toward midnight, Joyce sat curled up on the couch, a blanket draped over her legs, absently twisting a strand of her hair as the late movie rolled through its final scene. She hadn't even been paying much attention—just something to fill the silence. The end credits rolled, and she sighed. She clicked off the television, rubbing her arms as she stood. The house was plunged into darkness, all but the faint nightlight in the hallway.

She stretched, suppressing a yawn as she headed toward the guest bedroom. The staircase creaked beneath her feet, the sound loud in the hush of the house.

That's when she heard it.

A murmur.

Joyce stopped at the top of the stairs in the dim hallway; her pulse quickened. It was faint, but she knew she'd heard something. Tilting her head, she listened.

A voice.

Her eyes flicked to the closed door of Elizabeth's bedroom. Her mouth went dry.

Someone was in there with Elizabeth.

She stepped closer, her bare feet making no sound on the carpeted floor. The voice was muffled—it wasn't deep like a man's, but it wasn't soft either. It was…strange.

A cold prickle ran up Joyce's spine.

She took a step closer, heart pounding now, debating what to do. Should she knock? Throw open the door? Run and wake up Elizabeth's parents?

"Elizabeth?" she called softly.

No response.

She hesitated, straining to listen. The sound had stopped.

Maybe she'd imagined it. Maybe she was just tired.

She exhaled, shaking her head. Too many mystery novels. Too many crime stories. Everything that had been going on. That had to be it.

Still, as she turned and started for the guest room, a tiny voice in the back of her mind whispered, *"What if you're wrong?"*

Walking back to Elizabeth's door, she turned the knob slowly, pushing the door open just an inch, enough to see Elizabeth asleep in her bed, tucked under the blanket. The room was still, moonlight spilling in across the floor.

No one else was there.

Joyce let out a shaky breath, stepping back and shutting the door carefully.

She was being ridiculous.

But as she slipped into bed a few minutes later, she couldn't quite shake the feeling that someone had been in that room.

Chapter Twenty-One

A new day and the morning light filtering in through the curtains should have chased away the anxious feeling Joyce had when she woke up, but it hadn't. She sat at the kitchen table, a coffee cup warming her hands, staring out the window at the quiet street. She liked Wakeville, but was eager to get back to Parker City. Whenever that would be. It wasn't the big city Baltimore was, but it still made her feel alive. Wakeville was too much like the town where she'd grown up and was all too happy to move away from.

Elizabeth came down the stairs and into the kitchen, ready for work, looking tired. She yawned as she grabbed the coffee pot.

"You're up early," Elizabeth said, pouring herself a cup before sinking into the chair across from Joyce. "I'm usually the one dragging you out of bed."

Joyce hesitated, debating whether to say anything. She could let it go. She didn't want to sound paranoid. She could shake her head and force a smile.

"I didn't sleep that great," she finally admitted.

"Something keep you up?" Elizabeth asked, spooning sugar into her mug.

"I thought I heard something."

Elizabeth looked at her. "Something? Like what?"

Joyce set down her cup. The ceramic clinked against the table top louder than she'd expected, making her flinch. "Voices…a voice…I don't know. But it was coming from your room."

Elizabeth paused, the mug halfway to her lips. "My room?"

"I know it sounds crazy, but yeah. I mean, it could've been my imagination. Or maybe it was something outside. But I was heading to bed after the movie, and I heard you talking. Or…*someone* talking." She trailed off, nervously rubbing her arms.

Elizabeth was quiet for a moment. "You know, I woke up at one point and thought I felt something weird. Like something in the room was…different."

Joyce frowned. "Different how?"

Elizabeth stared into her coffee cup, as if looking for the answer, trying to put words to the feeling. "I don't know. It just felt…like something had been there. It didn't wake me up exactly, but I remember feeling…like I wasn't alone."

A shiver passed over Joyce. "But you didn't hear anything?" she asked softly.

Elizabeth shook her head.

The two of them sat there, the conversation hanging in the air between them. Joyce traced the rim of her coffee cup with her fingertip, trying to ignore the churning in her stomach. She *knew* she'd heard something. She wasn't crazy.

Their conversation was interrupted by the sound of Elizabeth's mother coming down the stairs, humming softly to herself. Joyce and Elizabeth exchanged glances, silently agreeing to drop the subject for now.

"Morning, girls," Marian Blakely said as she tightened the belt of her robe, walking directly to the coffee pot. "You two look like you're ready to start the day."

As her mother poured herself a cup of coffee and went on about her plans for the day, Elizabeth sipped her coffee, not able to shake the nagging thought in the back of her mind—had someone been in her room last night?

Chapter Twenty-Two

The small conference room next to the chief's office on the second floor of the PCPD had become their "War Room," the walls lined with photographs, notes, and copies of every letter received. Pictures of each of the women who'd been threatened stared down at them. Stale coffee, cigarette smoke, and frustration filled the air as Lieutenant Wallace Kerns, along with Officers Nick Caruso and George Wallenbeck, sat around the scuffed wooden table, reviewing the case that was slipping through their fingers.

Pressure was mounting.

The Parker County Sheriff's Department was breathing down their necks, itching to get involved. The mayor had fielded one too many calls from concerned citizens, and the city council was starting to murmur about whether the police department was handling things properly. Chief Stanley had made it clear—bring him a suspect, or he'd be forced to let the county take over.

And no one in that room wanted to feel the chief's wrath if the Sheriff's Department stepped in.

"Let's go through it again," Kerns said, massaging his temples. He hadn't slept well in weeks. None of them had.

Caruso exhaled, shifting in his chair. "We've got a dozen plus letters, all but one of them typewritten and sent through the mail. He pointed a pen at the photo of each woman as he went through the order in which the letters were received. "The letters all have the same style, same phrasing, same paper. No usable fingerprints or anything to identify the sender."

"And no damn leads," Wallenbeck muttered.

Kerns shot him a look but didn't argue. He felt the same way.

"Then, we have Elizabeth Blakely," Caruso continued. "Her letter was handwritten and delivered to her mailbox by, presumably, whoever wrote it. After she received her letter, someone got into her apartment. Again, we assume it was the same person who wrote the letter."

Kerns looked at the photos on the wall in front of him. "So, Blakely was the thirteenth woman to get a letter?"

"Between Stafford and Baxter," Caruso confirmed.

Kerns scratched his chin. "It doesn't make sense. This guy sends eight typewritten letters, then switches it up for Blakely, then goes back to the typewriter." He leaned back in his chair, brow furrowed. "Why?"

Wallenbeck stood and stretched. "I hate to be the one to say it, Lieu, even though we're all thinking it. But we're dealing with two different cases here. I don't think what happened to Elizabeth Blakely is connected to the other women."

"So, what?" Caruso asked. "We have a copycat-type situation? Some guy using the first letters as cover to scare her?"

"Alright," Kerns said, leaning forward. "Looking just at Blakely. What about suspects?"

Caruso tapped his fingers absentmindedly on the table. "I talked to Alfred Marsh, her boss. No indication he's anything other than concerned. Seems pretty squeaky clean. But sometimes it's the quiet ones, right? Then there's this guy named Dick Calhoun…" He trailed off, shaking his head. "A grade-A creep. Doesn't know anything about the letters and says he was at work when the break-in happened, but no one can say for certain whether they saw him or not."

"What if this is all about Elizabeth Blakely, and the *other* women are the smokescreen?" Wallenbeck asked, standing in front of the wall of letters and photos, hands on his hips.

"But he's still tipping his hand by sending a different kind of letter to Blakely," Caruso pointed out. "Not to mention breaking into her apartment."

"None of it makes any damn sense." The lieutenant slammed the palm of his hand down on the table.

"*Unless* it's two different guys," Wallenbeck said, taking Elizabeth's photo and the copy of her letter from its place amongst the rest and moving it to a space by itself.

"So, we got two cases to be working when we don't have enough time or manpower for one." Caruso leaned his elbows on the table and put his head in his hands. "You need to tell the chief."

A knock on the door to the conference room drew all three men's attention.

"Come in!" Kerns shouted, reaching in his pocket and pulling out his cigarettes.

The door opened, and one of the department's senior patrol officers walked in. Hank McMaster, an old-school street cop, was a favorite of Chief Stanley's and on his way up the PCPD ladder. Kerns knew he was next in line to make sergeant and that would only be the beginning.

"Sorry to bother you guys," McMaster said, a stack of papers in his hand. "But I was on my way in to see the chief, and Stull asked if I'd bring this up to you, Wally. It was on the front desk when he got back from the john." He tossed an envelope on the table and left.

As the envelope came to rest in front of him, Kern's eyes grew wide.

On the front of the white envelope, in bright red ink, with a jagged, deliberate hand, was written LIEUTENANT WALLACE KERNS. His eyes immediately flicked up to the copy of the letter Elizabeth Blakely had received. The handwriting looked identical.

Caruso and Wallenbeck exchanged glances. "What's that?"

Kerns flipped the envelope over and pulled out the letter inside. It was also handwritten in red ink.

Wallenbeck leaned forward to read it aloud:

LIEUTENANT KERNS,
    YOU THINK YOU CAN STOP ME, BUT YOU CAN'T.
    YOU HAVE NO IDEA WHAT YOU'RE DEALING WITH.
    BE CAREFUL.

CHAPTER TWENTY-TWO

Silence filled the room.

"Sonofabitch," Caruso muttered.

Kerns' jaw tightened. "It was waiting for me at the front desk."

Wallenbeck's expression darkened. "He walked right into the station and dropped it off. And Stull was in the john?" He ran a hand through his hair. "Now he's sending *you* letters? What the hell does that mean?"

Chapter Twenty-Three

1985...

Elizabeth Marsh stood in front of the Parker City Police Station with Alfred at her side, a flood of emotions washing over her as she looked upon the red brick building. Though it looked much the same as it did twenty years earlier—with its squat, square architecture and black iron lanterns flanking the front doors—the decades had clearly weathered it. The mortar between the bricks was darker and crumbling, and the limestone trim around the windows was stained with streaks from years of rain and neglect.

Stepping through the front doors, Elizabeth immediately noticed that the interior of the station had faired even worse. An entire swath of the linoleum flooring had peeled up from in front of the front desk due to the wear of visitors. And a musty smell filled the air.

As her eyes fell on the officer sitting behind the desk, Elizabeth flashed back to the first time she'd walked into that same building and been met by the friendly Officer Stull. It would have been too much to hope that it was him sitting there again after all this time. In his place was a fifty-something, graying-haired police sergeant with glasses and a wispy mustache, thumbing through a copy of *Sports Illustrated*. His name badge read SHEPARD.

Looking up at the pair in front of him, the desk sergeant laid the magazine down and gave them a friendly smile. "Can I help you, folks?"

"We need to speak with someone," Alfred blurted out, not even sure who to ask for.

Leaning forward, Shepard narrowed his eyes slightly, the smile disappearing. "Is everything alright? What exactly is the nature of your—"

Cutting him off, Elizabeth asked, "Is Lieutenant Kerns still here?"

"Wallace Kerns? I'm afraid not, ma'am. He passed away some time ago."

"What about Jim Stull?"

"Jimmy? He's a sheriff out in Ohio these days. Ma'am, what exactly is this all about?"

Elizabeth turned to Alfred, unable to say anything. Her eyes filled with tears as she clung to his arm for support. Seeing her distress, Shepard stood and looked to Alfred.

"My name is Alfred Marsh, and this is my wife Elizabeth," he began. As he explained the situation and who they were, Sergeant Shepard—who'd been with the PCPD for just over twenty years himself—began to recall the case. He'd only been on the job a matter of months, so was just a patrolman at the time. But he remembered, as more and more letters began showing up, everyone in the department was on edge because they had no idea what kind of crazy person was threatening the women of Parker City, or if it would go beyond simple anonymous messages. It had been a very tense time for everyone. But as he listened to Alfred, he realized he couldn't even imagine what Elizabeth Blakely, now Marsh, had really gone through.

"Mr. and Mrs. Marsh," Shepard said, coming out from behind the desk, "if you'll follow me this way. I'll get Detective Winters. He's the one you'll want to speak with. Please. This way."

Following him through a door, then down a couple of hallways, Alfred and Elizabeth were shown into the same interrogation room she'd been interviewed in twenty years earlier. Interestingly, she noticed the walls were now painted a different color. Some strange shade of green. Of all the things she'd seen that needed repaired or freshened up, she thought it was odd they'd taken the time and spent the money to repaint the interrogation room. And then she thought, with everything already on her mind, how strange it was that she'd even thought of that.

She perched stiffly on the edge of the uncomfortable metal chair, possibly the same one she'd sat on as a terrified younger woman. Only now, she was someone who had managed to build a peaceful life out of a nightmare. Or so she'd believed until the bright red handwriting appeared in her mailbox, snapping the locks off doors she'd spent twenty years trying to keep shut.

Alfred settled into the chair beside her and laid his hand over hers. She hadn't realized how tightly she was gripping the edge of the table until his warm skin made her unclench her fingers.

"You're alright," he whispered. "We're alright. I'm right here with you. I always will be."

She tried to nod, but her eyes kept drifting to the door. It was slightly ajar, allowing the muffled hum of the station in—phones ringing, footsteps echoing off scuffed floors, the low drone of officers swapping stories about their day so far. She hadn't noticed all of that before. Again, she wondered why thoughts like this were crossing through her mind. What difference did it make that she hadn't noticed the sounds of the station around her all those years ago? All she wanted was for someone out there to tell her she was safe.

But she knew no one could.

A knock at the door drew her and Alfred's attention. Before either of them could answer, a young man stepped in.

"Mr. and Mrs. Marsh?" he asked, his voice gentle and warm. He stepped forward and extended his hand to Alfred first, then to her. "I'm Detective Sergeant Ben Winters. Sergeant Shepard filled me in, but I'd like to hear everything from you, if you're up to it."

Elizabeth studied him. There was something trustworthy about his eyes. He might have been young, but she could tell he understood the severity of the situation. Just the way he carried himself and the expression on his face told her he was more experienced than she may have first thought.

"Thank you for seeing us, Detective," Alfred said, easing back into his chair.

Ben nodded and lowered himself into the seat across from them. He opened his notepad and set it next to a battered tape recorder that looked as old as the building itself.

"Mrs. Marsh," Ben said, addressing her directly, "take your time. There's no rush. Just start where you need to."

Elizabeth swallowed, her mouth dry despite the cup of tea she'd barely touched back at home. Her eyes flicked to Alfred, who squeezed her hand once more.

She drew in a slow breath. "Today," she began, her voice steady but verging on the edge of breaking, "I got a letter. In the mail. It…it looked exactly like the letters I received twenty years ago. The same red ink. The same handwriting."

"Alright," Ben said carefully. "Before we get to that. Take me back to the beginning. I'll admit, I was only ten at the time. So, I really had no idea about what was happening. I actually have my partner pulling the old files right now. Can you tell me exactly what happened to you back in…1965, was it?"

Elizabeth closed her eyes and gave a short nod of her head. Twenty years ago, and it felt like only yesterday. Which is why, as she told Ben the story of what had happened, it still felt so fresh in her mind. Every single detail. Occasionally, she'd make eye contact with him, and she could tell he was paying attention to every word she said. He'd been feverishly scribbling so many notes she thought he'd need a whole new notebook by the time they were finished talking.

When she'd finished, she felt a sense of relief that someone was taking her so seriously and not dismissing her. She could tell just by looking at the young detective that his mind was already working, dissecting every detail she'd just given him.

Finally laying his pen down, Ben asked, "The letter you received today, did you bring it with you?"

Alfred reached into his jacket and pulled out the folded letter and envelope it'd come in. Elizabeth couldn't help but look away, her chest tightening at the sight of it. Just seeing it again made her sick.

Ben pulled a handkerchief from his pocket and took the paper from Alfred. "Has anyone else handled this since you found it?"

"No one," Alfred said. "Just her and me."

"Good," Ben said, then lifted his eyes back to Elizabeth. "I'm very sorry, Mrs. Marsh. This must feel like a nightmare. But you did the right thing bringing this straight to us."

"Do you think it's the same person?" Alfred asked. His tone was calm, but the edge beneath it betrayed the fury—and fear—he was trying to hide.

Ben hesitated. "At the moment, there's no way for me to say. And I don't want to mislead you before I really have a chance to look into the old case files. But we'll treat it as though it could be until we know otherwise. I'll get this to the lab today. We'll check for fingerprints. We could get lucky."

Elizabeth pressed a hand to her chest, forcing herself to keep breathing. She didn't know whether to be grateful or terrified.

Ben continued, "I also want to be clear, this may not be the same person. It could be someone copying what they heard about years ago. And now that you've moved back to Parker, they thought they'd play a sick prank. There are people like that. But we'll look at every possibility. You won't be alone in this."

The room fell silent except for the hum of the fluorescent lights overhead. Elizabeth felt the cold metal of the chair beneath her, reminding her she wasn't that helpless girl anymore.

She lifted her chin and looked Ben straight in the eyes. "Detective Winters…please. I can't go through this again. Whoever this is…find him."

Ben's eyes softened, but the determination was still there. "I promise you, my partner and I will do everything we can, Mrs. Marsh."

Outside the interrogation room, the murmur of the station carried on—mundane and oblivious. But for Elizabeth, the world had shifted again. And somewhere out there, she knew—just as she had twenty years ago—someone was watching. But this time, after talking to this young detective, she felt this time might be different, and she felt something like…hope.

Chapter Twenty-Four

After showing the Marshes out, Ben stood for a moment on the front steps of the station watching the two walk down the sidewalk toward their car. It wasn't that he didn't believe the story he'd just heard; he just couldn't imagine it. What Elizabeth Blakely—at the time—had gone through…only to have the case go cold. Then, when she finally thought it was safe to return, it started all over again. Inconceivable.

Ben exhaled and let the summer sun warm his cheeks before turning and walking back inside. He'd placed the letter the Marshes brought with them, along with the envelope it arrived in, in a plastic evidence bag. As he passed the front desk, he asked Shepard for a piece of paper, which he scribbled a quick note on, and then asked the sergeant to have the evidence bag with his instructions sent over to the Maryland State Police. The PCPD didn't have the resources to maintain its own crime lab. So, like many of the jurisdictions around Maryland, they relied on the state police to assist them. The Parker City Police were lucky in the fact that the state's regional crime lab was based right there in the city, only a few minutes from the station. It was almost as good as having their own Crime Scene Unit.

The note Ben had written was addressed to the CSU supervisor, Lieutenant Clover, whom he'd become friendly with over the years. He asked if he would have one of his techs examine the letter for fingerprints. Ben added that this might turn into a priority case and he'd call to explain.

With the letter on its way across town to the State Police Barracks, Ben made his way back up to the Detective Squad's office. The second floor was feeling stuffy today with the heat, and had been making Ben tired. But now his mind was focused on the conversation he'd just had with Elizabeth Marsh and her husband. Could her stalker really have been lying in wait for the last twenty years?

He needed to read the original case file—assuming it wasn't one of the files that had been lost over the years. When Shepard walked in and gave him a quick summary of the situation, Ben sent Tommy down to the Records Room to pull whatever he could find on Elizabeth Blakely and the 1965 investigation.

As he walked into the office, he found Tommy sitting at his desk with a stack of brittle, aging brown file folders in front of him. One of them was open, and his partner was reading through a series of reports.

Looking up from the file, Tommy said, "What have you gotten us into?"

"That bad?" Ben asked, loosening his tie and tossing his notebook down on his desk.

"I'm not sure yet. I mean…this Lieutenant Kerns and his team that were on the case seemed to do everything they could. It was pretty slow going. They just didn't have much to work with at the time. And, the thing is, in some of these summary notes, there's references about the Elizabeth Blakely—now your Elizabeth Marsh—case possibly being completely separate from the much larger investigation. I'm still just digging in and trying to make sense of it all. These files aren't exactly as orderly as *you* would have put them together," Tommy said, motioning to the assortment of papers he had spread out all over his desk.

Knowing he needed to start somewhere, Ben reached over his own desk and took the top file from the stack on Tommy's. Getting comfortable in his chair and pulling a legal pad from his top drawer, Ben opened the folder and started reading the first page, ready to make notes.

It took them a couple hours to read through and review every report, note, and piece of evidence from the original investigation two decades earlier. During that time, the two detectives remained silent, focusing on what was in front of them. Every now and again, though, one of them would break the silence with a sigh or the rustling of papers as they flipped back and forth to compare information. When they were finally finished, they just sat at their desks and stared at each other without saying a word.

Tommy finally spoke.

"Kerns retired before we got here, but I remember some of the old timers talking about him," Tommy said. "He was supposedly pretty sharp."

"Yeah," Ben agreed, thinking back to some of the stories he'd heard when he was still a patrolman.

"At this point," Tommy said, leaning back in his chair and throwing his feet up on his desk, "I would have agreed with Kerns. Whoever was…stalking, for lack of a better word, Blakely, was not the same person sending letters to all the other women."

"Unless he was just trying to cover his tracks," Ben pointed out.

Tommy shook his head. "So cynical."

"Yes. *I'm* the cynical one," Ben said, raising an eyebrow, then continued. "But then we have this guy." He picked up a thick folder and dropped it back on his desk. The impact caused a few sheets of loose paper to flutter. "Ralph Sanderson."

"Changed everything," Tommy said. "When they—"

Tommy was interrupted by a knock on the office door.

The detectives looked over to see Captain Ken Nelson standing in the doorway. Surprised to see him in a tan suit as opposed to his uniform, both Ben and Tommy thought he was one of the most average-looking men they'd ever seen—average height, average build, average brown hair. He could have easily passed for an average middle-aged businessman if it wasn't for the badge hanging from his neck on a chain. Chief Brent's right hand, he was sharp and very good with numbers and analyzing trends. Both detectives agreed he was a good administrator, though they thought sometimes he let the numbers make his decisions for him. When all was said and done, though, he always had the officers' best interest at heart, even if some of the members of the department saw him as the most bureaucratic deputy chief they'd ever had.

"Sorry to disturb you guys," he said, stepping into the room. "I just ran into Shepard downstairs, and he said you might have caught a stalker case related to something that happened twenty years ago? Did I hear that right?"

Bobbing his head up and down, Tommy said, "You did indeed, Captain."

"Those the original files?"

"Yep. And they come with their own dust," Tommy said, picking up one of the folders and blowing a puff of the years' worth that had collected on it in Ben's direction with a devilish grin.

Crossing his arms and propping himself against the wall, Nelson said, "Give me the thumbnail version."

Tommy deferred to Ben as the head of the squad to lay the original investigation out for the captain. He figured Nelson would rather have it without his color commentary anyway. Though Tommy thought that was the best part, he was learning from Ben that being a smartass was not always the way to go.

After Ben's ten-minute summation of events back in the '60s, he wrapped up by saying, "She married Alfred Marsh—who was her boss at the time—and they moved to Virginia. Never got a letter while they were there. And they just recently moved back because they thought enough time had passed." Ben referred to his notes to make sure he hadn't missed any of the salient details.

Nelson shook his head. "And it all starts again. You think this is some sort of copycat? Someone playing a joke on her?"

Ben didn't answer immediately. He leaned back in his chair and put his hands behind his head. "It could be. But after seeing the letter she brought in today and looking at the pictures of the ones she got back in sixty-five, the handwriting looks identical to me. If someone's copying, they'd need access to the original files and evidence, or…they were involved back then."

Nelson knitted his brow.

Rubbing his chin, he then said, "Alright. Well, if you don't have anything else pressing, have at it. Not that I'm discounting the importance of a matter like this, but if something else comes in, the severity of the crime determines the priority of the case."

Ben nodded in agreement, understanding what he was saying. If he could have had his wish, this stalker case would have been the last case they ever dealt with. He'd love for there not to be the kind of crime in Parker City that required a pair of police detectives. But he knew the criminal element was going nowhere. And as Parker City grew, all the same growing pains other cities felt would soon be at their own door.

The captain began to leave, then stopped, turning back to Ben, and asking thoughtfully, "Do you think it's the same person? After twenty years?"

"I don't know what I think yet. But I know we don't have all the information. It says in there the Sheriff's Department got involved. We need to see their files on the case."

"I'll take care of that," Tommy said. Reaching for the telephone, he paused. "Let's say he—or she—was interrupted back then. They wait for twenty years, then pick it back up right when Elizabeth moves back to town? That's not a coincidence."

"No, it's not," Ben agreed. "Which means one of two things. Either this person never left Parker City…or they were watching her all this time from a distance. Waiting."

That thought left a cold silence hanging in the air.

Chapter Twenty-Five

After Ben called Lieutenant Clover to explain the situation with the letter he'd sent over and Tommy made the request for the Sheriff's Department's file on the Blakely case back in '65, they decided there wasn't much more they could do until the next day. They'd been so wrapped up in reviewing the old files and trying to make sense of everything that they'd lost track of time. It wasn't uncommon. There'd been many occasions over the last several years that they'd become so engrossed in what they were working on, they never bothered looking at the clock.

Tommy was first out the door after they decided they'd regroup in the morning and determine their next steps. He said he'd swing by the sheriff's and pick up the file on his way in so they wouldn't have to wait for it to be sent over.

"Tell Christine I said, 'hello,'" Ben said to the back of his partner as he organized the papers and folders on his desk. There was no way he'd be able to leave such a clutter behind. As it was, he had to force himself to ignore Tommy's desk and not walk over and start straightening it up as well.

Finally, after a few more minutes of fussing with the items on his desk, Ben grabbed his suit jacket from the back of his chair and closed his briefcase. On his way down to the ground floor, he said goodnight to the officers he passed in the hallway. Some were heading in, while others were on their way out like him. Soon, the building would be much less active with just the number of people required to run the night shift. He'd spent many evenings surrounded by that stillness as he worked late. He enjoyed the quiet. It let him focus without any distractions. But, as there wasn't much more he could do with the Marsh/Blakely case that evening, he wasn't going to sit in his office just to look like he was working. The chief was the first person to tell Ben to go home when he could and spend time with his fiancée. There would be plenty of nights he'd have to work late, so take the time for himself when he could.

As he pushed through the large metal door opening onto the parking lot behind the station, a strange feeling struck him. A feeling not unlike what Elizabeth Marsh had described to him earlier. He suddenly felt uneasy walking towards his car. As if someone was watching him.

He paused in the middle of the lot, looking across the street over a line of parked patrol cars. A man in a blue baseball cap was lingering at the opening of the lot, looking down at a newspaper.

Ben watched him for a moment, though with his hat pulled down, the shadow obscured his face. Something about the man felt...off. Not threatening, just not right.

Then the man looked up, met Ben's eyes for half a second, and turned away. He walked down the block without so much as a glance back over his shoulder.

Ben's pulse picked up a couple beats. It was just his mind playing tricks on him, he told himself. He'd just spent the afternoon reading about a stalker. It's what was at the forefront of his mind. That had to be the only reason seeing a man standing around on the street caught his eye.

Taking a deep breath, Ben tried to let the air clear his head. Even with the sun just beginning to set, casting a bright orange hue in the sky, the temperature had fallen enough to make it cool and refreshing.

But as he got into his car and started the engine, he couldn't help but feel it again—that anxious sensation. Was it the man he'd just seen or something nagging at the back of his mind? He still had a lot of questions after reading the case file. But was there something specific he'd seen that was now trying to dig its way out of his subconscious?

The drive home was short. It was after the usual rush hour, so there wasn't much traffic. And the apartment he shared with Natalie was just on the other side of town along a quiet residential street lined with elms that cast long shadows in the evening sun.

"You're later than I expected," Nat said with a smile. "I didn't know if you'd make it home for dinner. Did you catch a big case?"

Ben slipped off his shoes and set his briefcase down. "I'm sorry I didn't call. Tommy and I lost track of time again. You didn't have to wait for me."

"Leftovers make terrible conversation." She kissed him on the cheek and motioned toward the kitchen. "Go sit. I'll heat it up."

Ben sat at the table watching Nat move around the kitchen. He loved how easily she filled the space, how comfortable she looked. As far as he was concerned, there wasn't anything she couldn't do. He knew how lucky he was to have found her. Even though their initial meeting was not under the best of circumstances.

It had been his and Tommy's first big case as detectives. They were investigating a series of horrific murders. Two of the victims ended up being students of Natalie's—she was a History teacher at Tasker River High. But it hadn't been until sometime after the case was closed that they began dating. Now, their wedding was in just a matter of weeks, and in the back of his mind, Ben hoped he and Tommy would be able to determine exactly who was behind the latest letter to Elizabeth Marsh before he'd be leaving for his honeymoon.

One of the things he loved most about Nat was that she completely understood how important his job was to him. Just as he knew how important her students were to her. She never questioned him staying out late or gave him a hard time about his job being too dangerous. She wanted him to be safe, of course. But she knew Tommy always had his back. Plus, it wasn't like Parker City was a cesspool of crime to begin with. And, from time to time, Natalie's fresh perspective on a case came in handy.

As she set down the plates, she said, "So, tell me about it. What's got you two so worked up now?"

Between bites of beef stroganoff, he told her a simplified version of what had happened back in 1965. While he hadn't remembered any of it because he was too young, Natalie wasn't originally from Parker and had only settled there after attending Hammermill College and getting a job at the high school. Listening to every word he said, it was clear Natalie was hooked on the details of the red ink, the twenty-year-old letters, and the victim returning after all that time only to find the past waiting for her. By the end, Ben felt more like a storyteller than a police detective summarizing a case.

"You think it's the same person?" Natalie asked.

Ben hesitated. "That's what everyone keeps asking. I have no idea. But whoever it is…they've either been patient for two decades, or they've studied the case inside and out. Either way, it's not good."

She nodded. "You'll figure it out. You always do."

He wanted to believe that. But as he stood washing the dishes, listening to Nat on the phone with her mother—who always managed to call just as they were finishing dinner—that uneasy feeling returned. Not as strong this time. Just enough to annoy him.

Later that night, after Nat had gone to bed, he sat in the living room with the original Blakely file spread out in front of him on the coffee table. Something was still gnawing at him. A detail. A note. Something he saw in the records earlier that hadn't fully registered at the time.

He flipped back through the reports, focusing on the timeline. The dates of the letters. The gaps between them. But nothing was becoming any clearer.

Instead of trying to force the thought to make itself known, he decided to look at any possible suspects Lieutenant Kerns and his team had at the time.

Flipping through the pages, he removed two interview summaries written by an Officer Nick Caruso. While there'd been dozens of interviews conducted throughout the investigation, two stood out to Ben. As, apparently, they did to the investigators at the time.

The first was Alfred Marsh. As Elizabeth's boss at Upton's Department Store, Caruso wondered in his notes if he'd taken too much of an interest in one of his secretaries. That would certainly prove interesting if Marsh had been her stalker, considering she ended up marrying him. That certainly could have been motive—scare her into his arms, promising to protect her. But then why send a letter now? What sense did that make? Plus, Ben didn't get a bad feeling from the guy when they spoke earlier at the station. He trusted his gut, and Alfred Marsh seemed like a stand-up kind of guy. Very old school. Even a little stuffy. Ben just didn't get the devious stalker vibe from him.

He thought about having Tommy interview him separately to see what he thought. It was always good to keep an open mind and get a second opinion.

The person who Ben was most intrigued by—due to the comments from Caruso and his partner, Wallenbeck—was a Richard "Dick" Calhoun. Another manager at Upton's, but by all accounts, a real sleazebag. Ben wondered if Calhoun was still around. He made a note to run a check on him tomorrow.

As Johnny Carson was beginning his monologue, Ben decided to call it quits and head to bed. If nothing else, they had somewhere to start. He wanted to track down Dick Calhoun and have a conversation with him—assuming he was still around—and Alfred Marsh. They'd shake a couple of trees and see if anything fell out. If that didn't work, then maybe something in the sheriff's file would give them a lead. Ben wasn't even trying to delude himself into believing CSU might find fingerprints on the most recent letter. That would just be too much to wish for.

The beginning of any case was always exhilarating and frustrating at the same time. Ben's desire to charge ahead needed to be tempered by the lack of initial information. A true police investigation wasn't like what people saw on television. More often than not, it was slow and drawn out. And with this case seeming to have its roots in events that happened so long ago, Ben knew he was going to have to be patient as he and Tommy started to put the pieces together for themselves.

Chapter Twenty-Six

The next morning, Ben was awake well before his alarm clock was set to go off. Not an uncommon occurrence. Instead of lying there staring at the ceiling, he got up, took a shower, made coffee, and sat down to read the newspaper. He wasn't too concerned with waking Natalie as she'd proven to be a sound sleeper. Especially on her days off. And being that she was on summer break, she'd been sleeping in quite a bit.

Even with their wedding day just around the corner, Nat was showing no signs of stress. She was as calm and collected as ever. All of the wedding plans had fallen into place a long time ago because she'd had an army of bridesmaids to help put it together.

Tommy made fun of Ben for being organized to a fault, but when it came to the wedding details, Natalie had reached a completely different level. And though Tommy was right there witnessing the preparations, he never dared make fun of her organizational skills. He valued his personal safety too much for that.

Ben was glad his soon-to-be wife and best friend got along so well. That was important to him. When the three of them were together, they could have serious conversations or spend the evening laughing. Most of the time, they were having a good time and relaxing, not having too many deep philosophical discussions or trying to solve the world's problems. And Christine had fit into the mix so easily, he and Nat were beginning to wonder if she might be around on a more permanent basis. After all, Tommy had been spending so much time with her, and it really did seem like a completely different relationship than Ben had ever seen his friend in before.

Just as he was finishing the paper and laying it down on the kitchen table next to his empty coffee mug, Natalie emerged from the bedroom.

"Do I smell coffee?"

"Yes. You do."

"Do I smell bacon and eggs?"

Looking over to the empty stove, then back at Nat with a confused expression, Ben answered, "No…"

"Could I?"

Ben laughed.

"I'd be happy to make some for you," Ben said, standing and going over to pour her a cup of coffee, "but last I checked, we ate all the bacon this weekend."

"A girl can dream," she said, taking the steaming cup from his hands. "Thank you."

Taking the first sip, Ben watched as the wave of caffeine worked its way into her system.

"Did you make any progress in the case after I went to bed?" she asked, sitting down at the table and unfolding the paper so she could read the front page. "You weren't up too late, were you? I didn't hear you come to bed."

Ben sighed.

"I feel like there's something staring me right in the face, but I just can't put my finger on it." Then, after pouring himself a second cup of coffee, he went on saying, "But I do know where we're going to start. There're two guys that the original team investigating the case specifically noted. Tommy and I will start by talking to them."

"You think they're still around after twenty years?"

"Well…one of them definitely is. It's the husband."

"Wait a minute," Natalie said, lowering the newspaper. "They thought the husband was a suspect? That *he* was the one sending the threatening notes?"

"He wasn't the husband at the time. He was her boss at the department store."

"Uh huh." Then, after thinking for a moment, she asked, "Why would he send her another note now?"

"A very good question, Detective Kirkpatrick. I must be rubbing off on you. You're turning out to be a pretty good sleuth. I had the same question. I know it doesn't make sense, but I still want to talk to him. You never know."

"Maybe it's a Jekyll and Hyde kind of thing, and he doesn't even know he's doing it. What's that called? A split personality! There. I solved your case for you."

Smiling and shaking his head, Ben said, "If only that were true, I'd take the day off. You'd better be careful, though. Throwing out theories involving things like Dr. Jekyll and Mr. Hyde makes you sound a lot like Tommy."

"Oh, please! Tommy's first thought is always a ninja assassin," Natalie protested.

"Actually, last time I think he thought it was a *Soviet* assassin. But I could be wrong. It's hard to keep track of his theories," Ben said with an innocent shrug.

Chapter Twenty-Seven

Ben was usually one of the first people to arrive at the station in the morning. He liked to have the time to get himself organized and take care of any business that might have been left over from the previous day. Then, by the time the overnight incident readouts landed on his desk and he reviewed them to see if there was anything he and Tommy might find coming their way, he was ready to hit the ground running.

Most days, it was a toss-up as to whether he or Chief Brent would be the first one with an office on the second floor to show up. Whoever did, started the first pot of coffee in the upstairs break room. Then, at some point, as they were filling their cups, they'd spend a few minutes chatting about things outside of their official duties. Sports was always a popular topic. It had allowed Ben and the chief to become friendly over the years and get to know one another better.

Today, the chief's unmarked Crown Vic was already in its spot when Ben pulled into the parking lot. As he got out of the car and collected his suit jacket and briefcase from the backseat, he wondered if he should tell Brent about the Marsh case. The chief was by no means a micromanager. He trusted his people and let them do their jobs. He just wanted to be kept in the loop on the big cases or anything that might end up on the front page of the newspaper.

Right now, Ben wasn't sure if what he had rose to the level of taking it directly to the chief. Captain Nelson knew what the Detective Squad was going to be working on for the time being, and Ben would finish his report on the Marsh interview from yesterday and pass it up the chain. Then, if the chief had any questions, he'd be happy to brief him. By that point, he and Tommy may have made some headway once they compared the sheriff's case file with their own.

On his way in, Ben stopped by the Watch Commander's office to see if anything interesting had happened overnight. Other than a call for a possible prowler, a couple of boozers being hauled in on drunk and disorderly charges, and an arrest for shoplifting at the Highs convenience store on the south side of town, it had been a quiet night.

With that in mind, Ben climbed the stairs to the second floor and the Detective Squad's office. After hanging his jacket on the back of his chair and removing all the files he'd taken home from his briefcase, he started making notes on the chalkboard he and Tommy used to organize their investigations. He started with a timeline of the original incidents, then made a list of the key people they'd come across in the files. He then boxed off the right side of the board and at the top wrote BLAKELY/MARSH 1985 and underlined it. Beneath that, he drew a giant question mark. He had too many questions to write them all down at the moment. And he'd like to think through them and group them in some sort of order before adding them to the board.

When he was finished, he stood looking at everything he'd written, hoping by seeing it presented in a different way, a light bulb might go off like in the cartoons, and he'd have a brilliant idea. Nothing was coming to him.

Instead of continuing to stare at the chalkboard and frustrating himself, he decided to start the search for Richard Calhoun. If he still lived in Parker City, it wouldn't be too difficult to find him. But if in the intervening twenty years he'd moved away, it might take some more time and phone calls.

Reaching into the bottom drawer of his desk, he removed the latest edition of the Parker County telephone book. The thick directory seemed to get bigger and bigger with each new printing. Flipping through the pages, Ben ran his finger along the names beginning with the letter C. He found five telephone numbers associated with someone with the last name Calhoun—a Darlene, Frank, Jonathan, Leonard, and an R.H.

If the guy they were looking for was any one of these, he'd be R.H.

Ben wrote the address and phone number in his notebook, then reached for the telephone. He dialed a contact he'd made at the Parker County branch of the Motor Vehicle Administration.

"MVA, this is Brendan Yates. How may I help you?"

"Brendan, Ben Winters. How are you?"

"I'm doing well, Detective. What can I do for you?"

"I have a name I'd like to run by you if I could. I'm looking for a Richard Calhoun. Would be in his fifties. I found an R.H. Calhoun at three-forty-seven Grant Avenue. Anything you can give me on that?"

"Give me one second," he said, then Ben heard the sound of typing on a keyboard come over the line. After a moment, Yates returned, saying, "There is a driver's license issued to a Richard Henry Calhoun at that address with a birthdate of October fourteenth, nineteen thirty-five. That would make the guy…fifty…two. How's that?"

"That's great. Thanks, Brendan. I appreciate the help."

Hanging up, Ben circled the address in his notebook and leaned back in his chair. They had a place to begin. Sometimes, that was the most difficult part of a new case, finding the starting point.

Looking up at the clock on the wall, he noticed that Tommy was running late. He figured it was because he'd detoured to the Sheriff's Department on his way in. And if he got talking to his friends over there, who knew how long he'd be held up? The stories Ben had heard some of them tell bordered on unbelievable. But he knew it was all in good fun and camaraderie.

No sooner had the thought crossed his mind, Tommy strolled in with a stack of folders tucked under his arm.

"Our friends over at the sheriff's did not disappoint," he said, placing the files on Ben's desk, then removing his jacket and hanging it on the back of his chair. "I skimmed through some of that in the car, and it is one of the most detailed case files I've ever seen. It looks like they interviewed everyone in Parker City at the time. A guy by the name of Ray Noble ran the investigation. Turns out, Noble was something of a legend."

Ben knew the name. "I've heard the name. Next to good old Sheriff Samuel Tildon back during the Civil War, Ray Noble may be the most famous lawman in Parker County."

"And, according to my buddies, he's still alive and well and living over in Middleboro. Which means we can go talk to him about the case."

"That could be helpful. As can this," Ben said, holding up his notebook and pointing to the circled information. "I have Calhoun's address and telephone number."

"Well, look at that," Tommy said, dropping into his chair. "We've both been productive this morning."

"I've also added two people to our list to talk to." Ben pointed to the chalkboard. "The roommate, Joyce Osbourne."

"Are you thinking this is a Jill the Ripper kind of thing?" Tommy asked, referring to the theory that posited the legendary Victorian killer was actually a woman, and maybe that was the case with Blakely's tormentor.

"It's not unthinkable," Ben said. "But I'm keeping my mind open. Regardless, she was a firsthand witness to everything that happened. It can't hurt to hear what she has to say."

Sitting up in his chair and leaning forward with his elbows on the desk in front of him, Tommy's expression became somewhat serious.

"Exactly how hard are we going to run on this one? I mean, we're not even really sure what it is we're dealing with. If they couldn't figure out who was doing this twenty years ago, at the time it was happening, who says we can? I'm not trying to get out of work here. And, after reading the files, there's no question she went through something traumatic, but...what are we doing?"

"I get it. It's hard enough to solve a case after forty-eight hours have passed, let alone two full decades. But this is what we do. We owe it to Elizabeth Marsh. And you heard the captain. We work the case until something else comes up."

Tommy put his hands up. "I get it. I just thought it should be said. So, who's the other person?"

"What?

"You said you had two more names to add to the list. The roommate is one. Who's the other?"

"LuCoco," Ben said flatly.

Tommy dropped his head into his hands. "I was hoping you missed that. I should have known the minute you mentioned Osbourne, you would have seen his name on the interview summary."

Officer Buck LuCoco was Tommy's least favorite person in the entire department. The young, fresh-eyed detective found the longtime patrolman to be lazy, and a throwback to the time when cops would throw the book at a person—literally—just to get the answer they wanted to hear. In their time on the force, Ben and Tommy had seen LuCoco do as little as possible, which partially explained why he was never promoted out of patrol. That, and the fact he himself didn't want to take on any more responsibility.

"He's the only member of the original investigation team we have to talk to," Ben pointed out. "Besides, you just need to play nice with him for a couple more weeks. He's retiring, and I hear moving all the way down to Florida. You'll never have to see him again."

"Don't tease me like that," Tommy said.

"I'm no fan of Buck's either. But when he's out of here, you have to admit, we're going to lose a lot of institutional knowledge. He's been around longer than anyone else in the PCPD at this point. Think about how some of the things he was around for and remembered helped us before. That resource will be gone," Ben reminded.

Releasing a dramatic sigh, Tommy said, "Why do you always have to be so rational and make so much sense? It's really annoying."

Ben smiled.

"Anyway," he said. "After we go through the sheriff's files, let's—"

He was interrupted by a sharp knock on the door.

"Detectives, sorry, but the watch commander sent me up with a message," Officer Neil Thompson said, holding a piece of paper out to Ben. "There's been a call for police and paramedics to two-oh-five Willowdale Way. There's been a stabbing."

Actually scratching his head, Tommy asked, "Why does that address sound familiar?"

Ben was already on his feet, grabbing his jacket. "Because it belongs to

Elizabeth and Alfred Marsh."

Chapter Twenty-Eight

1965...

Lieutenant Wallace Kerns stood at the window of his office, staring out at the street. The cigarette he'd lit but hadn't begun smoking hung forgotten between his fingers. The letter sat on his desk in an evidence bag, its words still burning in his mind.

His name, written in the same jagged red ink as Elizabeth Blakely's letter, was scrawled across the envelope like it was taunting him.

Caruso and Wallenbeck had gone to grab some coffee and talk to Officer Stull down at the front desk. Returning to the second floor, they joined Kerns in his office across the hall from the War Room. Both men sat quietly, sipping their coffee, watching the lieutenant.

Then, the door burst open and Chief Edgar Stanley marched in.

"What in the ever-loving hell is this, Kerns?" he barked, jabbing a stubby finger at the letter on the desk.

Kerns didn't flinch. "Exactly what it looks like, Chief. He sent me a letter."

Stanley yanked the cigar from his mouth and blew a ring of smoke toward the ceiling. "So now the sonofabitch isn't just harassing women—he's playing with my department?"

Caruso shifted uncomfortably. "Looks that way, sir."

Stanley slammed a fist onto Kerns' desk, rattling the lamp. "This is exactly the kind of bullshit Sheriff Colsh is looking for to shove his damn nose into this case! You know he's been chomping at the bit, waiting for us to slip up so he can swoop in and make a spectacle out of this. The mayor's already up my ass about it."

Kerns exhaled, doing his best to keep his frustration in check. "We haven't slipped up."

"The hell we haven't!" Stanley growled. "We've got, what, a dozen letters, a break-in, a woman scared out of her apartment, and now our lead investigator gets a damn threat delivered right to his desk. Meanwhile, we got *nothing* to show for it. No suspect, no arrest, no idea who the hell we're even chasing. You think that's gonna fly when Colsh shows up in here demanding to take over? We're just lucky no one outside Parker City has gotten a letter yet. Because the minute someone does, Colsh sure as hell will take the whole thing away from us."

Silence filled the room.

Stanley jammed the cigar back between his teeth. "We have got one shot at this before it gets yanked out from under us."

Kerns glanced down at the letter again. "Do you want us to haul in every typewriter in the city? See if the typing matches the letters. Not that that would work for this one and the one Elizabeth Blakely got."

Stanley nodded sharply. "I want you to do whatever needs to be done."

Wallenbeck ran a hand through his hair. "Well, what about Elizabeth Blakely?"

Kerns exhaled. "If he's focused on me now, maybe he'll lay off her."

"Or maybe he's just adding you to the list," Caruso muttered.

Stanley's face darkened. "Then you better figure out which it is—and fast. Because I'll be damned if I'm letting that smug sonofabitch Colsh waltz in here and take my case."

The chief turned on his heels and stormed out of the office, leaving behind a cloud of smoke.

The three men sat in silence.

After a few moments, Caruso said, "So…it looks like the chief doesn't think we're talking about two different guys here."

"Yeah," Kerns said, shaking his head. "I'd hoped to be able to talk to him about that. Didn't work out so well. What did Stull have to say?" he asked, dropping into his seat and stubbing out the untouched cigarette.

"He feels real bad about not being at the desk," Wallenbeck said. "But he needed to go to the can and said he was only gone a couple minutes. It was a quiet morning. He didn't think anything would happen while he was gone."

"No one down there saw anything?" Kerns asked, a hint of desperation in his tone.

"Sorry, Lieu." Wallenbeck leaned forward, elbows on his knees.

Kerns tossed his glasses on the desk. "I'll type up the report about this," he said, motioning to the letter on his desk. "But we need to keep this as quiet as possible. If the papers find out about it… In the meantime, one of you get it dusted for prints."

"You think he's gonna mess up now?" Caruso asked. "We haven't gotten any usable prints yet."

"He's bound to screw up sometime," Kerns said, rubbing his eyes. "We just need him to make one misstep. Let's just hope it's sooner rather than later. Because the way it's going, that may be the only way we catch whoever's doing this."

Chapter Twenty-Nine

It had already been a busy day, and it wasn't even lunchtime. Alfred Marsh had run from meeting to meeting since he'd arrived at Upton's that morning. The end of the year was always a busy time. And even though there were still a couple weeks before the new year began, he was already heavily involved with plans for things that wouldn't even happen until *next* Christmas. He was in no way a salesman, which is why his place as one of the top executives at the city's largest department store always seemed unfitting. But he was a numbers guy. He was levelheaded, practical, and could see patterns in sales and ways to improve revenue in his sleep. That was why he was such a trusted advisor to Daniel Upton, the chairman of the company.

At the moment, though, Alfred found himself distracted. He was idly tapping his pen on his desk, his eyes flicking to the clock on the wall. Nearly an hour had passed since he'd last seen Elizabeth, and she still hadn't returned.

He'd noticed she wasn't at her desk in passing when he'd returned from all the early meetings and assumed she had stepped away for a few minutes to powder her nose. But when those minutes began adding up, he'd become concerned. He checked the break room and asked Donna to look in the ladies' lounge. None of the other secretaries knew where she'd disappeared to either, but Donna pointed out her coat was missing as well.

Just as Alfred was about to head downstairs to look for her, she appeared in the hallway, stepping out of the elevator.

"There you are," Alfred said. "I was starting to think you'd run off to the

Bahamas."

Elizabeth blinked at him as if she'd forgotten where she was for a moment. She forced a smile. "Oh. No, just needed some fresh air. Sorry."

She moved to brush past him, but Alfred wasn't about to let her go that easily.

"Are you alright?" he asked, lowering his voice and placing a hand under her elbow.

"I'm fine," she said quickly, tucking a loose strand of hair behind her ear. "Really."

Alfred frowned. He could tell when something wasn't right. She had a distant look in her eyes, as if her mind was somewhere else.

"Elizabeth," he said gently, stepping in front of her.

She let out a small sigh and looked up into his eyes. "I just needed to clear my head, that's all. I didn't mean to worry you."

Alfred studied her face for a moment. "Where did you go?"

She hesitated for just a fraction too long before answering, "Nowhere, really. Just...around the block."

Alfred crossed his arms. "You weren't at your desk for nearly an hour."

Elizabeth shifted slightly, gripping the strap of her purse. "I lost track of time."

Alfred wasn't convinced. She wasn't lying. Not outright, at least, but there was something else. Something she wasn't telling him.

"I'm sorry. I'll work through lunch to make up for it," she offered.

"I don't care about that. I just want to make sure you're okay. You're what I care about. Did something happen?"

"No," she said quickly—a little too quickly. "I just...needed to be alone for a little bit. That's all, Alfred. You really are so sweet. The way you've been looking after me."

Alfred sighed and stepped back. "Alright. But if something's wrong, you know you can talk to me, right?"

Elizabeth nodded, offering another small smile. "Of course I know. You really are wonderful."

He couldn't help but smile, looking deep into her beautiful sapphire eyes.

He'd come to realize over the last few days, he would do anything to protect her.

"You'll have to make up your time another day," he said, "because we still have reservations for lunch at the Derby Room today."

She smiled a genuine smile as she passed him, walking into the office and settling at her desk as though nothing had happened. But Alfred wasn't fooled. Something had happened while she was gone.

He was just walking through the door to his office when he heard a voice behind him.

"Excuse me, Miss Blakely?"

Alfred turned as one of the salesclerks from downstairs stepped into the office, a young woman in a smart navy dress. She held an envelope in her hand, looking nervous.

Elizabeth glanced up. "Yes?"

The clerk hesitated before walking over to her desk. "This was left at one of the counters downstairs. I…um…I thought you should have it right away."

As Elizabeth reached out to take the envelope, her fingers began to tremble. Alfred turned and began walking toward her desk, already sensing something was wrong.

"No one saw who left it," the salesgirl continued, wringing her hands. "I stepped away for just a moment to help a lady looking at coats, and when I came back, it was just sitting there on the counter."

Elizabeth stared down at the envelope.

Alfred could see her entire body tense. He didn't even think she was breathing.

Slowly, she turned the envelope over, instantly focusing on the bright red letters. Sliding a finger under the flap, she opened it and pulled out a single sheet of paper.

The handwriting was unmistakable.

ELIZABETH,
YOU THINK YOU CAN HIDE? YOU CAN'T.

I ALWAYS KNOW WHERE TO FIND YOU.

Elizabeth's throat tightened.

Alfred was making his way around the desk. "Elizabeth?"

She didn't answer. She just stared at the letter, the color draining from her face.

Chapter Thirty

Elizabeth's fingers trembled as she held the letter. Her heart was racing, and the office around her seemed to be closing in. She couldn't breathe. She was feeling as though her legs were going to go out from under her. But all of a sudden, Alfred's hand was on her arm.

"Elizabeth?" Alfred's voice was cautious, his brow furrowing as he looked over her shoulder, fearing he already knew what he would see. "What is it?"

She swallowed, willing herself to push down the rising panic. Without a word, she handed him the letter. He read it, his jaw tightening. Donna, who'd been working at her own desk, stood and craned her neck to see what the fuss was about.

"Oh my God," she whispered.

Alfred folded the letter carefully, his expression more intense than any of the girls had ever seen. "You didn't see who left this?" he turned and asked the clerk, who was looking on nervously.

She shook her head quickly, still clutching the small stack of sales slips she'd been carrying. "No. I was helping a customer, and when I came back to the counter, it was just… there." She exhaled. "I swear, it wasn't there…"

Alfred turned back to Elizabeth. "We're going to the police."

She opened her mouth to protest, but the look on his face stopped her. He wasn't asking.

Elizabeth felt weak, helpless, as though whoever was doing this to her was watching her at that very moment, waiting to see her reaction.

"I just need a second," she murmured, stepping away from them, turning slightly so no one could see her face.

Alfred didn't move. He was still gripping the letter, his hands tightening into fists. "This has to stop."

Elizabeth tried to steady herself. The letter could have been left by anyone. The store was busy, people coming and going. It could have even been left by someone who worked in the store. The thought horrified her. Could someone at Upton's be behind this?

She inhaled slowly. "I'll go to the police."

The relief obvious on Alfred's face. But before he could say anything, a voice interrupted them.

"Well, well. What's got you all worked up, sweetheart?"

Elizabeth turned and felt her stomach twist.

Dick Calhoun was standing there with his hands in his pockets, a lazy grin tugging at his lips. But there was something in his eyes—amusement, as if he knew exactly what was happening—that made Elizabeth recoil.

Alfred squared his shoulders, stepping slightly in front of her. "Not now, Dick."

Dick's grin widened as he took a slow step closer, ignoring Alfred. "You look a little pale, Elizabeth. Bad news?"

She didn't answer.

Dick glanced at Alfred's hand, at the folded letter. His smile didn't waver, but his eyes flicked back to hers, sharp and calculating. "Everything alright? I'd be happy to help if I can."

Elizabeth forced herself to stay calm. She wasn't about to let Dick Calhoun of all people see her shaken. "That won't be necessary."

Dick shrugged, his gaze lingering on her for a second too long before he turned, whistling softly as he sauntered into his office.

Alfred watched him go, his expression unreadable, then turned back to Elizabeth. "Come on," he said quietly. "Let's get out of here."

Elizabeth nodded, but as she followed him toward the door, she couldn't shake the feeling that someone was still watching her. That whoever had left the letter was still close. And that this was all just the beginning.

Chapter Thirty-One

Lieutenant Kerns sat at the head of the table in the cramped, smoke-filled conference room, tapping a pen against his notepad as cigarette smoke lazily circled above his head. The walls were still lined with photographs, letters, and notes—each one a piece of a puzzle that refused to come together. The coffee in his cup had gone cold, but he hadn't touched it in the last hour. His focus was entirely on the case sprawled out in front of him.

Receiving a letter at the station had changed things. It was a direct challenge to Kerns and the investigation as a whole. Then, when Elizabeth Blakely showed up with a letter left for her at Upton's that morning, it confirmed Kerns's worst fear—that this case was spiraling out of control. And in so doing, it sent Chief Stanley over the edge. The only good that had come from the recent developments was that Kerns's longstanding request for additional officers to help his already overstretched team was finally granted.

Chief Stanley had thrown two more men onto the case, realizing that if they didn't start making progress, the whole thing would be snatched out from under them. Sheriff Colsh had already spoken with the mayor, who would, no doubt, see the two newly arrived letters as an escalation and call in the Sheriff's Department. The PCPD needed a breakthrough—fast. This was probably their last chance.

Now, along with Nick Caruso and George Wallenbeck, two new officers sat at the table. Jimmy Stull, who was young, energetic, and still trying to prove himself in the department, and Buck LuCoco, a ten-year veteran of the PCPD who'd seen his fair share of incidents over the years and had already become numb to pretty much all of it.

Kerns leaned forward, his chair creaking as he shifted his weight.

"Alright," he said, looking at the men assembled before him. "Now that we have more hands on this, here's how we're moving forward."

He turned toward Caruso, who was already rubbing his temples. "I want you back at Upton's. You and Jimmy. Talk to *everyone*. Co-workers, executives, salesclerks, hell, even the janitors. I want to know if anyone was having problems with her or if anyone knows of someone *she* was having trouble with.

"And while you're there, see if they happen to have any security cameras that might have seen whoever left that letter for her this morning. I've heard some stores are starting to put them in. Maybe we'll get lucky."

"Don't you think that Marsh guy would have told us about any cameras when he was here with Blakely?" Wallenbeck asked innocently.

"He seemed real worked up," Caruso muttered. "Could've slipped his mind."

"Well, find out," the lieutenant said. "And that's another thing—Alfred Marsh—I want to know more about him, too. Is he really just a concerned boss, or is there a reason he's taken such an interest in one of his girls?"

"Same could be said for that Calhoun character," Caruso pointed out.

Kerns nodded. "Yeah, him too. I want a full rundown on both of them."

"That's gonna be a lot for just the two of us," Caruso said, glancing over to Stull sitting next to him.

"Tell me something I don't know," Kerns shot back.

Then he turned to LuCoco. "Buck, I want you to go over everything we have so far and get familiar with the case. Fresh eyes and all. Then, talk to Joyce Osbourne."

"She's the roommate, right?" LuCoco asked.

"Right. But I don't want you talking to her just about Elizabeth. I want to know about her, too. She's been involved in this since the beginning. Find out everything she knows. Who she's been seeing, where she's been."

The corner of LuCoco's lip curled into a smirk. "You think she could be the one sending the letters?"

Kerns shook his head, "That's what we need to figure out. Even if she isn't involved, maybe someone she runs with is. You know the kind of guys we're looking for."

"Creeps." LuCoco nodded. "Yeah. I've met a few. They're my specialty."

Kerns sat back in his chair and picked up his coffee cup, taking a sip, he instantly regretted it. "I'm going over to Wakeville to talk to Elizabeth's parents. I want to know if they've noticed anything strange. If they've had any unexpected visitors, or if she's been acting differently around them. Maybe they have some idea who could be doing this."

Stull leaned forward. "You think this guy followed her there?"

Kerns sighed, running a hand over his face. "I don't know. But if he's got the nerve to break into her apartment and show up at her place of work, not to mention *hand deliver* a threat to a police station, why couldn't he follow her?"

The room fell completely silent.

Wallenbeck cleared his throat. "What about me, Lieu? What do you want me doing?"

Kerns looked up at the wall of letters and photos. "We can't ignore the other letters. Go back to the post office. Start at the beginning. Talk to everyone there again. See if any of them can remember anything they didn't the first time we talked to them. Or if they've seen anything since. Someone acting strange, someone they don't usually see coming in. Anything that seemed off. I don't care how small of a detail it seems."

"We've already talked to everyone at the post office," Wallenbeck said, reaching for the folder that contained the statements they'd taken after the first letters began showing up.

"I know," Kerns said. "But it's been a couple weeks. See if any of them have thought of anything."

"You thinking the guy's taking the letters to the post office? Not just putting them in a mailbox?" LuCoco asked.

"We have no idea one way or the other," Kerns admitted. "Which is why we can't rule anything out."

LuCoco leaned back in his chair and stared up at the ceiling. "Doesn't seem like there's a lot to go on."

Kerns ignored the remark and turned back to Wallenbeck. "When you're done at the post office, head over to Upton's and help them. And where are we on finding out how the paper got a picture of that damn letter?"

Wallenbeck shook his head. "I don't have anything I can prove, Lieu. But there are a couple guys in the department who are close to the sheriff."

Kerns slumped in his chair. Getting that letter in the paper was Colsh's doing. He was trying to use public pressure to get his hands on the case.

Shaking it off, Kerns said, "Alright. Fine. I'll figure out how to deal with that later. We have more important matters to deal with right now. You all know what you need to do. Get to it."

Assignments handed out, orders given, a contemplative silence settled over the room again.

Finally, Kerns pushed back from the table and stood. "I want reports back by the end of the day on whatever you've got."

"How long do we actually have until Colsh takes over?" Caruso asked solemnly, standing and adjusting the holster on his belt.

"The clock's already ticking, boys," Kerns answered, his tone grim.

One by one, the officers gathered their notes and filed out. Kerns was left alone in the room, staring at the board of letters pinned against the wall. The one with his name written in jagged red ink stood out among the others. "Sonofabitch," he said under his breath.

Chapter Thirty-Two

Nick Caruso and Jimmy Stull unbuttoned the long wool coats they wore over their uniforms as they stepped through the doors of Upton's Department Store. The place quietly hummed as customers shuffled from counter to counter, looking at the variety of offerings. Despite the polished veneer, Caruso felt a tension lingering in the air. Employees and shoppers stole nervous glances at the two uniformed officers, their presence at odds with the festive holiday atmosphere surrounding them.

Remembering the direction to the executive offices from his first time speaking with Alfred Marsh, Caruso led the way toward the elevators. As they rode to the third floor, Caruso leaned over to Stull. "First rule of interviews, kid. Watch how people act before they even open their mouths. Half the time, their faces tell you more than their words."

Stull nodded, pulling out his notepad.

Once on the third floor, Caruso opened the door to the Accounting and Business Office, nodded to the secretary he remembered as Donna, and walked straight over to Alfred Marsh's office. He could feel the eyes of all the secretaries following him, but he ignored them. Police turning up in one's workplace tended to set people on edge. It was something he'd grown accustomed to. But there was a job to do. And if a person wasn't involved in something that would attract the police's attention, then they had nothing to worry about.

Knocking on the closed door, a muffled "Come in" came from inside.

Pushing the door open, the officers found Marsh sitting behind his desk, a printout in one hand, a pen in the other. His office, much like his appearance, was immaculate—papers stacked in neat piles, a polished brass nameplate gleaming under the soft light of the desk lamp.

"Mr. Marsh," Caruso said, stepping inside with Stull right behind him. "Lieutenant Kerns sent us over to ask a few more questions."

"Of course. Please, come in. Have a seat."

Caruso remained standing. "We'll keep it brief. We just need to go over some things again."

Alfred nodded, folding his hands on the desk. "Anything to help Elizabeth. This whole situation has been...terrible."

Caruso watched him for a moment before speaking. "You seemed pretty worked up when you brought her into the station this morning. You and she have a close working relationship?"

Alfred's brow furrowed slightly. "She's a valued employee. Like I told you before, I wish everyone working here was like her. She's one of the best we have. I feel responsible for making sure she's safe. I wouldn't want something like this to happen to any of the girls out there."

Stull scribbled in his notepad. Caruso wondered what the younger officer had found so important to make note of.

"I know I've asked you this before, Mr. Marsh, but maybe you've remembered something since the first time we spoke," Caruso said. "Have you thought of anyone who has a problem with Miss Blakely?"

Marsh sighed. "No. I mean, I've tried to think of anyone who could be doing this. But everyone here likes Elizabeth."

Caruso crossed his arms. "What about you, Mr. Marsh? You've taken quite an interest in her well-being. Just how far does that concern go?"

Leaning forward, resting his elbows on the desk, and clasping his hands together, Alfred asked, "Are you implying something?"

"I'm implying that we have to look at everybody," Caruso said coolly. "You're in a position of authority over her. Some men let that kind of power go to their heads."

"Elizabeth is an employee and yes...a friend. I *do* care about her. So...I guess...it is more than just professional. But I would never do something like this to Elizabeth. Or anyone, for that matter. You can't think I've been sending all those letters. Can you?"

Caruso was watching him closely. "Like I said, Mr. Marsh. We need to look at all the possibilities. I'm not accusing anyone of anything right now. I'm just trying to get all the facts." He paused to let that sink in.

In his gut, Officer Caruso didn't think Alfred Marsh was involved. It was obvious to anyone looking, the guy clearly had feelings for Elizabeth Blakely. But he wasn't the suave, charming, sweep-'em off their feet type. Sure, he was good-looking, but he came off as awkward and shy. Plus, Caruso had been on the job long enough to know to trust his instincts, and they were saying Marsh was one of the good guys in all this. But he still needed to do his job and check him out.

"One more thing," Caruso said, closing his notebook. "Does Upton's have any security cameras installed?"

Marsh hesitated for half a second, running a hand through his perfectly slicked hair. "Believe it or not, that is a project we have been discussing for next year—having cameras installed near the doors and cash registers. I wish we had them now. We'd be able to see who left that damn letter this morning."

Caruso exhaled, exchanging a look with Stull.

"Officers, I want to help however I can."

"Good to hear, because we want to talk to the staff. Everyone who works here," Caruso said. "We'll start with the people up here in the offices—the ones who interact with Miss Blakely the most, then we'll move on from there."

"Of course, but that's a lot of people. I mean—"

"Let us worry about that, Mr. Marsh. But it would help if there was somewhere we could talk to them…privately."

"Yes. Right. Well…there's a conference room down the hall you can use. I can have someone bring you some coffee. You can set up there. And Donna can help coordinate with the staff. Just tell her what you need," he said, reaching toward the intercom on the corner of his desk.

"We'd like to start by speaking with Dick Calhoun," Caruso said, leveling his gaze.

Alfred Marsh nodded and reached for the telephone.

After a few quick phone calls were placed to the store manager and several other department heads, and instructions given to Donna to provide them with whatever and whoever they needed, Officers Caruso and Stull were seated comfortably behind a long table in the store's conference room. Large windows behind them looked out over Commerce Street below, while a series of sales charts hung on the wall opposite. It was a much nicer conference room than the one back at the station, with its dark wood paneling and leather chairs.

As requested, Dick Calhoun was shown in shortly after Donna brought two steaming cups of coffee to the officers as they arranged themselves at the table.

The contrast between Alfred Marsh and Dick Calhoun was unmistakable.

Where Marsh was stiff and professional, Calhoun was arrogant and full of bravado. The man lounged in the high-backed chair, a look somewhere between annoyed and mildly indifferent on his face. In fact, since taking his seat, he'd kept his eyes focused out the window over Caruso's shoulder.

"Thank you for speaking with me again," the senior officer began, jotting down Calhoun's name and date at the top of a fresh sheet of paper in his notebook.

"I didn't really think I had a choice," he said, looking at the officers for the first time as he picked an imaginary piece of lint off his jacket sleeve.

Caruso wasn't taking the bait. "Well, we appreciate your cooperation."

"I don't suppose you're here to tell me I won the award for most eligible bachelor in Parker City?"

Gritting his teeth, Caruso wasn't going to allow the conceited little prick to get to him. "Mr. Calhoun, I assume you've heard that Elizabeth Blakely received a second threatening letter earlier today. Right here at the store."

Calhoun scoffed. "Still going on about that? I told you before, I've got nothing to do with it. But yes, I heard about it. It's all anyone can talk about."

"We just have a few follow-up questions," Stull said. He might be new to the force, but even he could tell his partner for the afternoon looked as though he was about to leap over the table and throttle this guy.

Calhoun smirked. "Alright, shoot."

"You spend a lot of time around Miss Blakely?" Caruso asked.

Calhoun shrugged. "I like to think she enjoys my company."

"Do you?" Caruso pressed. "Because from what we've heard, she finds you more irritating than charming."

Calhoun's slimy grin faltered for half a second before he laughed it off. "You guys have no idea how women work, do you? They say one thing, mean another. Classic dance."

Stull bristled. He was starting to think he should let Caruso take a swing at him. "So, you think Elizabeth secretly enjoys your attention?"

"I know she does," Calhoun said confidently. "Just hasn't admitted it yet."

Caruso's patience was wearing dangerously thin. "You ever send her any letters, Dick?"

Calhoun rolled his eyes. "No. I told you that before. And I am telling you again. I don't know anything about the letters. How many times you want me to say it?"

"You ever follow her outside of work?"

"Come on." He shook his head. "I don't chase women. They come to me."

Stull exhaled. "I don't know, you sound like exactly the kind of guy who doesn't take no for an answer."

Caruso was impressed to see the spark in Stull. Apparently, he just needed a real scumbag to get him wound up.

Calhoun's face darkened slightly, but he quickly masked it with another of his trademark smiles. "Look, fellas. I'm not your guy. If I wanted Elizabeth, she'd be mine already."

Caruso stared him down for a long moment. "Thank you for your time, Mr. Calhoun. We'll be in touch."

As he walked out of the conference room, Stull turned to Caruso and muttered, "That guy's a real piece of work."

"No argument there," Caruso said. "But being an arrogant jackass doesn't necessarily make him our guy."

Chapter Thirty-Three

Officer Buck LuCoco wasn't in any particular hurry as he made his way across town to the Potomac Telephone Exchange. He rarely hurried anywhere these days. Ten years on the Parker City Police force had dulled whatever enthusiasm he'd once had for police work. Crime was crime. People were people. And in his experience, most folks had something to hide.

As the city got all worked up over the threatening letters showing up in women's mailboxes, he'd been more than happy to stay far away from the investigation. He would have been just fine allowing Caruso and Wallenbeck to run themselves ragged trying to find the mysterious letter writer. If they were actually able to catch the guy, good for them. He didn't care about the press attention they'd get. He just wanted to work his beat, go home in the evening, crack open a cold beer, and watch the television.

But then the creep causing all the fuss went and started focusing his attention on Elizabeth Blakely and Lieutenant Kerns, and he got thrown onto the investigation squad by the chief. And as the assignments were being handed out, he drew the short straw, being given the task of interviewing Joyce Osbourne, Elizabeth Blakely's roommate. Maybe she had a lead, maybe not. LuCoco wasn't holding his breath. If nothing else, though, he might end up being able to put in for some overtime if this took him past the end of his shift.

Pulling into the employee parking lot of the phone company, he pulled the squad car into an open space and shut off the ignition. Finishing the cigarette he'd been smoking, he tossed the butt on the ground as he opened the door. Then, heaving himself out of the car, he adjusted his belt over his thick waist and made his way around to the front of the building.

LuCoco lumbered up the steps into the Potomac Telephone Exchange, a squat little building off Fifth Street. The place smelled like cigarettes, machine oil, and hot wires—the way every place did where women sat in rows plugging wires into flashing lights. He unbuttoned his coat as he approached the front counter just inside the main entrance.

"I'm here to see Joyce Osbourne," he announced to the petite blonde with big glasses seated behind the counter.

Looking up from the form she was filling out, she said, "Joyce's in the back, but she's working the board right now."

LuCoco sighed and leaned his large frame on the counter. "Well, go tell her she's got company. Police business." He gestured to the uniform under his coat.

The woman hesitated. "I'll have to talk to the supervisor, Mr. Janson."

"Sweetheart, talk to whoever you need to, but I'm here to see Joyce Osbourne."

With that, she scurried off. A moment later, a woman in a crisp dark green polka dot dress and a sharp expression came hustling toward him. Joyce Osbourne wasn't a delicate little thing like he pictured most of the girls working switchboards. She had a presence—broad shoulders, a firm set to her bright red lips, and a look that said she didn't suffer fools.

She crossed her arms. "You the cop?"

"That's what they tell me," LuCoco said, already tired of this. "Got a few questions for you."

"Is Elizabeth alright?"

After explaining that her roommate had received a letter that morning at Upton's and the investigation had taken on a new urgency, Joyce's demeanor changed. The edge vanished. Concern for her friend turning her pale and unsure.

Seeing how she took the news about the most recent developments, LuCoco's humanity made a surprising return to the surface. "Maybe we should find somewhere a little more private to have this conversation. I mean, unless you want to stand out here in the lobby."

"Alright. Mr. Janson's letting me take my break early. We can talk in the lounge."

LuCoco followed her down the hall, moving like a bear that had just woken from hibernation. The breakroom was small but private, a couple of chairs, a coffee pot that had seen better days, and a half-eaten box of donuts on the table. LuCoco eyed them but decided against it. Who knows how long they'd been there.

Joyce grabbed a cup of coffee and leaned against the counter, arms crossed. "Alright, Officer. Ask away."

He scratched the side of his fleshy cheek, then got right to it. "You and Elizabeth have been roommates for a while, yeah?"

"Three years," Joyce said. "And if you're about to ask if she's got a long list of enemies, the answer is no. She's one of the sweetest people I know. Which makes this whole thing even creepier."

"You were the one who found the dress?"

She nodded. "Came home with her to change so we could go see a movie— to take her mind off the letter…the first letter—went to borrow a sweater, and there it was on the floor in her room. Shredded. Like something out of a horror movie."

"No sign of forced entry?"

"None. Isn't this in some report?"

LuCoco exhaled heavily. "You change the locks?"

"My aunt's the landlord. Said she'd take care of it. But we're staying with Liz's parents right now just to be safe."

He scribbled something in his notebook, though truth be told, he wasn't writing much. "What about these letters? Elizabeth tell you anything?"

Joyce sighed, tapping her fingers against the coffee cup. "Like what?"

"Like who she thinks might be sending them?"

Shaking her head, she answered, "Liz has no idea."

LuCoco grunted. He'd seen it plenty of times before. People didn't want to believe the worst until it smacked them in the face. It was likely someone she saw every day that was behind all this.

"What about her boss? Alfred Marsh?" he asked, thinking about one of the first names he'd read in the file back at the station.

Joyce smiled. "I think they like each other, but they're both afraid to make the first move. Been out to lunch a few times now, but Alfred seems like he's on the level. I just don't see someone like him writing threatening letters and sending them all over town. He's…well, sort of square. But in a cute way."

"And Dick Calhoun?" he asked, watching her reaction.

Joyce made a noise he couldn't quite distinguish. A laugh and a scoff at the same time. "His name says it all. He's a creep."

"He's got a thing for Elizabeth?"

"Oh, he thinks he does," Joyce said. "But he's one of those guys who thinks women secretly love being chased. It's pathetic. He probably can't even get it up."

LuCoco couldn't help but smile. He was starting to like this broad. "Think he'd do something like this?"

Joyce tilted her head, considering it for a moment. "I don't know. I don't really know him. But I get the impression he likes himself too much to take a real risk. All talk, no action."

LuCoco studied her for a moment. She was sharp, no doubt about it. He leaned back in his chair, rubbing his chin. "You ever notice anyone hanging around your place? Anyone watching you two?"

"No," Joyce said. "But if I had, you'd be the second to know."

He raised an eyebrow. "And the first?"

"The guy, right before I kicked him where it counts."

LuCoco chuckled. "I'll bet." He tapped his pen against the notebook. "One more thing. You think Elizabeth's told us everything?"

Joyce hesitated just long enough for him to notice. "I think she's scared," she admitted.

"What about you? Anything else you can think of?"

For a moment, she wondered if she should tell him about thinking she'd heard a voice in Elizabeth's bedroom the night before. But she'd begun to convince herself she was just imagining it and didn't want to sound foolish.

"Miss Osbourne?" he said. "I asked if there was anything else you could think of that might be helpful to us?"

She shook her head.

He pushed himself up from the chair with a grunt. "Alright, Miss Osbourne. I appreciate your time."

Joyce finished her coffee and set the cup down. "Yeah, well, let's just hope you guys catch this creep before things get worse."

LuCoco paused at the door. "You worried things are gonna get worse?"

Joyce met his eyes. "A guy who breaks into an apartment just to destroy a dress? A guy who keeps sending letters? *One of them to a cop.* That kind of crazy doesn't just stop."

LuCoco chewed on that as he made his way back out to the street.

Damn if she didn't have a point.

Chapter Thirty-Four

The lieutenant guided his squad car down the quiet streets of Wakeville, the town where he had been born and raised. It had changed over the years, growing from a sleepy farming community into the epitome of what people were now calling "suburbia." Still a small town, but back when he was a boy, it had been even smaller.

His family once owned one of the larger farms in the area—acres upon acres of rolling pastures, cornfields, and a big red barn that had stood for close to a hundred years. Now, that land had been carved up into a neat little residential development with streets named Orchard Lane and Harvest Drive. As if slapping a farm-themed name on the roads somehow preserved the history that endured for generations. The Blakelys' home sat in the middle of what had once been his family's property, right about where the old barn stood. Kerns could still picture himself as a kid, climbing up into the hayloft with his brothers and sisters, hiding from chores, or just killing time in the summer, out of the heat.

His father always assumed one of his sons would take over the farm, but no one ever looked at Wallace for that role. Turned out, that was for the best. He had a talent for killing anything green. The grass in his own yard back in Parker City was only still alive thanks to his wife's dedicated attention and gardening. Left to him, it would've turned to dust long ago.

No, Kerns had never been cut out for farming. He liked order, control, and problem-solving. That was why police work suited him from the start. And for a long time, it had been simple. Parker City wasn't Baltimore or Philadelphia. The kind of crime they dealt with was graffiti on a wall downtown left by a troubled youth, stolen hubcaps, and, on occasion, there would be a callout for a bar brawl. On the weekends, maybe some teens out hot-rodding and causing too much commotion. Up until these damn letters began showing up in women's mailboxes, it hadn't been that difficult of a job. Sure, dealing with someone like Edgar Stanley on a daily basis could be beyond frustrating, but his days were mostly paperwork and reading reports. Then, when someone needed to take an active role in overseeing the investigation, Stanley immediately tapped him for the job.

Though now, much like the chief, he didn't want to see the sheriff come in and take the case away from them. What he would have liked would be to work *with* the Sheriff's Department to find the guy sending the threats. He didn't understand why it could only be the PCPD or the Sheriff's Department working the case. Actually, he did. It was politics. Plain and simple. Neither Chief Stanley nor Sheriff Colsh wanted to share credit for catching the guy. If either could. And right now, the way he was feeling, Kerns didn't know if they'd ever be able to find their man. *Or men.*

Kerns was fairly certain whoever was tormenting Elizabeth Blakely, and who'd delivered a letter to him, was not the same person sending the anonymous letters through the mail. These were two different cases, even if the chief didn't want to admit it.

He turned onto the Blakelys' street, lined with two-story brick houses, neat driveways, and modest yards. These were homes where families put up Christmas lights in December and where kids rode their bikes in the summer until well after dark. Not the kind of place where you expected someone to be living in fear.

The Blakely house was no different—green shutters, a trimmed hedge, Christmas lights strung around the windows. The kind of place where a girl like Elizabeth should have felt safe. But that was the problem, wasn't it? Safe wasn't guaranteed anywhere anymore.

Kerns parked on the street in front of the house, grabbed his hat from the passenger seat, and stepped out of the car. He walked up the driveway, his boots crunching the last remaining bits of snow from the week before. Most had melted away, but there were still white patches here and there.

At the front door, he paused a moment to look up and down the street, then knocked. The door swung open almost immediately, as if they'd been waiting for him. A small woman, probably around his own age, with tired eyes, stood there.

"Oh, God. What's happened?" she said when she saw the police uniform beneath his long, heavy coat.

Introducing himself, he said, "I'm Lieutenant Wallace Kerns with the Parker City Police. I've been speaking with your daughter about…I'm in charge of the investigation. You're Mrs. Blakely. Yes?"

Her eyes showed a combination of relief and fear. "I thought something else had happened. Has something else happened? Oh, yes. I'm Marian, Elizabeth's mother. Please, come in. Come in."

He stepped inside, removing his hat. The house smelled like coffee and something baking in the oven. The kind of homey scent that should have been comforting, if not for the feeling of fear hanging in the air.

Elizabeth sat curled up on the couch in the den, a blanket draped over her shoulders, a cup of tea clutched in both hands. She looked up at him with wary eyes, dark circles underneath them.

Clifford Blakely stood near the fireplace, arms crossed, his jaw set. He was a broad-shouldered man, built like a bricklayer, though Kerns knew from his speaking with Elizabeth that he'd been a businessman of some sort before he retired. He was a man who'd been accustomed to being in control. Kerns figured the helplessness of the situation was eating at him.

"Good afternoon," Kerns greeted each of them with a nod, then introduced himself to Clifford.

"You here to tell us you caught the bastard?" he asked, his words clipped.

Kerns ignored the sharp edge in the man's tone. He couldn't blame him. "Not yet, Mr. Blakely. I wanted to check on your daughter after what happened this morning."

"Alfred brought me home after we saw you at the police station," Elizabeth told him. "He gave me the rest of the day off. Told me not to come in for the rest of the week."

"That was nice of him," Kerns said, scratching his cheek.

"That Alfred is a real gentleman," Elizabeth's mother offered emphatically.

The lieutenant made a mental note that Alfred Marsh had seemed to ingratiate himself with the Blakelys, then turned his attention to the reason for his visit. "I'd like to speak to all of you. Ask a few more questions. I won't take too much of your time."

"What do you want to know, Lieutenant?" Clifford asked.

Taking out his notebook, Kerns opened to a new page and prepared to take down anything he thought might be useful. "Miss Blakely, Elizabeth, can you think of anyone who could be sending these letters? Or, Mr. and Mrs. Blakely, might you have any ideas? Anyone been around lately acting strange, asking questions about Elizabeth?"

Looking to his wife, who was standing next to Kerns, Clifford shook his head. "We've been talking about it. Trying to think of anything that seems out of place. But neither of us can think of anything. We go to church every weekend—Saint Joe's in Parker. We play cards with the neighbors a couple of times a week. We've been getting ready for Christmas like everyone else."

"Other than our younger daughter's wedding," Marian added, "things have been completely normal."

"This wedding was last week?" Kerns asked. He already knew from speaking with Elizabeth, but wanted to confirm. "And nothing out of the ordinary happened at the wedding?"

"No," Clifford said. "Besides, these letters first started showing up weeks before the wedding. According to the papers, at least."

Casting his eyes over to Elizabeth, Kerns could see the toll that was being taken on her. "I have officers at Upton's this afternoon, questioning everyone. We'll find whoever's behind this," Kerns said. He just wasn't sure if he fully believed it, but it was what needed to be said. "I really am sorry about all of this, Miss Blakely."

Elizabeth swallowed, setting her cup down on the coffee table.

"She's a good girl," Marian Blakely added, sitting on the arm of the couch, placing a protective hand on her daughter's shoulder. "She hasn't done anything to deserve this."

Kerns nodded. "We're not saying she has, ma'am. But sometimes, people hold grudges over things that don't make sense. A misunderstanding. A perceived slight."

"Do you think it could be Dick Calhoun?" Elizabeth asked, her voice not much more than a whisper.

Kerns turned to her. "Do *you* think it could be?"

She rolled her eyes, a sudden spark appearing in them. "He's an arrogant bastard who doesn't like being told no. He thinks women are just supposed to fall at his feet."

"The police need more than just that to arrest someone," Clifford Blakely pointed out, though his words and tone didn't match.

"Yes, we do," Kerns agreed. "But it gives us reason to keep looking at him."

Elizabeth shifted, gripping the blanket tighter. "I just—I keep thinking, what if it's someone I don't even know? Someone who's just been…watching me?" Her voice wavered, the fire gone as quickly as it flared.

"We're going to find out," Kerns assured her.

Elizabeth gave a small nod, but her expression said she wasn't sure she believed it.

"Thank you for your time, everyone. If anything comes to mind—anything at all—you let us know."

The telephone rang just then, and Marian jumped up and darted toward the kitchen to answer it.

As he turned to leave, Elizabeth's father followed Kerns to the door. "Lieutenant," he said in a low voice, "if you find the sonofabitch doing this…you make damn sure he never does it again."

Kerns met his gaze. There was nothing more dangerous than a father who felt powerless to protect his daughter. And nothing more determined. He completely understood, having a daughter of his own.

"We will," Kerns said, tipping his hat.

"Lieutenant Kerns!" Marian called from the kitchen, her hand covering the mouthpiece of the phone. "It's for you—the police station."

Something must have happened if someone from the station called him here at the Blakelys'.

Stepping into the kitchen and taking the phone from Marian, he said,

"Lieutenant Kerns here."

Chapter Thirty-Five

1985…

The minute Ben and Tommy pulled out of the parking lot, Ben hit the siren as Tommy stuck the bubblegum light on the roof of the car. The unmarked Crown Vic made a sharp right onto Rockwell and sped past the front of the station in the direction of the Marshes' home. Late morning, there was very little traffic clogging the city streets, making it easy for Ben to maneuver around the cars that did cross their path.

As Ben kept his eyes on the road ahead of him, his pulse picked up speed as the car accelerated out of the downtown area.

In the seat next to him, Tommy lit a cigarette and said, "Okay. So, obviously, this is not nothing, and we may need to start looking at the case in a different light."

"You think?" Ben asked.

"It's one hell of an escalation if this guy went from dropping off a letter one day to murder the next."

"He's had twenty years to stew," Ben offered half-heartedly.

Neither spoke for the rest of the drive, the sound of the wailing siren filling the space between them. Tommy finished his cigarette as Ben watched for oncoming traffic.

Elizabeth and Alfred Marsh lived in the relatively new Gardenbrook Lake Estates neighborhood on the east side of town. In fact, it was the furthest east one could go before passing out of the city limits. Strangely enough, there was no lake anywhere in the neighborhood. But there was a fountain as Ben turned into the housing development.

After several more turns, they found themselves on Willowdale Way. The sight of two city squad cars and an ambulance down the street in front of them showed them where they were heading.

Pulling the car to a stop on the street behind one of the cruisers, Ben and Tommy jumped out of the car at the same time a team of paramedics were quickly wheeling a stretcher out of the house. On it, Alfred Marsh lay with an oxygen mask covering his face, his wife running by his side, sobbing hysterically. The men handling the stretcher looked grim as they loaded him into the back of the ambulance.

"Detective Ben Winters, PCPD. What happened?" Ben asked one of the medics as he helped Elizabeth Marsh into the back of the ambulance and closed the doors.

"Stab wound. Lost a lot of blood. We've stabilized him for now, but we've got to get him to the hospital."

"Is he conscious? Did he say who did it?" Tommy asked, following him around to the front of the ambulance as the guy jumped into the driver's seat.

"No to both questions." He slammed the door and put the ambulance into gear.

Ben tossed the car keys to Tommy. "Go with her to the hospital. Stay by her side."

Jogging back to their car, Tommy jumped in and made a quick U-turn. Ben watched as the Crown Vic picked up speed to catch up with the ambulance. After both vehicles disappeared around a turn, Ben focused his attention on the house.

The Marshes lived in a beautiful one-story, red brick home with cream shutters and a forest green front door. The rancher sat on a decent-sized lot, Ben noted, seeing how far back from the street the house was.

Walking up the driveway, Ben was met by Officer Larry Bronson. A big fella with broad shoulders and a nose that looked as though it had been broken several times over the years, Bronson had joined the PCPD around the same time as he and Tommy, but was at least ten years older. He'd come straight from the Army and several tours deployed overseas. A nice guy all around, there was still a great deal of rigidness and discipline left in him from his years in the military.

"Sergeant Winters, sir," he said with a quick nod of his head.

"Larry, I've told you. You can call me Ben."

"Yes, sir."

Ben smiled. "Tell me what we've got."

As they started toward the house, Bronson said, "I was the first responding officer on the scene. When I arrived, the front door was open, and I could hear a woman screaming inside. I made my entry and found a middle-aged woman on the floor of the kitchen cradling a man of a similar age in her arms. They were both covered with blood. I couldn't see any weapons, so I tried asking the lady what happened. The man appeared unconscious."

"What did she say?"

"It was pretty hard to understand with the way she was crying. But I managed to figure out that she said her husband had been attacked."

"Did she say who did it?"

"No, sir. She didn't say much else. She was hysterical. The call that went out was that there'd been a stabbing, so she must have been able to tell Dispatch. I'm sorry I wasn't able to get any ID on either of them."

"That's alright, Larry. I actually know who they are. Unless you believe in serious coincidences, this is most likely connected to a case Tommy and I are working."

As Ben stepped through the front door, he was immediately struck by the sharp, metallic smell of blood. Looking to his left, he saw into the kitchen where Officer Dean Jackson was trying to avoid stepping in any of the pools of it on the floor. The bright red a stark contrast to the white ceramic tiles.

"What do you have, Dean?"

"A real mess." Then, pointing to the area on the floor with the most blood, he said, "This is where the victim was lying. Over there, just under the cabinet, is a bloody kitchen knife. I didn't touch it, but it looks like it's part of the set over there on the counter by the stove. There's also an empty coffee cup on the table there, and another one broken over here on the floor by the sink."

Ben turned back to Bronson. "When you got here, did you check his pulse?"

"I did. It was barely there. But he had one."

Moving carefully through the kitchen, Ben took it all in. Nothing about the scene looked premeditated. No sign of forced entry. No ransacking. It didn't feel like a break-in. It felt personal.

He crouched down near the fallen cup, examining the broken pieces. What little coffee that had remained inside had splattered out, mixing with the blood. He glanced toward the kitchen table where the second cup sat.

"Someone else was here," he muttered.

"What was that, Sarge?" Bronson asked.

Ben stood up. "Two cups. Did he have coffee with his attacker? Or were he and Elizabeth interrupted? And if she'd been here, why didn't the attacker go after her, too? I need her statement," he said, trying to play through the various scenarios in his head.

Jackson nodded. "Could've been a visitor and she wasn't here."

Ben didn't reply. His eyes were already scanning the kitchen table, the counter, and the hallway beyond. If someone had been here, they hadn't left much behind—no coat, no bag, no easy trail to follow.

But something didn't sit right. It just felt *wrong*. Not that any crime scene felt *right*.

Was this the work of Elizabeth Marsh's stalker? Had he finally struck out at the man who took her away from him?

Ben instructed Officer Jackson to start the crime scene log, in which anyone who entered or exited the house would be recorded, as he and Bronson did a quick sweep of the house. They checked the doors and all the windows. All locked. Nothing broken. No one hiding anywhere. No sign of a struggle outside the kitchen. Whatever happened, happened fast.

"Bronson, go radio in and have them roll CSU. I want them to do a full work-up," he announced. "Prints, fibers, all of it. And ask for a few more units to be dispatched to canvas the neighborhood. Somebody had to have seen something. I don't care if it was just a shadow in the window or a car parked the wrong way on the street.

"We need to figure out exactly what happened here," Ben said. "And I need a ride to the hospital."

Chapter Thirty-Six

Additional patrol units arrived at the Marsh home on Willowdale Way within minutes, their lights flashing silently as officers stepped out to help secure the scene. Yellow crime scene tape unfurled across the yard, fluttering lightly in the warm midday breeze.

Though most residents were still at work at this time of the day, those who were home began to trickle outside—drawn to the flashing lights and official activity. A few watched from porches, coffee cups in hand. Others clustered on sidewalks in pairs, whispering to each other. In neighborhoods like this, everyone usually knew everyone else's business.

Ben moved methodically, assigning officers to perimeter watch and door-to-door canvassing, but his eyes scanned the street just as carefully. He didn't know who belonged on Willowdale Way and who didn't, but if anyone lingered too long, looked too interested, or seemed out of place, Ben wanted to know their name and why they were there. The idea that the person responsible might be watching from among the onlookers wasn't just a theory—it was a possibility he'd seen before.

A few minutes later, the familiar white van of the Maryland State Police Crime Scene Unit rolled to a stop in front of the house. The back doors opened, and the forensic team piled out, equipment cases in hand.

Ben felt a flicker of relief when he spotted Aaron Clover climbing down from the passenger side. Not that he didn't trust the other supervisors, but Clover's reputation carried a certain gravitas. When he showed up, people didn't cut corners—they dug in and paid attention to the smallest speck of dust.

"Lieutenant," Ben greeted him with a nod.

Clover returned it with a brisk one of his own. One of the thinnest men Ben had ever met, Clover's gangly frame made his beige uniform hang on him like it belonged to someone else. With his oversized round glasses, angular face, and long black mustache, he looked like a cross between a Civil War cavalryman and a cartoon scientist. But there was nothing funny about the way he ran his team—tight, meticulous, and efficient.

Ben pulled him aside and quietly filled him in on what they knew so far: the stabbing, the couple's connection to an old case from '65, and the threatening letter that had appeared in Elizabeth Marsh's mailbox just a day earlier. Clover listened intently, nodding occasionally as he adjusted his glasses and wiped them clean with a handkerchief from his pocket.

"Well," Clover said at last, slipping the lenses back on. "If this is connected to your letter, it's no longer just an old mystery. It's an active case again."

"The timing's hard to ignore," Ben answered, shaking his head.

"Mmmm," Clover muttered in agreement. "We lifted two sets of prints from that letter you sent over. Neither matched anything we had on file. If I can get fresh samples from both Mr. and Mrs. Marsh, we can at least eliminate them."

"They were printed back in sixty-five. Originals are in the case file," Ben said. "I'll have copies sent over within the hour."

"Good. In the meantime, we'll run a full sweep of the scene here—print, fiber, blood analysis. If there's anything to find, we'll find it."

As Clover turned to begin giving orders to his team, Ben stepped back and watched the technicians move into position like chess pieces—snapping photos, placing evidence markers, preparing test swabs, and fingerprint dust. It was a process he was becoming accustomed to. But for some reason, today felt somehow different. Maybe it was because he'd met Alfred Marsh and seen him as a warm and caring husband. Previous scenes like this, when he was called in, he'd usually never met the victim.

After checking in with the officers canvassing the neighborhood and taking another walk through the house, Ben felt comfortable enough to turn over the scene to the patrol supervisor who'd been sent out. He wanted to get to the hospital and check on the Marshes. It'd been a few hours since the ambulance had pulled away, and he hadn't heard anything from Tommy.

Needing a lift over to Tasker Valley Memorial, Ben found Officer Bronson, who was ready to head back to the station so he could write and file his report as first officer on the scene. Jumping in the car with him, the two men sat quietly as Bronson navigated the squad car out of the Marshes' neighborhood. A serious expression on the big patrolman's face caused his brow to furrow into a deep V.

"Do you think he made it?" he asked, turning to Ben. "That was a lot of blood."

Ben exhaled. "We can only hope. I would think if he hadn't, Tommy would have come back by now. Hopefully, the reason he's still at the hospital is *because* Alfred Marsh survived the attack, and he's waiting for an opportunity to talk to him."

Bronson gave a small nod but said nothing else.

Ben leaned back against the headrest, staring out the passenger-side window as houses and storefronts passed by in a blur. His mind was racing—not just with questions about who had attacked Alfred Marsh, but why now? After twenty years of silence, why start again?

And why go after Alfred?

It didn't feel random. Not even close. The coffee cups, the lack of forced entry. Whoever had come into that house had likely been let in—or was someone who didn't need to force their way inside. Would Elizabeth's stalker have just been asked in? He would if they didn't know he *was* her stalker.

Or, Ben thought with a sinking feeling, this had nothing to do with the letters and who was sending them. And this was a crime unto itself.

Ben rubbed his temple with his fingers. There were too many possibilities, and not enough answers.

The cruiser pulled up to the main entrance of Tasker Valley Memorial, and Ben was out before Bronson had come to a complete stop.

"Thanks for the lift," Ben said, shutting the door behind him.

Bronson gave him a short wave and pulled away from the curb.

Ben took the hospital steps two at a time and stepped through the sliding doors. The antiseptic smell of the lobby hit him immediately, crisp and sterile, completely at odds with the coppery blood he'd smelled just hours earlier.

Spotting a familiar figure seated near the far corner, Ben made his way toward Tommy, who stood as soon as he saw him approach.

"She's in with the doctor," Tommy said in a low voice. "Been in there a while. I don't know what that means. Her sister and that Joyce Osbourne are in with her. She asked me to call them a little while after we got here."

Ben nodded and looked toward the hallway leading to the ICU. Everything about it—the quiet, the stark white walls, the faint hum of machines behind closed doors—made his stomach tighten.

"All right," he said, voice low. "Let's find out what the hell happened."

With that, the two detectives turned and walked toward the Intensive Care Unit.

Chapter Thirty-Seven

Ben followed Tommy down the corridor, their footsteps soft against the heavy linoleum floor. Pushing through the door into the ICU, they came to a raised desk, manned by a stern looking nurse Ben thought reminded him of their late chief, Edgar Stanley…if he'd been a woman. The reason for that was explained when the detective saw the nurse's name badge, which read A. STANLEY.

Waiting patiently for Nurse Stanley to acknowledge them, Tommy also recognized the resemblance. Nonchalantly, grabbing Ben's arm, he motioned with his head toward the shiny name tag affixed to her white uniform. Without saying anything, Ben gave a quick nod and pried his partner's hand from his elbow.

"Can I help you?" Nurse Stanley asked, finally setting aside the papers she'd been filling out, looking down at the men in front of her through the glasses perched at the edge of her nose.

"I hope so," Ben said, taking out his badge. "I'm Detective Winters, and this is my partner, Detective Mason, with the PCPD. We're here about Alfred Marsh. He was brought in with a stab wound."

"Mrs. Marsh was brought back a little while ago to speak with the doctor," Tommy added.

"We'd like an update on his condition," Ben said. "And to speak with the doctor when possible."

Surprisingly, without arguing or putting up any sort of resistance, Nurse Stanley picked up a clipboard and ran a finger down the top page.

"You'll want to talk with Dr. Baxter. But I can tell you that Mr. Marsh is out of surgery. He's in room three. If you'll wait here, I'll see if the doctor's available."

"Thank you," Ben said with a smile.

"I'm happy to help, Detectives. My sweet big brother used to be the police chief. Did you know him? Whenever I have a chance to help, I try to."

As she disappeared down the hall and through a door marked AUTHO-RIZED PERSONNEL ONLY, Tommy turned to Ben. "There's no way she's really related to the chief. She was too helpful…and didn't swear once. And what was that about her *sweet* big brother?"

Ben shrugged. "She obviously saw a different side of him than we did."

Leaning against the desk as they waited, the sounds of the medical unit filled the air. The low beeping and humming of equipment coming from behind the closed doors up and down the hallway were only drowned out by the conversations of doctors and nurses as they passed.

After fifteen minutes, Nurse Stanley returned, followed by another woman wearing surgical scrubs under a white doctor's coat, with a stethoscope hanging around her neck. Her dark hair pulled back into a tight bun, she spoke to the nurse without looking away from the clipboard she was carrying.

"Detectives, I'm Dr. Charlotte Baxter. Sorry to keep you waiting. It's been an unusually busy day. I understand you're here about the stab wound that came in earlier. Why don't we talk over here?"

They followed the doctor to what looked like a small consultation room, very similar to the interrogation room back at the station. The only difference was that the furniture was nicer. Taking their cue from Dr. Baxter, Ben and Tommy sat at the small table in the middle of the pale blue room.

Ben couldn't help but wonder if this was the first chance she'd had to sit down in a while, judging by the look on her face as she began rubbing her temples. In front of her lay the clipboard with what Ben assumed was Alfred Marsh's information.

"The patient came in with a single stab wound to the abdomen—left upper quadrant," she began, referring to the notes. "It was a deep, penetrating injury. He'd lost a significant amount of blood before arriving. We're talking life-threatening hemorrhage.

"The blade hit the stomach. There was active internal bleeding. We had to get him into surgery immediately. If the ambulance had been five minutes later, we might be having a very different conversation.

"We've got him stabilized for now, but he's not out of the woods yet. Injuries like this can cause complications—internal infection, sepsis, peritonitis. However, there was a further complication while in surgery, which makes things all the more uncertain."

"A complication," Ben repeated.

"Yes. While I was trying to stop the bleeding, Mr. Marsh went into cardiac arrest. It was touch and go, but like I said, right now, he's stable but still in critical condition."

"Is there any chance we can speak with him?" Tommy asked, trying not to sound too over-eager.

"I'm afraid not. He's being kept heavily sedated for the time being. I'm not saying we had to put him into a medically induced coma, but he's not going to be fully awake and cognizant of his surroundings for a couple of days.

"He'll be here in the ICU so we'll be able to monitor him."

As Dr. Baxter was talking, Ben had been jotting down notes. He'd need a copy of the medical records at some point. But for now, he wanted to speak with Elizabeth Marsh.

"Where is Mrs. Marsh at the moment?" Ben asked, closing his notebook.

"She's in a private waiting room down the hall. I can take you to her if you don't have any other questions for me."

"Thank you, Doctor. I appreciate it. We'll just need copies of all Mr. Marsh's charts. And if there's any updates on his condition, please notify the station."

"If you leave your information with Nurse Stanley at the desk, she'll make sure you receive the updates we're able to provide. But for privacy reasons, you really should speak with Mrs. Marsh."

"Of course," Ben said, not wanting to point out this was all part of a *police investigation* to find out who was responsible for putting Alfred Marsh in the hospital in the first place. But he wasn't going to press the issue.

Following her down one hallway to the next, they found themselves outside yet another hospital door, behind which they could hear the faint murmur of voices. Knocking gently, Dr. Baxter entered the room, followed by Ben, then Tommy.

When Elizabeth Marsh saw the doctor, her eyes widened and began to fill with tears.

"Has something happened?" a woman with bright red curly hair asked, jumping to her feet.

"No. Everything is fine," Dr. Baxter answered with a quick shake of her head. "Mr. Marsh is still stable and resting. These are police detectives who would like to speak with Mrs. Marsh."

"Is now really the time?" asked another woman who Ben noticed bore a striking resemblance to Elizabeth. Most likely the sister Tommy mentioned.

Before Ben could respond, Elizabeth put her hand on her sister's arm and said, "No. I need to talk to him. Alfred and I talked to him yesterday when we got the letter. Detective, this is my sister, Patty, and my best friend, Joyce."

"Thank you, Mrs. Marsh. I'm Detective Ben Winters," he introduced himself to the other women. "This is my partner, Tommy Mason."

"Anyone ever tell you you look like Magnum, P.I.?" Joyce asked in that way that only she could at the most inappropriate time.

With that, Dr. Baxter excused herself, and the detectives took seats on a small, uncomfortable sofa opposite Elizabeth Marsh and her sister.

"I'm so sorry about Mr. Marsh," Ben began. "But we do have a few questions we need to ask you. The sooner we have all the information, the quicker we'll be able to get the investigation moving."

"Of course. I understand." Elizabeth straightened slightly, steeling herself for whatever she may be asked.

"There's no other way to put it," Ben said, trying to be as delicate as possible, "but do you know who did this? Were you there when the attack occurred?"

"No," Elizabeth answered quickly. "I found him that way. With all the blood..."

"Alright," Ben said, his voice calm. The last thing he wanted to do was upset her even further. He knew the questions he needed to ask were going to be difficult, but they needed to be asked. Moving quickly at the beginning of an investigation was paramount. If too much time passed before they had all the necessary information, they'd be hampered from the start. Unfortunately, this meant sometimes they could not afford to be gentle. "Can you tell me exactly where you were when this happened?"

"I was out running errands. At the mall."

"Was there a reason Alfred was home in the middle of the week on a workday?"

"He just didn't go into the office today. He said he didn't want to leave me home alone. Not after getting that letter. He was going to work from the house. He said his business partner was going to stop by to drop off some papers for him. I don't care much for Todd, so I thought I'd go out for a while." She wiped a tear away as it began to roll down her cheek.

"Todd?" Ben asked, his pen hovering over his notepad.

"Todd Kimble. Alfred's partner in the accounting firm." Elizabeth said, looking at Ben through puffy, bloodshot eyes.

If his business partner stopped by, that could explain the two cups of coffee, Ben thought. Then just as quickly, he wondered if this was some sort of business dispute and had nothing to do with Elizabeth's stalker at all.

Without conferring, Tommy knew exactly what Ben was thinking. He could read the subtle expression on his face, which prompted him to ask, "Why is it you don't care for him, Mrs. Marsh? Todd Kimble?"

"What? I mean… I just… He's young and arrogant…smug even. He thinks he knows more than anyone else. And was always trying to get Alfred to use *new* accounting methods. I never understood, but Alfred said they were questionable and he cared more about the firm's reputation than saving a few dollars."

Following up, Tommy asked, "Did this cause problems between them?"

Elizabeth's forehead wrinkled. "I don't think so. Alfred never said there was a problem. They just had different ideas about running the firm from time to time."

Ben scribbled down the name Todd Kimble, then underlined it twice.

He glanced up at Elizabeth, her face pale and drawn, her hands tightly clasped in her lap like she was holding something in. Her sister sat protectively close, her body angled toward her, ready to step in if needed. Joyce, unusually quiet, looked like she was biting her tongue.

"When exactly did you go out this morning?" Ben asked.

"I think I left around nine."

"And you got back…?"

"Around eleven. I wasn't gone long."

"Was there anyone you can think of who might want to hurt your husband for any reason? Any clients or associates who might have been angry or upset with him?"

"Everyone loves Alfred. He's the first person people turn to when there's a problem."

"Has anything unusual happened recently?"

"No. Just the letter yesterday."

"Of course," Ben said. "Is there anything else you can remember about today?"

She hesitated. Her eyes darted toward her sister, then to Joyce, and finally landed back on Ben.

"I don't know if this means anything," she said, her voice barely above a whisper, "but when I pulled into the driveway… I think there was a car parked across the street. Not one I recognized. A dark color. It was gone by the time the ambulance arrived."

Ben and Tommy exchanged a quick look.

"Thank you, Mrs. Marsh," Ben said. "That might help more than you think."

He rose from the sofa and tucked his notebook back into his pocket.

"If you remember anything else—anything at all—you can call the station. They'll always be able to find us."

Elizabeth gave a slight nod.

Outside in the hallway, the two detectives walked in silence until they reached the main lobby. Finally, Tommy looked over at Ben.

"Arrogant business partners make for good suspects."

"Yeah," Ben said quietly. "It's starting to look less like a stalker and more like someone close to them."

Tommy nodded slowly. "Unless it's both."

Chapter Thirty-Eight

Sitting on a bench in the warm summer sun outside the hospital, Ben squinted against the bright glare, watching Tommy pace like a restless animal, a curl of cigarette smoke trailing behind him. Both men had removed their jackets, but Tommy had gone further by rolling up his sleeves to the elbow and loosening his tie. He always argued that he thought better when he was dressed more comfortably.

"Is there any chance this Kimble guy could've sent the letter?" Tommy asked, taking a drag on his cigarette as he turned mid-step.

Ben didn't answer right away. He'd been tossing that question around himself.

"Well," he finally said, stretching out his legs and leaning back against the bench, "for that to make sense, he'd have to know about what happened back in sixty-five. Alfred could've told him, I guess. It sounds like he's too young to have been around at the time."

"Sure," Tommy said, exhaling smoke through his nose. "But why would he try to scare Elizabeth in the first place? What's the angle? Especially when he turns around and stabs Marsh the next day?"

"Maybe Alfred figured out he sent the letter. Confronted him. Things got heated." Ben let the idea sit for a second, but even as he said it, it didn't feel right.

"No," he said. "That's not it. It's off. Doesn't make sense if the stabbing had anything to do with business."

Tommy gave a slow nod, flicking the last of his cigarette to the ground and crushing it with the heel of his shoe.

"So…we have two options. One, Marsh and Kimble get into it, things go sideways, and Kimble stabs him. Two, Elizabeth's stalker decides after twenty years to kill her husband."

"Technically," Ben said, "there's a third option."

Tommy raised an eyebrow. "Random act of violence?"

Ben nodded.

"C'mon," Tommy said. "You don't even believe that. Guy's at home, middle of the day, you said there were *two* coffee cups. This wasn't some stranger off the street."

"I agree," Ben said. "But until we can prove it wasn't random, we can't rule it out completely."

Tommy sat down beside him on the bench with a groan, brushing his palms on his knees.

"My gut says it's either the stalker or Kimble. And they're not the same guy. No way."

"Yeah," Ben said. "But we're still going to ask him about the letter."

"Oh, absolutely. I've got this irritating commanding officer who insists we cover all the bases. Total pain in the ass."

Ben cracked a smile. "Well, maybe the people he supervises are the ones causing the problem."

Tommy gave a thoughtful nod. "Hmm. No. That's not it."

Ben glanced at his watch. "We've still got time to swing by Marsh's office. If Kimble's there, we'll catch him before he leaves for the day."

Tommy stood and shrugged into his jacket. "Fine. But we're hitting McDonald's first. We missed lunch again, and if I have to interview a pompous accountant on an empty stomach, I might accidentally shoot him in the foot."

Ben was halfway into his own jacket when his gaze drifted to the hospital entrance.

He paused. "Hold that thought."

Tommy followed his eyes.

Coming through the automatic doors, red curls catching the sunlight, was Joyce Osbourne. Stepping away from the doors, she took a pack of cigarettes from her purse and began shaking one out.

Ben gestured in her direction. "Let's have a chat with Miss Osbourne first."

They crossed the parking lot toward her, their pace quick but casual.

Joyce spotted them before they reached her. Lighting her cigarette, she then placed a hand on her hip and let out a sigh like she was wondering what took them so long.

"If you're here to arrest me, Detective Magnum," she called out, "at least let me finish my smoke."

Tommy grinned.

"What can I do for you boys?" she asked.

"Just a few questions for you. Should only take a couple minutes," Ben answered, taking out his notebook.

Joyce eyed them warily, then blew a stream of smoke into the air. "Ask away. But I warn you, I have a very low tolerance for stupid questions."

Tommy smirked. "Then we're in luck. We left all our stupid questions back at the station."

Joyce gave a sarcastic smile and motioned for them to walk with her. "Good. Because this whole thing…*twenty years*, Detectives! Someone needs to catch this guy."

They strolled slowly along the sidewalk, shaded by the canopy of a tree-lined drive. Ben kept his voice calm and steady.

"You've known Elizabeth and Alfred a long time, right?"

"Longer than either of them would probably like to admit," she said. "Elizabeth and I have been best friends for as long as I can remember. We were roommates back in the day."

"Roommates back in sixty-five? So, you were around when she was receiving the threatening letters?" Ben asked.

Joyce gave a short, sharp nod of acknowledgement. "Yep. I was there for all of it. Right by her side."

"Did she ever say who she thought sent them?" Tommy asked.

"At the time, we all thought that one of the guys at Upton's was behind it. Dick Calhoun," Joyce said. "I still remember him. A real slime ball."

Ben and Tommy exchanged a glance. Dick Calhoun seemed to have been at the top of everyone's list back then. So far, he was definitely turning out to be the frontrunner on the stalker side of the investigation.

"Do you know if Elizabeth has seen Dick Calhoun recently?" Ben asked.

Joyce scoffed. "If she has, she didn't tell me, and there's no way she *wouldn't* tell me, Detective. So, no, I'm sure she hasn't seen that creep."

"Alright. You know anything about this Todd Kimble?" Tommy asked. "Alfred's business partner?"

Joyce made a face like she'd just smelled sour milk. "Ugh. Todd. Well, only what Liz has told me about him. She tries not to talk about him much, but she can't stand him."

"Would you say he and Alfred got along?"

She hesitated. "They got along the way you get along with someone you can't fire. But like I said, I only know what Liz has said. He seems like he's a bit ethically slippery, if you know what I mean."

Ben's brow furrowed. "Slippery how?"

Joyce shrugged. "I don't speak accountant, but it didn't sound like the kind of stuff you'd brag about to the IRS."

Tommy rubbed the back of his neck. "Could he have been in trouble? Gotten the firm in a jam in some way?"

"No idea." Then suddenly, as if someone had flipped a light switch, she stopped and turned to them. "Hey. Wait a minute. Do you think he did this to Alfred? That it doesn't have anything to do with the letters? Because that seems a little too coincidental for me to believe."

"Miss Osbourne, it's our job to look at every possibility. We're following both lines of inquiry," Ben offered in response.

Joyce shook her head. "Do you realize what it means if Kimble's the one who stabbed Alfred? You still have Elizabeth's stalker to find!"

Ben hadn't wanted to say it out loud, but there it was.

"No," she went on. "This is that sick person who came after Liz. He's the one who did this. You boys need to figure this out. She's been through enough."

Ben couldn't agree more. "That's what we're going to do, Miss Osbourne.

If I could just ask you one more question." Ben hesitated. He had to ask, "Where were you this morning?"

Her eyes narrowed, and the corner of her lip curled. The look in her eyes told Ben he didn't even want to know what she was thinking of him at that moment.

But instead of releasing a tirade about how they should be looking for the real attacker and not questioning Elizabeth and Alfred's friends, she said in a tone that could freeze a campfire, "I guess you did bring one stupid question with you, Detective. But if it helps you find who really did this…I was showing a house to some prospective buyers in Wakeville. I'd be happy to give you their telephone number to verify. Or do you already have the number for *Judge* William Randall Scott?"

"I think we'll be able to track that down," Ben said. "Like I said—"

"You have to look at all the possibilities. Yes, Detective. I understand," she said, a distinct chill in her voice.

"Thank you for your time. If there's anything else you think of, please let us know."

As she walked off, she tossed what remained of her cigarette into the street.

Tommy let out a low whistle. "She's a lot."

"She actually reminds me of your Christine," Ben said. "If she was twenty years younger."

They turned and started walking toward the car.

"I'm not calling Judge Scott," Tommy said. "He scares me."

Chapter Thirty-Nine

The Big Macs and French fries helped to give Ben and Tommy a boost of energy after departing the hospital. This wasn't the first time they'd worked through lunch, and they knew it wouldn't be the last either. But after letting the fast food fill their stomachs, they were ready to interview Alfred Marsh's business partner. They'd been fortified by greasy goodness for whatever direction their conversation with Todd Kimble would lead them.

If they were lucky, they'd walk out with a killer in handcuffs, ready to be booked and locked up. Money was one of the oldest and most common motives. Right alongside love and revenge, when it came to the kind of crimes most detectives were called in to investigate. Even though every crime could be considered unique in its own way, ultimately, they all fell into one of several categories. So the term "unique" became slightly less meaningful.

As they'd sat in the drive-thru, Tommy radioed in and got an address for Marsh, Kimble, and Associates, Public Accountants. The offices turned out to be on the third floor of a slate gray, pre-World War II building at the edge of downtown. To its left was a travel agency and to the right, a dental practice. Stepping through the door with the firm's name etched into the frosted glass window, the outer office had a pale green carpet with darker green leather chairs for clients to wait. A reception desk sat in the corner next to a large Ficus plant.

Ben rang the small brass bell on the desk. A woman with thick glasses and even thicker lipstick appeared from the back room. Several pencils were stuck haphazardly into her helmet-shaped hair.

Presenting his badge, Ben said, "Good afternoon. We're here to speak with Todd Kimble."

"Mr. Kimble?" she asked. "May I tell him who's calling?"

"Detectives Winters and Mason. Parker City Police," Ben answered. "We just have a few questions for him."

The woman's eyes widened slightly. It was a common reaction. Most people could go their entire life without a pair of detectives showing up, flashing their badges at them. But when they appear at one's place of work looking to ask questions, it's only natural to wonder what it's all about.

Seeing the curiosity in her eyes, Ben knew it was only a matter of waiting for her to ask, "Is everything alright? Mr. Kimble isn't in any sort of trouble, is he?"

Giving her his best reassuring smile, the one that always put women at ease, Tommy answered, "We just need to ask him some questions. He might be able to help us with a case we're working on."

That seemed to appease her.

"His office is down the hall there. Last door on the left," she said, pointing towards a series of doors running down a wood-paneled hallway.

A gold plaque on the door read TODD M. KIMBLE, CPA.

Tommy knocked and opened the door when he heard a voice call, "Come in."

Todd Kimble stood behind a heavy oak desk, dressed in a crisp white shirt and matching paisley tie and suspenders, sleeves rolled halfway up, dark hair gelled back within an inch of its life. He looked like a slick operator, Ben thought with one look. A fan buzzed quietly in the corner, stirring the hot afternoon air.

"Can I help you gentlemen?" he asked, coming around the desk and extending a hand. "I'm Todd Kimble."

"Detective Sergeant Winters. This is Detective Mason." Ben shook his hand. "We're here about Alfred Marsh."

Kimble blinked, confused. "Alfred? What about him? Is he all right?"

Tommy watched him carefully. "You haven't heard?"

"Heard what, exactly?" Kimble questioned, a tone of concern making its way into his voice. "He said he was working from home today. I've been here. Why? What happened?"

"When was the last time you saw Alfred?" Ben asked, not wanting to mention the stabbing just yet.

"Well…yesterday. I was supposed to stop by his house this morning, but I was running late after I left an early morning meeting with one of our clients to get back here for another meeting. I called Alfred from the car to tell him I couldn't make it."

"You called him from the car?" Tommy asked, raising an eyebrow. "Do you have one of those fancy car phones?"

"No. I have a new cellular phone," Kimble said with a smile, then lifted what looked like a large gray brick with an antenna sticking out of it off the corner of his desk. "It's made doing business so much easier."

Ben had seen advertisements for the new phones that you could take anywhere and weren't tethered down by a wire. It was impressive to see one in person. He noticed the device was attached to a black case with a strap on it—the battery that kept the thing charged.

"So, you never made it to the Marshes' home this morning," Ben confirmed, focusing back on Kimble rather than the new piece of technology that he desperately wanted to examine further.

"Right."

This new bit of information caused something to click in Ben's mind. Thinking back, he hadn't seen any sort of business documents or folders lying around at the crime scene. There was always the possibility that Kimble could have picked them up after he stabbed Marsh to cover his tracks. But he must have known that Elizabeth knew he was supposed to be there, and the scene didn't look premeditated, so he might not have thought to take the papers with him.

They'd need to confirm that Kimble was at a meeting in the morning and exactly what time he'd left, and when he'd arrived here at the office after that meeting. They'd also need to confirm with his cellular telephone provider if he had, in fact, made a call to the Marsh house that morning and when. A lot of details to follow up on. But if they all checked out, Ben was starting to wonder if Todd Kimble might not be their guy.

But the time had finally come to see how he reacted when he found out his business partner was in the hospital.

"This morning," Ben began, watching him intently, "Alfred Marsh was attacked in his home. He's currently in critical condition at Tasker Valley Memorial."

Kimble's brow creased, and he looked genuinely stunned—or was doing a good job of faking it. "Good Lord. I...I had no idea. Is he going to be alright?"

"He's stable," Ben said. "But it was close. They're monitoring his condition. We're all hoping he pulls through."

Kimble rubbed the back of his neck and shook his head slowly. "I was supposed to go to his house this morning. If I'd been there, maybe...or maybe..."

"Who's the client you were meeting with this morning?" Tommy asked, trying to keep him from going down the what-if path.

"What? Sorry. Um...Caldwell Financial Investments. I was meeting with Ron and David Caldwell. They brought us in to audit their books and make sure everything was meeting the latest regulations. I can't believe someone attacked Alfred."

"What time did you leave the Caldwells' this morning?" Tommy pressed.

"It was almost nine-forty-five, and I needed to be here by ten."

If they were able to confirm that timeframe was true, there would be no way he could have been the one to attack Marsh. He physically couldn't have been there.

Ben looked up from his notebook. "What kind of relationship would you say you and Alfred had?"

Kimble sat back on the edge of his desk. "Professional. We weren't exactly buddies, if that's what you're asking. He was a little too old school for me. But we worked well together."

"You sure about that?" Tommy asked, crossing his arms.

Kimble narrowed his eyes. "Something you're not telling me?"

"There were some concerns that the two of you didn't always agree on how to run the business. That true?"

Kimble gave a tight smile. "Alfred was…conservative. I tried to modernize a few things. Take advantage of a few new provisions in the tax code. He didn't always love my ideas."

"Did those disagreements ever get heated?"

"Never. He always got the final say. I might've vented a little now and then, but I didn't have any reason to hurt him, if that's what you're implying."

"What about anyone else?" Tommy asked. "Did Alfred have any unhappy clients who might—"

"Detective, our clients are not like that," he snapped, cutting Tommy off. "We are one of the most respected accounting firms in the city. We're not some shady mob accountants. If anything, the types of people and businesses we have on our client list, they'd sue us. Not physically attack us."

"Fair enough," Tommy said, easing off a bit. He'd wanted to push the account to see if he'd lose his cool.

"What about Elizabeth Marsh?" Ben asked, changing the angle. "How well do you know her?"

"I guess I know her as well as I can. We've never spent that much time together. A few business dinners, a couple social events. She's nice but keeps her distance from the business."

Ben nodded. "Were you aware she received a threatening letter yesterday?"

Kimble looked genuinely taken aback. "No. From whom? Why?"

"Did Alfred ever mention anything about her being stalked in the past?"

"No," Kimble said firmly. "That's not something I ever heard about. Someone was stalking her?"

"Are you from the Parker area, Mr. Kimble?" Tommy asked.

"No. I moved here a few years ago."

"So, you never heard about what happened back in the sixties with women receiving anonymous letters?"

"No. I was in college in Philadelphia. I'd never even heard of Parker City then."

Ben studied him. He couldn't tell if Kimble was lying or just a damn good actor. Either way, they were going to have to verify every word of this conversation.

"If you think of anything else," Ben said, tucking his notepad inside his jacket, "or remember anything odd about the last few days, please call us."

Kimble nodded. "I will."

Outside on the sidewalk, the heat rising off the pavement, Ben waited as Tommy caught up with him.

"Secretary said Kimble came barreling in right before the meeting started at ten this morning. She didn't think he was going to make it," Tommy reported. "Says he didn't look upset or like a guy who'd just committed attempted murder."

Ben nodded, running a hand through his hair. "If we can verify that phone call, it's looking less and less likely that Kimble was the one with the knife."

Tommy let out a slow breath. "Damn shame. That guy's definitely guilty of something. But…"

"…not the kind of something we're after," Ben finished the thought.

They stood in silence for a moment, the city humming around them. From the moment they'd gotten the call about Alfred Marsh, a part of them had already known.

This wasn't about business deals or professional grudges. It was about something older and more personal.

It was about obsession.

Whoever had come after Elizabeth Blakely all those years ago hadn't lost that obsession.

The truth about who stabbed Alfred Marsh didn't rest in any of the accountant's numbers or spreadsheets. It was buried in the past. And they were going to have to dig it up before whoever the figure in the shadows was made another move.

Chapter Forty

1965...

With the sun having fallen below the horizon hours earlier, Parker City was gripped by a bitter cold that sent people hurrying indoors. The streets empty, the warm glow of televisions flickered behind closed curtains as families settled in for the evening's Christmas specials following a hearty dinner.

But at the Parker City Police Department, the night was just beginning.

In the brightly lit interrogation room, Ralph Sanderson sat hunched over the metal table, his sweater too big, his corduroy slacks baggy and wrinkled. His dark, curly hair needed a trim, and his thick glasses teetered on the tip of his nose. Normally, he would've pushed them back up, but with his hands cuffed to the metal ring on the table, he was left to scrunch his nose repeatedly in a useless effort.

Watching from the other side of the one-way mirror, Chief Stanley exhaled, blowing a stream of cigar smoke toward the glass, shaking his head. "A damn hippie," he muttered.

Lieutenant Wallace Kerns, standing next to him with his arms crossed, didn't respond. Instead, he kept his gaze locked on Sanderson. The kid looked small in that chair—nervous, twitchy. They had spent weeks chasing down leads, piecing together a puzzle of terror and confusion. And now, if all was to be believed, they had their man.

Kerns wasn't so sure, though. But since he'd received the call at the

Blakelys' house, everything began falling into place faster than anyone expected.

Behind him, Officers Nick Caruso and George Wallenbeck leaned against the wall, both holding cups of lukewarm coffee from the breakroom.

Wallenbeck had been the one to nab Sanderson, and he'd given Kerns the rundown in his office an hour earlier.

As instructed, he'd gone to the post office that afternoon to reinterview the clerks. The postal employees had been cooperative, but no one was able to share anything new that could get them any closer to identifying their suspect.

Then, as he was finishing up, Wallenbeck noticed Ralph Sanderson enter the post office.

The young man walked in like any other customer, but something about him made the police officer take notice. The second Sanderson's eyes landed on Wallenbeck in his uniform, his whole demeanor shifted. His shoulders tensed, and his eyes began darting around.

That's when Wallenbeck really started paying attention.

Sanderson awkwardly turned, moving too quickly, and knocked into a man carrying a stack of packages. The boxes went flying, and as Sanderson stumbled backwards, his foot caught on a trash can, sending it clattering across the floor.

Instinctively, Wallenbeck was already moving.

Sanderson took off, bolting for the door, but he wasn't fast enough. Wallenbeck was on him before he made it five feet outside, tackling him to the sidewalk. Sanderson struggled, kicking and twisting, but Wallenbeck was able to subdue him. And on the ground next to the man were two envelopes. Each had a typewritten address on it. Neither had a return address. While typed words all looked pretty identical, Wallenbeck had been looking at this exact typesetting for weeks. They looked identical to the others.

Once he got Sanderson back to the station and briefed Kerns, Officers Caruso and Stull were immediately sent from Upton's to Sanderson's apartment across town to have a look around. Wallenbeck did a dive into the man's life to find out whatever he could about him.

When Caruso and Stull returned with a typewriter from Sanderson's place, the team gathered in the War Room and, on a clean sheet of paper, typed out a copy of the last letter that had been received. The two looked identical. The state's attorney would surely want to run his own tests to take into court, but as far as Kerns and his men were concerned, they'd found the mystery man who'd been terrorizing the women of Parker City.

Officer Wallenbeck was then able to answer the question of why Sanderson had chosen the women he'd sent letters to. Ralph Sanderson worked at the Parker County Library right down the road from the police station. And after making a few inquiries at the library, Wallenbeck was able to confirm each of the women had checked out books at some point over the last several weeks. Each woman—every single one.

Including Elizabeth Blakely.

Armed with this information, Lieutenant Kerns quietly entered the interrogation room and settled into the chair across from the suspect. As he lit a cigarette, Sanderson shifted in his seat. Kerns looked down at the file folder he'd carried in with him.

"Mr. Sanderson, you work at the library," Kerns said. His voice was calm but firm.

Sanderson nodded slowly. "Yeah."

"What is it you do there?"

"I…um…I work at the desk, checking books out."

"So you see a lot of people come through?"

Sanderson shrugged and looked away.

From the folder, Kerns then removed a set of photographs. They were the pictures of the women from the wall of the War Room. "You ever see any of these women at the library?"

When Sanderson didn't look at the photos spread out on the table, Kerns shook his head. He didn't need Sanderson to confirm they'd been there; they'd already printed out the record from the library proving each of the women had been there in recent weeks. He was more interested in seeing Sanderson's reaction to the photos.

"Mr. Sanderson," he said again, "please look at the photographs and tell me if you recognize any of these women."

Slowly, Sanderson looked down and gave a hesitant nod. "I guess I've seen 'em."

Kerns exhaled slowly, a stream of cigarette smoke floating across the images laid out on the table. "Let's cut the crap, Sanderson. We know you saw all of these women at the library. Then you used the library records to find their addresses, and you sent them little notes. Threatening them."

Sanderson swallowed hard. "I...I..."

Kerns leaned forward. "We have your typewriter. It matches all the letters."

Sanderson pressed his lips together, his shoulders tightening.

"But here's what I don't get," Kerns continued. "What makes Elizabeth Blakely so special? Why hand write her letters? Why break into her apartment and tear up that dress? What was that all about? Something about her special to you?"

"I don't know anything about a break-in. Who's Elizabeth Baker?"

"*Blakely*," Kerns said, separating her photo from the rest.

Sanderson tilted his head as he looked at the picture of the young woman staring up at him. "I don't know who that is."

"That wasn't you, was it?" Kerns stubbed out his cigarette.

Sanderson's eyes darted to the mirror behind Kerns, as if expecting someone to step in and save him. "I told you. I didn't break in anywhere. I don't know what you're talking about."

Kerns sat back.

Silence filled the room.

The lieutenant watched the young guy for a long moment. He was guilty of some things—but not everything. But this was just the beginning of the questioning. There was a long night ahead of them.

Kerns stood, tossing a glance toward the mirror before heading to the door.

In the hallway, Chief Stanley was waiting. "Good work, Wallace. We got him."

Kerns shook his head. "I don't think so."

Stanley frowned. "The hell are you talking about? We got the typewriter. The library connection. He wrote those letters. You'll get him to admit it. You can see he's gonna break. He looks like he's got something wrong in his head to me."

"Yeah," Kerns agreed. "He does. And I'm sure he sent all those letters. But he's not the guy who *hand-delivered* those letters to Elizabeth Blakely...and me."

Stanley's scowl hardened. "It's him, Lieutenant. Be happy. We got him. It's over."

Kerns exhaled. "We might have the guy who wrote the letters. But we don't have the guy who's after Elizabeth."

Stanley shook his head. "Close the case! Let the state's attorney handle the details."

Kerns felt a knot tighten in his gut. Sanderson was definitely guilty. But there was someone else out there. He was certain of it.

Chapter Forty-One

The *Blue Ridge Herald*'s headline practically shouted at readers from newsstands across town: **POLICE PREVAIL: HOLIDAY TERROR ENDS WITH ARREST OF MYSTERY MAN** The article beneath it detailed the "triumph" of the police in capturing the person responsible for the wave of fear gripping the city's women. Ralph Sanderson, a library employee, who it turned out, had a few minor charges for trespassing in his youth, had been taken into custody, and with Christmas just days away, the city could now celebrate in peace.

At City Hall, Mayor Richard Worthington, beaming with satisfaction, stood before a gathering of reporters, flanked by Chief Edgar Stanley on one side and Lieutenant Wallace Kerns on the other. The mayor's elegantly appointed office in City Hall was filled with the scratches of pens on notepads, the click of camera flashes, and the hum of hushed voices.

"The Parker City Police Department has done an outstanding job ensuring our community remains safe," Worthington proclaimed. "With the suspect in custody, the city's holiday festivities can continue without a dark shadow looming over them."

The reporters, eager for a good quote, pressed forward, throwing out questions.

"Chief Stanley, can you confirm that Ralph Sanderson acted alone?"

"Absolutely," Stanley replied without hesitation. "We have every reason to believe he was solely responsible for the letters. With him off the streets, women have nothing to fear."

Off to the side, Kerns bristled.

After a few more questions, as the reporters left to file their stories, the mayor turned to Stanley and Kerns, clapping them both on the shoulder. "Fine work, gentlemen. The people of Parker City can rest easy now, and they have both of you to thank. I hope you and your families have a very Merry Christmas."

Stanley, soaking up the praise, nodded in agreement. But Kerns was lost in thought. His mind kept circling through the details—the ones no one else wanted to acknowledge.

He knew Sanderson had been responsible for the typed letters mailed to women across the city. The typewriter matched. The timing made sense. The evidence was solid. The state's attorney had him dead to rights on those charges.

But Elizabeth Blakely's case was different.

Her letters had been *handwritten. Delivered in person.* And someone had broken into her apartment. None of the other victims had experienced anything like that. The only link between Sanderson and Elizabeth was that she, too, had borrowed books from the library during times he'd been working.

That wasn't enough. At least not for him.

Stanley, sensing his hesitation as the mayor left, turned to his deputy with an exasperated sigh.

"How many damn times do you need to solve the case to be happy, Wally?"

Kerns didn't respond. He just watched the chief walk out of the office and head down the hallway.

Which is what he did a few minutes later. But instead of heading back to the station, he climbed in his car and drove north to Wakeville.

When he knocked on the door to the Blakelys,' it was Elizabeth's father, Clifford, who answered.

"Lieutenant," he said, stepping aside to let him in.

Marian Blakely appeared from the kitchen, wiping her hands on a dishtowel. "Is it really over?" she asked, her voice hopeful. "That's what the radio's saying."

Kerns nodded, choosing his words carefully. "We have a suspect in custody.

The man responsible for the letters has been arrested."

Clifford exhaled, relief washing over him. "That's good news."

Elizabeth and Joyce joined everyone in the entry hall, the younger women exchanging a look.

Joyce, never one to hold back, spoke first. "*The* man responsible for *the* letters," she repeated. "You're sure it's him?"

Kerns met her sharp gaze. "We're confident that Ralph Sanderson was behind the letters."

Elizabeth studied him, her arms crossed tightly. "And he's the one who broke into our apartment."

It wasn't a question.

Kerns let out a slow breath. "We have not been able to confirm that."

Marian's hand went to her chest. "What exactly does that mean?"

Kerns looked from Marian to Elizabeth, then cautiously admitted, "There is a possibility Sanderson isn't the one who threatened you. He claims he didn't break into your apartment and knows nothing about the letter you received."

"Then why is the police chief saying it's over?" Joyce demanded.

Kerns glanced at Clifford and Marian before answering. "Because as far as the department is concerned, it *is* over. The mayor wants people to feel safe again. Especially with the holidays coming up. Everyone wants it to be over."

Joyce scoffed. "Politics."

"But it doesn't mean he *isn't* the guy either," Kerns offered. "We just can't prove he broke into your apartment."

Elizabeth's voice was quiet but firm. "So what do I do?"

Kerns considered his answer carefully. He had already taken a risk by admitting his doubts. If Stanley got wind of this conversation, there'd be hell to pay. But he couldn't lie to her. That wasn't the kind of cop he was. Sure, it would have been the easy thing to do, but then how could he look himself in the mirror every morning?

"Stay vigilant," he said. "Keep your doors locked. And if anything— *anything*—feels off, call me."

She nodded, but Kerns could see the disappointment in her eyes.

"Thank you for everything you've done, Lieutenant Kerns," Elizabeth said, a slight tremble still hidden in her voice.

A few minutes later as he stepped outside, the December air bit at his face. He hesitated on the porch, scanning the quiet street. Snow had started falling, dusting the houses and yards in white. The town of Wakeville was peaceful, but Kerns couldn't shake the feeling that something was still wrong.

As he walked toward his car, a sudden movement caught his eye.

A man, standing at the corner of the street, just at the edge of the streetlamp's glow. He was bundled up with a scarf wrapped around his face and a knit cap pulled down low. Kerns stopped, narrowing his eyes. But before he could get a better look, the figure turned and disappeared into the darkness.

Chapter Forty-Two

Four months after the arrest of Ralph Sanderson, Parker City was happily settling back into its routine. The holiday season came and went with a renewed sense of celebration, and now, as Easter approached, the city had all but forgotten the fear that had gripped it just a short time earlier. With each new day, the front-page headlines in the city's two main newspapers became more and more forgettable.

The only newsworthy event that had residents of Parker City talking was when President Lyndon Johnson made a brief stop in Downtown Parker City during one of his visits to Camp David, the presidential retreat situated in the Catoctin Mountains north of the city. The president and his entourage had stopped into none other than Upton's Department Store, where he spent his time browsing around the Sporting Goods Department.

All across the city, with Easter around the corner, the pastel-colored decorations in shop windows, the scent of chocolate and hot cross buns filling the air, and the promise of warmer days ahead had erased the lingering unease of the dark winter of 1965.

Lieutenant Wallace Kerns had been among the last to let his guard down. At first, he'd remained skeptical that Sanderson had been responsible for everything. The typewritten letters? No doubt. But the ones delivered to himself and Elizabeth Blakely? The break-in at her apartment? Those had always felt different.

And yet, in the months since Sanderson had been locked away waiting for trial, there had been no more letters. Eventually, even Kerns was forced to admit that maybe, just maybe, they had gotten the right man after all.

Needless to say, Chief Stanley, when talking about it, was more than happy to claim most of the credit for the capture. Though he did mention Kerns and his team when talking about the investigation, one would think by listening to him, he'd been in the War Room every single day, solely focused on finding the man threatening the women of Parker City.

Elizabeth and Joyce had finally moved back into their apartment in February. They had taken every precaution—new locks on the doors, a chain installed, even a baseball bat propped up next to Elizabeth's bed. But as the weeks passed without incident, their initial anxiety faded, and soon, life had begun to feel normal again.

For Elizabeth, part of that return to a normal life came in the form of Alfred Marsh.

What had started as occasional, polite visits—him checking in on her after work, bringing her small gifts like a book he thought she'd enjoy or a sweet treat from the bakery down the street—had slowly grown into something more. They went to the movies, had dinners at cozy restaurants, and even took walks through Jefferson Park when the weather was nice. Though neither of them had said it outright, it was clear to anyone paying attention that they were becoming more than just acquaintances.

Even Joyce had taken notice.

"I'm just saying," she'd told Elizabeth one evening while setting the little table in their kitchen, "if Alfred isn't already your boyfriend, he's putting in an awful lot of effort for a guy who isn't."

Elizabeth had rolled her eyes, but couldn't hide the smile.

"Well, he *is* nice," she admitted, placing a bowl of mashed potatoes down.

Joyce shook her head. "Nice? Liz, the man practically trips over himself to open doors for you."

Elizabeth didn't argue. And she didn't deny that she liked the attention and felt good when she was around him.

Now, as Parker City bustled with preparations for Easter Sunday, Elizabeth found herself fully immersed in the festive atmosphere. Upton's, like all the other stores in town, had transformed into a pastel wonderland. The front windows boasted an elaborate display featuring stuffed rabbits, baskets overflowing with candy, and mannequins dressed in springtime finery.

Inside, the store was as chaotic as ever. Customers filled every department, women scouring the racks for the perfect Easter dress, children tugging at their mothers' skirts, begging for chocolate eggs from the candy counter.

Elizabeth had even been asked to help with a new spring fashion display near the front of the store, which was why she was carefully adjusting a mannequin's dress when the sound of a familiar voice made her shoulders tense.

"You know, you should be a model, honey."

Without turning around, she could tell by the overpowering scent of Aqua Velva that it was Dick Calhoun.

Elizabeth stiffened but kept her focus on the mannequin, refusing to give him the satisfaction of a reaction.

"I bet Alfred would agree with me," he continued, sauntering up beside her. "I understand you two've been spending plenty of time together."

Elizabeth turned to face him, her expression cool. "Is there something you need, Dick? Or are you just here to waste everyone's time?"

He grinned, unbothered by the clear disdain in her voice. Disdain she wasn't afraid to hide any longer.

"Now, now, don't be like that, sweetheart," he said, adjusting his tie and smoothing his slicked hair using the reflection in one of the store's mirrored columns. "I'm just making conversation."

Elizabeth folded her arms. "Unfortunately, I'm not the boss's nephew, so I don't have the luxury of standing around *making conversation*. Some of us have to work for a living."

Calhoun chuckled, shaking his head. "You know, that sharp tongue of yours might scare some men off." He leaned in slightly. "Good thing I like a challenge."

Before Elizabeth could respond, another voice cut in.

"She's not interested, *Dick*."

Alfred seemed to materialize out of thin air. Elizabeth hadn't even noticed him approach, but there he was, standing beside her, his expression unreadable but his tone carrying an unmistakable warning.

Calhoun scoffed but took a step back. "Relax, Marsh. Just having a little fun."

Alfred's gaze remained steady. "Go have your fun somewhere else, or I'm going to have words with your uncle."

For a moment, it was like Calhoun might have something cutting on the tip of his tongue, but then he thought better of it. Raising his hands in mock surrender, he said, "Alright, alright. No need to get worked up." He winked at Elizabeth before turning and strolling away in the direction of a couple female salesclerks standing together behind the jewelry counter.

Elizabeth let out a deep breath. "I swear, that man is a—"

"I know," Alfred agreed, even without her finishing the sentence. "You should never have to deal with him. I think it might be time someone finally tells Mr. Upton just how useless Dick really is."

"You think he doesn't already know?" Elizabeth asked with a smile. "Thanks for stepping in."

He nodded, then glanced toward the display she'd been working on. "Need a hand?"

She laughed. "Only if you know anything about adjusting mannequin dresses."

Alfred shrugged. "Can't be that hard."

Elizabeth couldn't help but smile.

That evening, after another busy day, Alfred walked Elizabeth home so they could enjoy the crisp spring air.

As they approached her building, Elizabeth hesitated.

"Something wrong?" Alfred asked.

Elizabeth shook her head. "No…just tired, I guess."

Standing in front of the door to the apartment building, they said goodnight—Elizabeth giving him a kiss on the cheek. With a tip of his hat, she watched him walk off down the street as she opened the door.

Inside the apartment, everything was as it had been when she left that morning. Yet, as Elizabeth set down her purse and slipped off her coat, she couldn't shake a strange feeling.

Stepping to the front window, she stared out into the darkening street. Just the usual evening traffic and people walking past.

Shaking her head, she forced herself to relax, turning on the television set so there was some noise filling the apartment.

It was over. Sanderson had been the guy. It was just her nerves playing tricks on her.

Still, as she got ready for bed that night, Elizabeth made sure the baseball bat was within reach.

Chapter Forty-Three

As the sun rose on Easter Sunday, Parker City was bathed in a brilliant golden glow. Little did anyone know it would become one of the most beautiful days of the year. With a crystal-clear sky stretching on forever, pleasant spring temperatures, and the scent of freshly blooming flowers wafting through the air, the city hummed with joy and excitement. Those celebrating the holiday could not ask for a more exquisite day as they headed off to church in their Sunday finest with colorful hats adorned with silk ribbons and polished shoes catching the morning light. A city whose skyline was dotted with towering steeples, its bells rang out in harmony, welcoming one of the holiest days of the year for the faithful. Easter had arrived, and with it, a day of celebration that felt almost impossibly perfect.

Marian and Clifford Blakely led their family out the front doors of Saint Joseph's Episcopal Church into the bright sunlight, where they paused at the top of the steps to greet their longtime pastor. Marian, filled with excitement, could barely contain herself as she introduced him to Elizabeth's "handsome new boyfriend," Alfred Marsh, who'd accompanied Elizabeth to church that morning and would be joining the family for lunch back at the house.

A devoted member of the church's Ladies Auxiliary, Marian knew every member of the congregation, and she made it her mission to parade Alfred around like a prize. Wearing a bright yellow flowered dress, she looked like a little bumblebee buzzing from group to group as she mingled with everyone outside St. Joe's, making certain they all knew who Alfred was.

Elizabeth, meanwhile, made several attempts to rescue him, but it was a losing battle. Once Marian had grabbed onto something—or someone—there was no escape. To his credit, Alfred handled the attention without putting up a fuss, though occasionally he would glance toward Elizabeth with pleading eyes. In return, she would simply smile and shrug her shoulders. Secretly, she enjoyed the attention she was getting—even though it was through him.

After all the needling from Joyce and Patty, and a few choice comments from Donna at lunch one day, Elizabeth finally admitted how she really felt about Alfred. The next night after dinner, as Alfred was opening the car door for her, she summoned up all her courage—hearing Joyce's voice encouraging her in her head—leaned in and kissed him. The feeling of exhilaration that surged through her was something she'd never felt before. She'd never done anything so bold. And the best part was that Alfred kissed her back. Elizabeth blushed just thinking about that moment as she watched him with her mother.

A few feet away, Clifford leaned against a stone column, lighting his pipe as he watched the show unfold. Marian was in her element. With an amused grin, he turned to see his youngest daughter and her husband, Kenneth, walking toward him. Married now for four months, Patty still had that newlywed glow about her. He was happy for his baby girl. Kenneth was a good man and good for her, and that was all a father could ask for. They seemed to be the perfect fit for one another. He'd noticed them holding hands in church that morning. It was sweet. As much as he loved Marian, he couldn't remember the last time they'd held hands.

"Look at how happy Mom is," Patty said, shaking her head.

"Of course she is. She's showing off your sister's boyfriend." Clifford smiled, watching her drag Alfred over to the next group of ladies.

"It's about time Liz finally fessed up about how she felt about him," Patty said with a smile.

"There's nothing wrong with taking it slow," Kenneth said with a shrug.

"Oh, hush," Patty said, smacking her husband playfully on the stomach. "I just want to see Liz settled down and happy. Plus, he's pretty dishy, if you ask me."

"Hey!" Kenneth protested, wondering if he even sounded remotely serious.

"Don't try it. I know you look at the secretaries at the bank."

Opening his mouth to respond, Kenneth saw the look Clifford was giving him over Patty's shoulder and took his wordless advice not to respond.

"That's better," Patty said with an impish grin.

"Why don't I go get the car?" Kenneth offered.

"Safest thing you can do," Clifford advised, watching his son-in-law head off toward the parking lot behind the church.

Turning back to her father, Patty suddenly began fidgeting with the buttons of her coat. In that split second, Clifford had seen her entire attitude change. The playful demeanor vanished, replaced by a look of nervousness.

"What's wrong, kiddo?"

"Why do you think something's wrong?"

"Because you're pursing your lips like you do when you've got something on your mind."

"I don't do that."

"Sweetheart, I've known you your entire life. I know every face you make, and what each one of them means."

It was true. Growing up, she and Elizabeth could never keep anything from their father. It was uncanny how he could always tell when they had something on their mind or were worrying about something. Even worse, he could always tell when they'd done something they weren't supposed to do. He'd just have to look at them, and he'd know. And they knew he knew. But that supernatural ability was also what had made him such an amazing father. They both adored him. If either of them was having a bad day, he'd know what to say to cheer them up, and when something exciting happened at school, he was the first person either of them wanted to tell.

"So?" He asked again, "What's on your mind?"

Patty took a deep breath, then looked up at him with a smile. "Well…since it's Easter, a day for new beginnings and all of that…we kind of figured today would be a good day to tell you and Mom."

Clifford raised his eyebrows. "Tell us what?"

Hesitating for only a second, Patty blurted out, "I'm pregnant."

The pipe nearly fell out of Clifford's mouth. His eyes widened as he took a step back and looked at his little girl. For the briefest of moments, he thought she might just be teasing him, that this was a joke, but looking into her bright eyes, all he could see was a mixture of excitement and nervousness.

"Pregnant," he repeated.

Patty bit her lower lip and nodded. "Yeah. Kenneth and I just found out last week. We wanted to wait for the right moment to tell everyone. I guess this is kind of it." She shrugged her shoulders, her smile growing even wider.

"Well, I'll be damned," Clifford finally said. "I'm going to be a grandfather!"

"Yeah. You are. You're gonna be a grandfather," she said into his chest as his arms wrapped around her. She'd always felt so safe when her father hugged her.

Clifford suddenly pulled back, placing his hands on her shoulders. "Wait a minute. Does your mother know?"

Patty shook her head. "Not yet. I wanted to tell you first."

"Well, brace yourself. Once you tell her, she'll have the baby's entire wardrobe picked out by dinner tonight." Looking back over to his wife, watching as she dragged Alfred Marsh behind her, he said, "Guess you better tell her before she starts planning your sister's wedding first."

As they walked toward the chattering crowd, Clifford Blakely took one last look at his daughter, the little girl he used to carry around on his shoulders, now about to become a mother herself. At that moment, he couldn't even begin to explain how he felt. His heart was full of so much love and pride.

Chapter Forty-Four

The Monday after Easter was going to be a blur for Elizabeth. She already knew this as Joyce pulled up in front of Upton's, halfway through a sentence about some nonsense at the telephone exchange. A stack of quarterly reports that needed to be typed up were awaiting her at her desk. Those were all on top of her usual beginning-of-the-week tasks. She was resigned to being chained to her typewriter all day. Which, she realized as she stepped into the employee elevator and hit the button for the third floor, was alright with her. She wasn't feeling very much in the mood to talk to people today, even though she knew all the girls in the office were going to be excited to hear that she was going to be an aunt. For whatever reason, today, she'd much prefer just to keep her head down and focus on her work.

Walking into the Accounting and Business Office, the few secretaries who'd arrived ahead of her were all clustered around Donna's desk, fresh cups of coffee in hand, chatting about their weekends. It was a pretty standard scene for the first day of the week. Elizabeth saw none of the office's executives had gotten in yet. Except, of course, for Alfred. His door was closed, but she could see movement in the office through the frosted glass.

Elizabeth smiled to herself, thinking about him in there pacing back and forth—as he did—with a sheaf of paper printouts in his hand, making mental notes. Alfred liked his numbers. And she liked Alfred. It was a big step asking him to join her and her family for church on Easter. And, until Patty had sprung the news on them that she was pregnant, she'd barely had a chance to talk to Alfred because her mother had been monopolizing him. But once she heard about the baby, Alfred was released from being the center of her mother's attention, and they were able to spend a little time together, just the two of them.

Alfred had been such a good sport through all of it. First, her mother's fixation on him and introducing him to every single person they knew at church, then the loud family meal where there'd been enough food to feed a small army, followed by the even louder reaction and aftermath of Patty and Kenneth's announcement. Throughout the entire day, whenever she'd caught Alfred's eye, he'd blush and smile. It was sweet how he still seemed so nervous around her. Even with all the time they'd been spending together.

"How was your Easter?" Donna asked as Elizabeth put her purse in the bottom drawer of her desk and removed her jacket—it was still just a little too cool in the mornings not to wear one.

"It was very nice," she said with what she felt was a forced smile.

Before she sat down, she stepped over to Donna's desk with the other girls and told them about her sister's news. As she expected, they all hooped and hollered, saying how happy they were for her sister…and her, since she was going to be a new aunt and all. After a few more minutes of idle chitchat, during which the rest of the office began trickling in, Elizabeth sat down at her own desk to get to work.

The office quickly began to fill with the sound of clacking typewriter keys and the ringing of telephones. Elizabeth found herself falling into a nice rhythm, and before she knew it, Alfred was standing in front of her desk, asking if she was ready to go to lunch.

Looking at the pile of papers sitting on the side of her desk, it didn't look like she'd made any progress, even though she hadn't taken a single break since she started that morning. The minute she looked back up into Alfred's eyes, he could tell she was going to say she wasn't able to go to lunch today. Which was exactly what she did.

"I'm sorry. I just have all these reports that need to be taken care of."

"I know," Alfred said, the disappointment in his voice evident. "I should be glad you want to get all of those finished. That's definitely going to be helpful. But all things considered, I'd rather spend time with you."

"You're so sweet. But you're my boss. You should want me to get my work done."

Alfred thought for a moment. "You're right. I am your boss. I could tell you that you *have* to take a lunch break and join me across the street for a sandwich."

"But you're not going to do that," Elizabeth pointed out, "because you know I take my job seriously."

That was just one of the things he'd found he liked about her. Though, if pressed, he would have to admit, as he and Elizabeth had been getting closer, it was becoming a little more awkward around the office. Not that she seemed to mind, but he felt bad when he needed to give her a last-minute assignment or asked her to handle a tedious task. But she was good at what she did, and he knew he could count on her. Not only to get the job done right, but usually to do it better than anyone else could.

He hadn't discussed it with Elizabeth yet, but he'd been thinking it may be time to make a change. As much as he'd come to rely on her, he didn't feel it was right for her to be his secretary any longer. Upton's didn't have any specific rules about co-workers dating…but was it right for him to be dating his secretary? He knew any of the other executives would snap her up to work in their department, but that would mean he wouldn't get to see her as much. He felt as though he were walking a tightrope. He'd never needed to balance his professional and personal life like this before.

Looking down at her, he smiled and said, "This means we're not going to get to spend any time together today. I have my game with the fellas tonight."

Once a week, Alfred would get together with some of his buddies to play poker. It turned out numbers weren't the only thing Alfred Marsh enjoyed and was good at. He liked card games. Poker was just an excuse to hang out with the guys. Other card games were all about probability and statistics, which were two things he was able to calculate almost instantaneously in his head.

"I'll make it up to you tomorrow. Why don't you come over after work, and I'll cook dinner. Joyce said she has plans, so we'll have the apartment all to ourselves."

Alfred's face flushed when he saw the twinkle in her eye.

"Alright. Tomorrow night it is then."

Elizabeth's heart sank just a little bit as she watched Alfred put his hat and coat on and leave the office for lunch without her. But she told herself she needed to be responsible and finish her work. She didn't want to take advantage of her relationship with Alfred.

Sighing and shaking her head, she pulled the next stack of papers in front of her. The numbers were all starting to blur together. Maybe she should have taken a break and gone to lunch. If nothing else, just to help clear her head. Instead, she decided to take a walk to the breakroom and get a cup of coffee. Even a few minutes away from her desk might help to refocus her, she thought as she made her way down the hall.

The breakroom was empty, but she was glad to see there was still half a pot of coffee sitting on the warmer. And next to the coffee machine on the counter was a plate of cookies someone had brought in. Grabbing a couple of sugar cookies and her coffee, Elizabeth got back to work.

Before she knew it, an hour had passed, and Alfred returned carrying a small box and a bottle of soda pop. "I thought you'd need to eat something. Turkey sandwich and a Coke to get you through the afternoon."

He smiled and set the food down on the edge of her desk. She hadn't realized how hungry she was until she opened the box and saw the sandwich, smelling the fresh lettuce and tomatoes. She thought it was so sweet that Alfred thought to bring her something. He really was one of the good guys.

By the time six-thirty rolled around, Elizabeth only had one last report to go, but knew she'd be able to finish it the next day. As it was, she was the only person left in the office. The executives had all taken off the minute the official workday was over, with all of the secretaries leaving a few minutes later. Even Alfred had left earlier than usual. Though his departure time was always well after most of the others. But he was looking forward to his card game tonight.

Turning off the lights, Elizabeth made sure the door was closed behind her and walked to the elevator. As she pressed the button and waited for the doors to open, she thought she heard a cough from somewhere down the hall. Turning to see who was still working as late as she was, the hall was empty, and all the doors were closed. She figured she'd imagined it.

Making her way along the sales floor, Upton's wasn't quite as busy as it had been in recent days. She figured most people weren't out shopping the evening after a holiday. Waving goodnight to a couple of the salesclerks, she walked outside and immediately felt a chill. The air was cool—it was still early April—but there was a strong breeze. Elizabeth wished she'd worn a warmer coat.

As she pulled her jacket around her a little tighter, she noticed a man standing across the street in front of the diner where Alfred had gotten her lunch. He was wearing a dark trench coat and matching hat pulled down low so it was difficult to see his face. She couldn't be certain, but she thought he was looking in her direction. Being that she was standing in front of the main entrance to Upton's, though, she realized he could be waiting for anyone to come out. It wasn't hard to imagine he was a husband who'd ducked into the diner for a cup of coffee or piece of pie rather than shop with his wife.

It wasn't until she started walking down the street and glanced back over her shoulder that she saw he was also now moving along the sidewalk in the same direction. Picking up her pace just a little, she turned the corner and was glad to see all the other pedestrians out and about. It had actually been quite a while since she'd walked home by herself. She'd gotten used to Joyce taking her to work and picking her up, and then after they'd moved back into their apartment, Alfred tended to walk her home or give her a lift when Joyce couldn't. Being amongst the crowd also made her realize how silly she was being. There were so many people out on the street. And just because a man walked in the same direction didn't mean he was following her. She was getting herself all worked up over nothing.

But then, at the end of the block as she was waiting for a bus to pass, she looked back and saw the man in the dark coat again. This time, he'd crossed the street and was on the same side as her, coming straight towards her.

Her heart began to beat faster. Maybe she wasn't imagining it. The minute the intersection was clear, she darted across, pushing her way past a group of construction workers, their hard hats tucked under their arms, metal lunch pails in hand. If any of them paid her any attention, she didn't take the time to notice. As she reached the sidewalk and turned, she saw the man had made it to the intersection she'd just crossed and was turning in her direction.

A trickle of sweat formed at the base of her neck. Her heart pounded.

Her apartment was only a few blocks away. She'd be there in no time. She just needed to keep going and not look back. That was easier said than done, though. Elizabeth couldn't help looking over her shoulder every few feet. Each time she did, the man was there.

By the time she reached the front door of the apartment building, her heart was thundering against the inside of her chest. Jamming the key into the lock, she thought she might rip the handle from the door, so she yanked so hard to open it. As she practically leapt into the small entryway, she looked out to the street one final time. A little old lady was walking along on the other side of the street, and a couple of teenage boys were playing ball. The man in the dark hat and coat was nowhere to be seen.

Elizabeth leaned against the door jam, shaking like a leaf. Resting her head against the cool varnished wood, she tried to regain her composure. How ridiculous she'd been. Parker City was a big enough town. That man could have been going any number of places that happened to be in the same direction she'd been going. He wasn't following her. She made the whole thing up.

She needed to steady her nerves.

Dinner and a glass of wine would help. Maybe two glasses. Then she would curl up on the sofa and watch the television. Deep down, she wished Joyce was going to be home or that Alfred didn't have his card game with the boys. She would welcome the company.

Not only had this been the first time she'd walked home by herself in months; it was the first night she was going to be by herself for the evening. That realization didn't sit well with her as she let herself into the apartment and kicked off her shoes. Her feet were aching, but not nearly as bad as her head.

Locking the door behind her—checking it twice—she walked into the bathroom to splash some cold water on her face. As she turned the lights on in the apartment, the windows lit up with a warm amber glow. Outside, as Elizabeth's shadow moved gracefully behind the drawn shades, a man wearing a dark hat and overcoat passed, pausing at the front door to the apartment building.

Chapter Forty-Five

Elizabeth woke with a start, her breath coming in sharp gasps. The room was dark with only the faintest trickle of light coming from the streetlamp outside her window. Sitting up, she rubbed her temples, wincing at the dull throbbing behind her eyes. The clock on her nightstand said it was only five o'clock. It was too early to be awake, but she knew there was no chance she'd be able to fall back asleep.

Her dreams had been strange and unnerving—flashes of red ink swirled in her head. The more she tried to remember, the faster the memories slipped away. She shook her head, trying to push the uneasy feeling away, but the sensation held her tight.

Even though it had been all over the news that Ralph Sanderson was on the verge of pleading guilty to the charges against him, and she'd received no more letters following the arrest, she couldn't shake the feeling that it wasn't over. The case was closed. But she didn't feel any safer. And then there was last night—the man in the dark coat, his slow, deliberate steps behind her, and the way he had vanished the moment she reached the front door of her apartment building. Had she imagined it? Or had she really been followed?

Elizabeth was shivering even with the blankets pulled up around her. Whether it was because of the memory of the man from the previous evening or the early morning chill, she wasn't sure. The longer she sat there in the dark, the more anxious she became. Swinging her legs over the side of the bed, she reached for the robe draped over the chair. Then, slipping her feet into her slippers, she made her way down the hall, the floorboards creaking beneath her.

In the kitchen, she put a kettle on the stove and reached for the bread, dropping a couple of slices into the toaster. Maybe tea and toast would help settle her stomach. But as she stood at the counter, watching the water slowly come to a boil, she realized her hands were trembling.

She exhaled sharply. She needed to get a grip on herself.

As she sat down at the small table in the kitchen, her appetite vanished. She picked at the toast absentmindedly, her mind slipping back to the flashes of terrifying red ink in her dreams. The images had been so vivid. Like she was looking at those terrifying letters she'd received all over again.

She rested her head in her hands, massaging her temples, trying to force the thoughts into some kind of order. The headache wasn't helping, and neither was the anxious energy coursing through her.

After a few moments, Elizabeth reached for her tea with both hands. She'd convinced herself that her mind was still dealing with everything that had happened—that she'd been on edge, jittery from a long day at work and too much wine with dinner.

She glanced toward the small window, looking out toward the building's back yard. Outside, the first hints of dawn were creeping over the rooftops. It was too early for many people to be out, but she suddenly wished Joyce were home. Even the noise of her friend moving around the apartment would have been comforting. Or just knowing she was asleep in the room next to hers.

Instead, the silence was deafening.

She needed to get out of her head. A warm shower might help, and she still had time before she needed to get ready for work. Standing abruptly, she left her half-eaten toast and lukewarm tea on the table and made her way back down the hall.

The hot water felt good against her skin, washing away some of the tension, but it didn't completely erase it. As she wrapped herself in a towel and caught her reflection in the mirror, she barely recognized the face staring back at her. Dark circles appeared under her eyes, and a slight flush to her cheeks from the heat of the shower. She looked...tired.

She got dressed slowly, choosing a simple navy pencil skirt and white blouse, and pinned her hair back neatly. By the time she was ready to leave, the sky had brightened, and the city was waking up. People were starting their morning routines, and for a moment, it felt silly to have been so upset.

Still, when she stepped outside, she couldn't help but glance down the street, scanning for any sign of the man in the dark coat.

Nothing.

Maybe she really had just imagined that he'd been following her.

By the time Elizabeth arrived at Upton's, the office was already coming to life. Typewriters were clacking away as the scent of fresh coffee filled the air. Donna was at her desk, chatting with one of the other girls, but she waved when she spotted Elizabeth.

"You alright?" Donna asked, eyeing her closely. "You look a little pale."

Elizabeth forced a smile. "Didn't sleep well," she admitted, slipping off her jacket and draping it over the back of her chair. Her purse, as always, went into the bottom drawer of her desk.

"Not feeling well?"

"Might be coming down with something," Elizabeth said. It was easier than explaining what was really on her mind.

Donna shook her head and went back to talking with the other secretary.

Elizabeth settled into her seat and pulled a stack of papers toward her, ready to lose herself in work. But before she could even roll a fresh sheet of paper into her typewriter, the door to Alfred's office opened, and he stepped out, scanning the room until his eyes landed on her.

For a moment, he hesitated, then made his way over.

"Good morning," he said, his voice warm, his eyes bright. "How are you today?"

"I'm fine," she said without much enthusiasm.

Alfred studied her for a moment, and she could tell he didn't quite believe her. "You sure?"

She nodded, offering him the best smile she could muster. "Just tired. Didn't sleep very well."

"Right," he said, but something in his expression told her he wasn't entirely convinced.

He glanced down at the papers on her desk. "I was actually going to see if you wanted to step out for coffee before the day gets crazy, but I can see you've already got your hands full."

The idea of fresh air and coffee was tempting, but she shook her head. "I should really get started on these. And I still have one more quarterly that I need to finish."

Alfred nodded, but she could see the disappointment in his eyes. "Alright," he said, slipping his hands into his pockets. "But let me know if you change your mind."

She watched him walk back to his office, the door closing softly behind him.

She exhaled slowly. Why did she feel like she was coming undone?

With a shake of her head, she turned back to her work, forcing herself to focus.

Chapter Forty-Six

The sound of paper jamming in the enormous copy machine ripped Elizabeth from her thoughts. The harsh crunch of crumpling pages was almost violent, yanking her back to reality. She had no idea how long she'd been standing there, watching the reports she'd spent yesterday typing spill out onto the tray, one after another.

Over the grinding of the copier, she could still hear Donna saying, "—and after making such a big deal about needing me to take dictation, the guy doesn't even bother to show up."

Elizabeth blinked, trying to remember what Donna had been talking about. "What?" She frantically pressed buttons on the control panel, desperate to silence the loud buzzing that filled the room. "I'm sorry...I can't—"

Finally, the machine was silent.

"Sorry," she said again, shaking her head. "I was off in my own little world. What were you saying?"

Donna sighed, leaning against the copier. "*Dick.* He made such a fuss about me being here early, and now it's almost ten, and he's nowhere to be found."

Elizabeth glanced at the clock on the wall. "Not like him to pass up the chance to boss someone around."

Donna snorted. "Exactly. He acts like he's the king of this place just 'cause he's the boss's nephew, but he can't even be bothered to keep his own schedule." She reached for the stack of papers Elizabeth was juggling. "Here, let me help. Seeing as I suddenly have all this free time."

Elizabeth handed over half the pile, and together, they walked back toward the Accounting and Business Office. As they entered, her eyes darted toward Dick Calhoun's office. The door was closed, no lights on behind the frosted glass.

Strange.

She didn't remember seeing him leave yesterday. And she was the last one out of the office. But then she did remember thinking she heard someone down the hall while she was waiting for the elevator. Could that have been him? Then again, Dick wasn't the type to stick around after regular business hours. He barely worked *during* regular business hours.

She stapled the last set of reports and slid them into a folder on her desk. As she did, she couldn't ignore the feeling she felt in her stomach. She told herself it was nothing—probably just her mood from this morning—but something about this felt…off.

Her gaze drifted back to Calhoun's office.

Before she realized what she was doing, she was standing in front of his door. She knocked softly, though wasn't expecting an answer. Something made her reach for the doorknob anyway. It turned easily.

Elizabeth hesitated. Dick was notorious for locking his office when he wasn't in. The man didn't care about other people's personal space or privacy, but he guarded his like a pirate did his treasure.

Maybe he had come in early and was working on another floor, and just forgot to lock up?

No. The only thing he did less than stay late was arrive early.

Elizabeth pushed the door open, reached in, and flipped the light switch. The fluorescent bulbs sparked to life. Looking around, at first glance, everything appeared normal. She'd been in the office countless times and couldn't see anything out of place. Then she saw a dark gray raincoat and matching hat hanging next to the door.

Her breath caught in her throat, her mind instantly flashing back to the man she thought had been following her last night. Could it have been Dick Calhoun? Was he waiting outside for her? Elizabeth realized her hands were shaking, the paper she was holding quivering like a leaf.

"Can I help you with something, sweetheart?"

Elizabeth nearly jumped out of her skin.

Turning, she found Dick Calhoun standing a mere couple of inches from her, so close his cologne made it difficult for her to breathe. The grin on his face turned her stomach.

"You don't look too good, Elizabeth. Everything alright?" he asked as he brushed past her, making sure his shoulder rubbed against her own, forcing her to take a slight step back.

"I was just…um…Donna said you needed her this morning, but no one had seen you."

Her eyes kept darting back to the coat and hat.

Dick dropped into his chair and kicked his feet up on his desk. "Oh, yeah. Forgot about that. My uncle called me into his office for a meeting as soon as I got here this morning. I know you'll all be sorry to see me go, but I might be moving down the hall to the senior executive offices pretty soon. Is there something about my hat and coat that's interesting to you?"

"What?" Elizabeth jump. She hadn't realized how obvious she'd been. "No. I just…is it a new coat?"

"Nice of you to notice. It is," he said with a smile.

Inside, Elizabeth was kicking herself. Now he was going to think she'd been paying attention to him and what he wore. Knowing the way his mind worked, with his overinflated ego, he'd probably assume he was all she ever thought about.

The knot in Elizabeth's stomach tightened.

"Sorry," she mumbled. "I still have some reports to get together."

Without waiting for a response, she turned and walked back to her desk.

Half an hour later, when Alfred stepped out of his office to grab a cup of coffee, he noticed Elizabeth wasn't at her desk, and that her jacket wasn't hanging on the back of her chair like it usually did. Must have had to run an errand, he thought as he turned heading in the direction of the breakroom. But for the briefest of moments, he paused and looked back at the empty desk. He didn't know why, but a sudden feeling of anxiety washed over him.

It wasn't that he required any of the secretaries in the office to inform him if they needed to run out for a few minutes—he was a very lenient boss in that regard—but with everything that had gone on with Elizabeth, and their current relationship, he wished she'd have told him where she was going. But he was sure everything was alright.

Wasn't it?

Chapter Forty-Seven

L ieutenant Wallace Kerns sat at his desk, the telephone receiver in one hand and a half-smoked cigarette in the other, as he stared down at a pile of official papers begging for his attention. Even in a small city police department, there was a lot of paperwork. He was interrupted when Officer Jimmy Stull—who'd been manning the front desk—rushed into his office. The young man was out of breath, and judging by the expression on his face, Kerns knew immediately that something was wrong.

"I'll have to phone you back, Irv," Kerns said, hanging up the receiver and stubbing out his cigarette. "What is it, Jimmy?"

"Sir, you need to come down to the interrogation room. Now. A couple just brought Elizabeth Blakely in. They found her up by Jefferson Park. She's saying a man kidnapped her outside Upton's."

"Sonofabitch," Kerns muttered, standing so abruptly his chair rolled backwards into the wall.

As he jogged down the stairs, Stull just a few steps behind him, his mind raced. This was exactly what he'd feared. Yes, Ralph Sanderson was behind bars, but he'd never truly believed Sanderson was the man tormenting Elizabeth Blakely. He'd known all along they were dealing with two different suspects. But once Sanderson was caught, he'd let himself be convinced— like everyone else—that he was responsible for all of it. For the last four months, that seemed to be the case. Elizabeth Blakely had gone back to her life, and there had been no more incidents.

Until now.

Stopping outside the interrogation room, Kerns took a moment to compose himself. If Blakely had been abducted, she was already scared. The last thing he wanted was to charge in and upset her even further. He needed to proceed carefully and not push her, but still get all the details of what happened while they were fresh in her mind. He reached for the doorknob, then hesitated.

"Jimmy, go get us two cups of coffee and a glass of water," he instructed. "Then find Caruso and Wallenbeck."

"Should I let Chief Stanley know—"

"No," Kerns cut him off. "Not yet. I want to find out exactly what happened before we talk to the chief. He's going to have questions, and I want to make sure I have the answers. And the couple who brought her in—where are they?"

"I put them in there with her. I thought she could use the company." Stull shrugged.

Kerns nodded. Under the circumstances, he couldn't disagree.

Taking a deep breath, he opened the door. Inside, three people sat around the metal table in the center of the room.

Elizabeth Blakely sat with her arms wrapped around herself, a man's suit jacket draped over her shoulders. She was slowly rocking back and forth in her chair. Across from her sat an older couple, at least ten years older than Kerns, likely in their late sixties. The man—dressed in a shirt and tie, his jacket now being used to keep Elizabeth warm—held his wife's hand. The woman, in turn, was focused on Elizabeth, her expression one of a mother's concern.

As soon as Kerns stepped into the room, the man stood, giving him a quick nod.

"Lieutenant Wallace Kerns," he introduced himself.

"Marty and Jan McGreevey," the man replied.

"Please, have a seat, Mr. McGreevey."

Taking the chair beside Elizabeth, the lieutenant's expression softened as he studied her. Her face was pale, and the eyes that looked back at him seemed hollow. He looked at her like a father would his own daughter. He had prayed this was over. But deep down, he'd known better. He should never have allowed Chief Stanley to convince him that Sanderson was responsible for everything. They should have kept investigating. At the very least, they should have *confirmed* Sanderson had been the one sending those letters to Elizabeth. But when the chief spoke, orders had to be followed.

"Elizabeth," Kerns said gently. "Can you tell me what happened?"

Slowly, she looked down at her lap, and Kerns noticed the scratches on her cheek.

After a moment of silence, she finally spoke. "Last night, after work, while I was walking home, I thought a man was following me. I didn't see his face. He had his hat pulled down low and his collar up. Then, this morning, I saw a coat just like his hanging in Dick Calhoun's office. I know that sounds ridiculous—it was a dark raincoat. Lots of men have coats that color. I just…I don't know. It scared me. I needed to get out of the office, get some fresh air. So I decided to take a walk around the block. That's all. I just needed to clear my head.

"When I got outside…I was turning onto Third Street when a man came up to me. I hadn't seen him. He was just…there all of a sudden. He was wearing a dark overcoat just like… He grabbed my arm and shoved me into his car. He told me he had a knife. That if I screamed, he'd kill me."

She paused, trying to catch her breath. The room was silent. All eyes were on Elizabeth, waiting for her to continue.

"What happened then?" Kerns asked gently.

"He drove us up to Jefferson Park. He parked on the road and pulled me out. He took me into the wooded area—the side with all the tall trees. Not the part with the bandshell and playground. The other side."

Kerns nodded. He knew the exact part of the park she meant.

"I didn't know what he was going to do to me," she continued. "He just kept looking at me. Then we heard a noise behind one of the trees. He looked away for just a second. I saw a big branch on the ground and grabbed it. I swung it at him. I hit him in the head. He yelled, and I ran. He grabbed my coat and tried to pull me back, but I slipped out of it. I ran through the trees." As she spoke, she reached up, touching the scrapes along her face. "When I got through the trees, I was out on the road."

"That's when we saw her. We were driving home from the market," Marty McGreevey said. "She ran right into the street. I slammed on the brakes just in time."

"I was so scared," Mrs. McGreevey added, wringing her hands. "But I could tell she needed help. You could see it plain as day. We got her into the car, and when she told us what happened, well, we knew we had to bring her here."

"It's good you were there," Kerns said reassuringly.

Elizabeth swallowed and took a deep breath. "If they hadn't been there…" Her voice trailed off as a tear streaked down her cheek.

At that moment, there was a tap on the door. Officer Stull had returned with the coffee and water.

"Mr. and Mrs. McGreevey," Kerns said, "would you mind waiting in my office? I'd like to speak with you a little more, but I need to talk to Elizabeth first. Officer Stull will take you there. And Jimmy—get Caruso to take their statement."

When the couple had left, Kerns took out his notepad.

"Elizabeth, I want you to go over everything again, starting with your walk home last night. Every detail you can remember. Nothing's too small."

She recounted her story without interruption. Kerns jotted down notes as she went, waiting until she was finished before asking, "Let's talk about the man who grabbed you. What did he look like?"

She hesitated. "He was taller than me, but not as tall as Alfred. He wore a dark trench coat. And…he had a mustache."

"Do you know the man? Had you ever seen him before today?"

Elizabeth shook her head.

Kerns made a note. Then asked, "Did he try to hide his face in any fashion?"

"He had sunglasses on."

"What color was his hair?"

"Brown."

Kerns tapped his pen against his notepad. "Any marks on his face or hands? Scars? Birthmarks?"

She shook her head.

"Other than the sunglasses, he wasn't trying to hide his face?"

"No." She frowned. "Does that matter?"

"It means you've seen him," Kerns said carefully. "Think, Elizabeth. Did you recognize him at all? Was anything about him familiar?"

She was quiet for a long moment, then shook her head again.

"No," she whispered. "I've never seen him before."

Kerns wasn't sure if that was better or worse.

Chapter Forty-Eight

1985…

Ben shot upright in bed, the haze of sleep vanishing in an instant as the thought that had jolted him awake came sharply into focus.

Two coffee cups.

There had been two coffee cups on the table at the Marsh house.

Not one. *Two.*

Who had Alfred Marsh been sharing coffee with that morning? Who had he invited into his home? Clearly feeling comfortable, completely unconcerned for his safety. Which turned out to be a mistake.

Ben turned toward the clock on his nightstand. Just after three.

Outside the window, the streetlamps cast a dull glow over a thick blanket of fog that hung low over the ground. The warm summer air of the previous day had surrendered to a sudden cold snap, and the meeting of the warm ground and cold air had created an eerie image outside. At this hour, it looked more like a dream than the real world—ghostly and deadly quiet.

The apartment was completely still, except for the soft, rhythmic breathing from Natalie on the other side of the bed. Ben exhaled slowly and leaned back against the headboard, running a hand through his hair.

After leaving Marsh's office, he and Tommy had called it a day. That had given him the rare opportunity to spend the evening with Natalie like a "normal" couple. She always knew when he needed a break. So, she convinced him to shut his notebook, change clothes, and go out to dinner at their favorite restaurant. Just the two of them. Good food, a couple of glasses of wine, no crime scenes or interview notes.

It had worked.

For a little while.

Now, the gears in his head were grinding again. Every time he closed his eyes, he saw the pieces of the puzzle, scattered and just out of reach. The two coffee cups kept hovering near the center of it all. They had to mean something.

He had half a mind to throw the covers off and head straight for the station. But even he had to admit it was too early for that. There was nothing he could do at this hour except sift through the files again. He still hadn't gone through the materials Tommy brought over from the Sheriff's Department. They hadn't had time, with Alfred's attack, to even crack the case file open.

There might be something in those old pages that could shake something loose and give them a solid lead now that they were nearly certain Alfred's stabbing was connected to what had happened to Elizabeth.

He also needed to go back and do a more thorough reading of the PCPD's original reports. Their first pass had been just that, a quick read-through to get an idea of what had happened back in 1965. If they'd known that a cold case would lead to a violent, present-day attack, they'd have studied every word a little more closely.

Somewhere in all that paperwork, they'd find the answer to all of it.

Staring up at the ceiling, he suddenly heard Natalie's muffled voice.

"I can hear you thinking."

Ben looked down as Natalie rolled over to face him, one eye open.

"Sorry. Didn't mean to wake you with my thinking," he said, instantly realizing how ridiculous that sounded.

Natalie gave him a faint smile. "You assume I can't detect the almost inaudible sound of obsessive detecting."

"Guilty as charged, I guess. I didn't realize *detectiving* had a sound," he said.

"It does. Trust me."

"I'm just trying to figure something out."

Natalie closed her eyes again. "I'll make you a deal. Go back to bed. If you still haven't solved this case by tonight, you can bring the files home, and I'll solve it for you."

Ben raised an eyebrow. "You'll solve the case?"

"I'm very clever. You knew that when you proposed."

"You are. And I did." He smiled and pulled the blanket up around her shoulders.

"I'm going to be an incredible wife."

"Yes, you are," he said, sliding down and wrapping her in his arms.

But even as he closed his eyes, his thoughts didn't stop.

The puzzle was still there. Scattered in front of him.

And at the center of it, still unexplained, were those two damn cups. Someone had been there with Alfred that morning—someone close enough to be let in without hesitation. Someone who sat down for a casual conversation...*before* everything turned violent.

Ben didn't know who it was yet.

But he was determined to find out.

Chapter Forty-Nine

Three yellow slips, all with messages from Lieutenant Clover, were waiting for Ben on his desk when he arrived that morning. Flipping through them, Ben instantly felt a sinking feeling in his stomach. After he and Tommy finished with Todd Kimble, he never came back into the office. When they'd gotten back to the station, he dropped Tommy off next to his Bronco and went straight home.

"Dammit," he said, picking up the telephone and punching in the direct number for the State Police Crime Scene Unit supervisor. Ben knew he also arrived at the office early, so hopefully he'd be there to answer.

After several rings, the distinctive nasally voice of Aaron Clover came on the line, "This is Clover."

"Lieutenant, Ben Winters. I got your messages. I'm so sorry. I never made it back into the office last evening."

"How's your victim doing, Detective?"

"Critical. But stable as of last evening," Ben said, taking a seat at his desk and moving some papers around. "I'm going to have those fingerprints brought over to you for comparison this morning."

"Thank you. That will be helpful. But that's not why I was calling you. It's about something we found at the crime scene after you left."

Ben sat straight up in his chair.

"As we were going through the kitchen, one of my guys found a piece of paper that had slid under the refrigerator. It was another letter. It looked like the one you'd already sent over."

Ben was back out of his chair, pacing behind his desk.

"There was blood on it," Clover continued. "So…I can only surmise that it was out in the open somewhere in the kitchen when the attack occurred. I could speculate that the victim was holding it and dropped it when he was stabbed, and that's when it slid under the refrigerator. But that would only be guessing. I can't prove that."

"What did it say?" Ben asked, his hand holding the receiver so tight he thought he might snap it in half.

On the other end of the line, Ben heard the lieutenant shuffling some papers. "It reads, 'Did you miss me?'"

After rattling off several more questions and giving Clover his pager number so he'd never miss him again, Ben hung up and slouched down in his chair. If he'd only come back up to the office yesterday and gotten the messages… Then what, he asked himself. They'd still have talked to Todd Kimble. Wouldn't they?

Of course they would, Ben told himself. They needed to look at all possibilities. And now, they were able to rule Kimble out as the attacker. That, and they certainly had no reason to believe he was the one who sent Elizabeth the letter the other day. But this new bit of information confirmed for him that their theory was correct that Alfred Marsh was attacked by Elizabeth's stalker was correct.

The look on his face obviously gave away his feelings because Tommy stopped in the doorway when he saw him.

"What's wrong? Please don't tell me we've got a body?"

After filling his partner in on what he'd just learned, Ben stood in front of the chalkboard quietly contemplating what they knew so far.

"Are we completely clearing Kimble then?" Tommy asked.

Slowly turning, Ben shook his head. "We still need to confirm when he left the meeting at…where was it…Caldwells? And get our hands on his cellular phone record for yesterday morning. I want his alibi locked down tight before we officially clear him. Even though I think it's safe to say—"

"—he's not our guy," Tommy finished.

"Call Caldwell Financial and find out if he left when he said. And I'll call Andrew Fields over at the State's Attorney's Office and see if we need to go through the same process for mobile phone records as we do for regular phones."

"Yes, sir," Tommy said, reaching for the telephone directory on Ben's desk.

As he called his contact at the Parker County State's Attorney's Office, for the first time, Ben felt as though he'd lost control of the case and made a mistake. Learning there'd been a key piece of evidence found at the crime scene hours after the fact had thrown him. But again, how would knowing there'd been another letter change anything they'd done? If nothing else, they knew they were on the right path, focusing solely on finding Elizabeth's stalker. Because when they found him, they'd find who attacked her husband.

"David Caldwell says that Kimble left their office sometime after nine-thirty yesterday morning," Tommy announced, hanging up the telephone. "That, combined with the secretary at Marsh, Kimble confirming he ran in just before ten, proves there was no time for him to have gone and stabbed Marsh. Let alone join him for a cup of coffee."

Ben shook his head. "Andy says he'll take care of getting the phone records. He's had a couple of cases that have involved mobile telephone information, so he has a contact over at Cellular One that he can talk to."

"Okay. Alright. So, we're back on track," Tommy said, rubbing his hands together. "What's the next—"

There was a knock on the door. Officer Bronson entered.

"Morning, Sarge. I have the canvassing reports from yesterday," he said, handing Ben a stack of papers. "Not many people were home, it being the middle of the day. And the ones who were didn't see much."

Ben took the reports and started flipping through them feverishly, looking for one key piece of information.

Raising an eyebrow, Tommy asked, "What are you looking for?"

Ben was chewing on his lower lip as he quickly went page by page. Finally, he looked up and said, "None of these say anything about a strange car being seen in the neighborhood. Remember, Elizabeth said she saw a dark car parked outside when she got home."

"It's possible no one noticed it," Tommy offered.

"Right. But it would have been nice if someone else had seen it."

"It would also have been nice if whoever stabbed Alfred Marsh would have waited at the scene for us and turned himself in. But here we are."

"Thank you, Larry," Ben said, turning back to the patrolman.

"Let me know if there's anything else I can help with, sir," he said with a stiff nod before turning and leaving the office.

"Is he on your list to join the Detective Squad?" Tommy asked, motioning toward where Bronson had just been standing.

Ben nodded. "I like him. I think he and Thompson could be good. But until we know for sure what the chief's plan is going to be, I really don't want to think about it."

"Alright, so what's *our* plan for the morning?"

"I'm thinking one of us can start going through the sheriff's files and the other can go have a conversation with Dick Calhoun. See what he remembers and what he's been up to all these years."

"And where he was yesterday morning," Tommy added.

"Exactly."

"I'll flip you for it," Tommy said, reaching into his pocket. "Heads, I go talk to Calhoun, and you dig through these dusty files, tails you dig through these dusty files, and I go talk to Calhoun."

Before Ben could answer, his partner pulled an imaginary coin from his pocket and tossed it in the air. Pretending to catch the nonexistent piece, he said, "Oh, looks like I'm going to go have a chat with Calhoun."

As he watched Tommy cross toward the door, Ben asked, "Just out of curiosity. Which was it? Heads or tails."

With a devilish grin, Tommy shrugged and said, "You pick."

Chapter Fifty

Ben hadn't argued with sending Tommy to talk to Richard Calhoun. If anyone could handle a personality like the one the officers from the first investigation described in their twenty-year-old interview notes, it was his partner.

By late morning, Tommy was pulling up in front of 347 Grant Avenue. The street was quiet, shaded by tall oaks and lined with tidy homes, most of them built sometime around World War I. The one he was looking for stood out, slightly larger than the rest—solid stone, well-kept, American flag hanging off a bracket by the door, and a white mailbox shaped like a miniature barn. Someone had put some love into the place.

In the driveway, he noticed a shiny black Mercedes-Benz coupe.

"Well, that's a dark car," Tommy said, walking by and admiring it on his way to the front porch.

Straightening his jacket and tie, he approached the front door. He knocked once, then again. Finally, the door swung open.

The man who answered was trim for his age, early fifties, dressed in khakis and a crisp golf shirt with a country club logo on the chest. His silver-streaked hair was combed back, his smile was too big to be genuine. The hairs on the back of Tommy's neck immediately stood up.

"Yes?"

"Richard Calhoun?" Tommy asked.

"Yes."

"Detective Mason. Parker City Police." He held up his badge. "Just want to ask you a few questions about something we're working on, if I could."

The smile faded just a fraction. "Something I did?" he asked cautiously.

"It's a case you were interviewed about some time ago. Related to a woman named Elizabeth Blakely? Do you remember her?"

Calhoun's jaw tightened.

"Oh. That," he said. "Well, I don't know how much help I can be. You're right. That was a long time ago. I don't even know the last time I saw her."

"I understand," Tommy said, "but I'd appreciate just a few minutes of your time."

Calhoun stepped aside and gestured for him to enter. The inside of the house was clean and well-decorated. Just as he'd expected from the way the outside had been kept up. Tommy was impressed. The guy had obviously done well for himself.

"Nice place," Tommy said, taking in the polished hardwood floors and paintings on the walls. A collection of porcelain figurines displayed in a glass cabinet caught his eye on the way into the formal living room off the entry hall.

"Thank you," Calhoun said. "Can I offer you something to drink? Water? Iced tea?"

"No, I'm good. Thank you," Tommy said, taking a seat on the edge of an armchair next to the fireplace, and opening his notebook. "You worked at Upton's Department Store back in the sixties."

"I was one of the executives. Yes," Calhoun said with a bit of a smirk. "Family business. My mother was an Upton."

"I see. During that time, you were interviewed by the police. Do you remember that?"

"I do. Vaguely. Like I said, it's been a long time," he said, waving a hand dismissively.

Tommy leaned in slightly. "You remember Elizabeth Blakely?"

Calhoun gave a thin smile. "She worked in the office. Sweet girl. Quiet. Seemed a bit... full of herself."

"Really?"

Calhoun shrugged. "She was very attractive, and she was always trying to use her *feminine wiles* to get ahead."

Tommy jotted a note. "Really?"

"But then, she suddenly became very high-strung."

"How so?"

"She started getting agitated easily. Anxious. Seemed like she was always looking over her shoulder like she thought someone was watching her."

Leveling his gaze, Tommy asked, "Was someone?"

"I wouldn't know. I minded my own business."

"Uh huh."

This guy was as phony as a three-dollar bill, Tommy thought to himself as he looked over at the pompous little yuppie sitting in his big leather chair.

Tommy flipped to a clean page in his notebook and said, "So, you remember that someone started sending Miss Blakely threatening letters?"

"It was hard not to know about it. She made sure everyone knew."

"That so?"

Calhoun shrugged. "The girls in the office gossiped all the time. It was hard *not* to know what was happening."

Everything out of Calhoun's mouth was contradicting the official reports and summaries. And the grin plastered on his face made Tommy want to slap it off him.

"Alright. What was your relationship with Elizabeth Blakely?"

"My relationship? I didn't have one. I was a manager with a lot of responsibilities. I didn't have time to mix business with pleasure."

"Interesting. Because what I read, you really liked the ladies. Had something of a reputation with the female staff."

Calhoun cocked an eyebrow. "I'm not sure what you mean."

"I'm not judging. I'm just trying to understand your connection to the case."

"I didn't have one," he said sharply. "And it certainly isn't my fault the women in the office took a shine to me? I was an attractive, successful man. Why wouldn't they be interested in me? Hell, even now, the girls at the club fall all over me. I live in a big house, drive an expensive car, and have lots of money. It's only natural."

"You're definitely a catch," Tommy said, not sure if the self-absorbed former store manager picked up on the sarcasm. "At any rate, Mr. Calhoun, someone back then was doing their damnedest to scare Elizabeth Blakely. If you were friends, I'd think you'd want to help us out here."

"First of all, we weren't friends. I was an *executive,* and she was a *secretary.* Not that that stopped some people," he said offhandedly.

Tommy narrowed his eyes. "What exactly do you mean by that?"

"Well, she and Alfred Marsh—*her supervisor*—were very close. Alfred was head-over-heels for her. It was very unprofessional."

"Wait. Are you saying you think Alfred Marsh may have been the person stalking Elizabeth Blakely?"

"I'm not saying anything. I don't really know why he'd have had to stalk her, as you say, considering the way she threw herself at him."

So far, none of what Richard Calhoun was saying made any sense. He did not like this guy and understood why he'd been a suspect back then.

Tommy leaned back in his chair. "That's an interesting perspective because that isn't how anyone else saw it."

"I can only tell you what I saw, Detective."

"Alright. Let's go with that. What did you see? Other than Alfred Marsh—as you say—was there anyone else who paid Elizabeth Blakely a lot of attention?"

Calhoun shrugged. "Not that I can remember. She was pretty, but beauty fades."

"Did you know that she and Alfred Marsh got married and moved away from Parker City?"

"I might have heard something. They both disappeared at the same time, as far as I remember. My uncle put me in charge of the Business Office when Alfred left. It was a massive headache having to take on all his responsibilities in addition to my own. It was completely unacceptable the way he left things."

"I'm guessing you didn't know they'd moved back to Parker City?"

"How would I?"

"Then you haven't been in contact with either of them?"

"No. Of course not," Calhoun said with a firm tone of indignation in his voice. "Detective, I don't understand why you're even here. This all happened twenty years ago."

"Well, Mr. Calhoun, one thing I've learned as a detective is that the past sometimes comes back to haunt us."

Tommy's statement was sharp, to the point, and seemed to have the desired effect. The smile had disappeared from Calhoun's lips.

Standing abruptly, Calhoun said, "If you don't have any further questions, Detective, I have a tee time at the club that I need to be leaving for."

Tommy followed him into the hallway and saw a set of expensive-looking golf clubs propped next to an equally expensive-looking sideboard.

"You play golf, Mr. Calhoun?"

"I do. Have a ten handicap," he answered.

Not having any idea what that meant, Tommy didn't say anything.

"I just got back from a golf trip to Las Vegas with some friends, in fact."

Tommy smiled. "Did you? Just got back, you say? When exactly was that?"

Trying to understand why Tommy was asking, Calhoun countered with his own question. "You never said, Detective. Why *are* you asking about a twenty-year-old case? I thought this had all been settled years ago."

"There have been some new developments in the matter since the Marshes moved back to Parker."

"I see. And somehow knowing when I got back from Las Vegas will help?"

"Believe it or not, Mr. Calhoun, it will."

"Fine. My friends and I flew back into Baltimore yesterday."

Tommy made a quick note in his notebook before slipping it into his jacket pocket. "What time yesterday?"

"What time?" Calhoun repeated, sounding irritated. "Just before ten. We took a red eye."

"I don't suppose you happen to have your airline ticket handy?"

Clearly annoyed, but eager to get the detective out of his house, Calhoun walked past Tommy and through the door opposite the living room. He returned a moment later with a handful of papers. Shuffling through them, he found his airline tickets from his recent trip and handed them over.

Noting that Calhoun had in fact arrived back in Baltimore yesterday morning, Tommy knew he couldn't have been the one who attacked Alfred Marsh. Or the one who put the letter in Elizabeth Marsh's mailbox the day before that. And there was no doubt he'd been in Vegas as he claimed because Tommy also had in his hands the ticket for his flight out to Nevada, his bill from the hotel, and a handful of receipts from restaurants and two golf courses.

Returning the stack of papers to Calhoun, Tommy said, "Thank you for your time. I hope you get a slam dunk on the golf course today."

"I think you mean a hole in one," Calhoun corrected.

Tommy gave him a tight smile. "Right. Hole in one. I guess I was thinking of a different kind of game—one where people don't get to rewrite the score after twenty years."

Then he tipped an imaginary cap and let himself out.

Chapter Fifty-One

Ben stood alone in the office, staring at the sprawling mess on the chalkboard. Names. Dates. Notes. A timeline that was starting to look more like a spider's web than a clean investigative thread.

He rubbed his temple with the side of his hand as the door opened and Tommy walked in, carrying a brown paper bag and a couple of sodas. Ben could already tell by the look on his partner's face how the interview went.

"The interview with Calhoun was that good?" he asked dryly.

Shaking his head, Tommy set the food on the desk. "If we ever need to convict Calhoun of being a smug jackass, I've got everything we need. But if we're looking for someone who stabbed Alfred Marsh…he's not it."

Ben accepted the club sandwich gratefully, popping the tab on the soda can Tommy handed over.

"What did he have to say?" Ben asked.

Tommy plopped into the chair across from him with a groan. "Claims he barely remembers Elizabeth Blakely, but couldn't wait to tell me how she 'threw herself' at Alfred Marsh and how terrible that was. But according to him, he thinks *he's* God's gift to women."

Ben raised an eyebrow. "Really."

"Oh yeah. One thing I'll say for *Dick* Calhoun is that his name fits him perfectly. He's just as bad as Caruso and Wallenbeck made him out to be—maybe worse. He talks like a man who thinks a restraining order is just a sign he's making progress."

Ben snorted into his sandwich. There was a certain irony to hearing Tommy Mason complain about a womanizer. Back in the day, Tommy had his own reputation. The difference was, women actually *liked* Tommy. Ben had lost count of how many times he'd seen a woman slip a phone number into his partner's coat pocket without a word. Tommy had what women wanted. Calhoun just thought he did.

"He's also got a solid alibi," Tommy continued, mouth half-full of chicken salad.

"Airtight?" Ben asked, bracing for the answer.

"Airtight. Flew home from Vegas yesterday morning. Had airline tickets, hotel receipts, credit card slips, you name it. Couldn't have stabbed Marsh even if he tried to hitchhike straight from the runway."

Ben let out a breath, deflating slightly. "So, we're right back to where we started."

Tommy looked toward the chalkboard and studied the tangle of information. "Not exactly. We're narrowing it down. That's something."

"Is it?" Ben muttered, the frustration creeping into his voice. "Feels more like we're eliminating every possible lead while the guy we *should* be chasing is sitting somewhere out there laughing at us."

He turned to the board, pointing at the increasingly crowded timeline. "We've got to be missing something. Someone who was there back then that no one thought of."

Tommy tossed his sandwich wrapper into the trash. "Let's run it again. Calhoun's out. Kimble's out. I don't think Alfred Marsh was the stalker either. Doesn't make sense. If he wanted Elizabeth, he married her. Why send her letters now? And then stabbing yourself...why? To throw off suspicion? Makes no sense."

Ben nodded, chewing thoughtfully.

Tommy leaned forward. "Alright. Let me throw something wild out there."

"That's so unlike you," Ben replied with a sarcastic grin.

Pursing his lips in mock offense, Tommy ignored Ben's crack and said, "What if it's not a man?"

Ben blinked. "What do you mean?"

"I'm saying... what if we've been looking for *him* and it was really a *her* the whole time? Could be a jealousy thing. Maybe someone who hated

Elizabeth for being so pretty. I don't know how women think."

Ben considered it. "Joyce Osbourne? I already thought of that. Plus, she was showing a house to Judge Scott at the time Marsh was stabbed. Her alibi's solid."

Tommy sighed. "Damn. Is it too late to suggest Alfred was a Soviet secret agent and got knifed by a CIA assassin? Maybe the letters were coded messages from Moscow?"

Ben shot him a look.

"I know, I know," Tommy sighed. "Even *I* don't buy that one."

Ben looked at the chalkboard. "I've been trying to flesh out the entire investigation using both sets of case files. The PCPD's and the sheriff's." He pointed to the first cluster of notes on the left side of the board. "In November and December of sixty-five, Lieutenant Kerns and his guys are looking into multiple anonymous letters being sent to women across the city. They think Elizabeth is just one of them. Then they arrest Ralph Sanderson. He confesses to writing the letters to the others, but he *denies* ever targeting Elizabeth."

Tommy frowned. "Why confess to everything but that?"

"Exactly. Doesn't make sense. But the letters stop once he's behind bars, so everyone thinks it's over. Four months later, Elizabeth is abducted. That's when the sheriff swoops in and takes over."

Ben picked up the folder containing the Sheriff's Department's documents. "Detective Noble hit the ground running real hard, it looks like. They interviewed everyone who worked at Upton's, everyone at Elizabeth's church, all her friends. The list of people they *didn't* talk to would be shorter."

"But they came up empty, too?"

"Yep. After Elizabeth and Alfred got married and moved away, nothing else happened. There wasn't any more for Noble to work with, so the case went cold. It was never officially closed, just put up on a shelf."

Tommy took the folder from Ben and started flipping through the pages. After a moment, he pulled a report out, held it up, and said, "Noble got a letter from this guy, too? That's gutsy."

"Just like Kerns did," Ben pointed out, motioning to that bullet point on the chalkboard.

Leaning back in his chair and putting his hands behind his head, Tommy said, "I'm not going to lie. It's a pretty damn good mystery if you ask me. Because you're right. There's got to be someone right there that we've all missed. It's a shame there's not a butler."

"A butler?"

"Yeah. Isn't it always the butler that does it in your British mystery novels?"

Ben rolled his eyes. Though, for the briefest moment, he couldn't argue with his partner. There did seem to be a serious rash of homicidal butlers in British mysteries.

"There's one person who could solve all of this for us," Tommy offered, shooting his empty soda can into the trash like a basketball. "Alfred Marsh. Once he comes to, all we have to do is ask him who stabbed him."

"Assuming he does wake up," Ben said. "But I don't want to sit around waiting for that. Especially if there's a dangerous suspect out there who may try and go after Elizabeth Marsh. I spoke with the security office at the hospital while you were at Calhoun's. Asked them to put a guard on Alfred's room. And I'm waiting to hear if the captain will approve a car to sit on the Marsh house for a few days."

"That costs money, dear Benjamin," Tommy chided. "You know Nelson doesn't like unexpected expenditures."

"I know. But it's worth it."

Taking the sheriff's file back, Ben started to collect all the documents spread across his desk. After he'd reorganized everything and tucked it all back in the large folder, he said, "I think we need to go talk to Ray Noble. You have his address?"

Tommy searched his cluttered desk for the scrap piece of paper he'd written the information for the former sheriff's detective on. "Right here. He lives in Middleboro."

"Let's go see if eliminating Dick Calhoun as a suspect makes him think again about anyone else."

At this point, Ben was looking for anything that might give them a new lead. Having eliminated their two best suspects, they didn't have much to go on. It was possible CSU would turn something up from their search of the Marshes' house, but Ben wasn't holding his breath. He had a feeling that the letter under the refrigerator was going to be the biggest discovery at the scene. And while he wanted to stay optimistic, he had the sinking feeling they weren't going to find any prints on it or the first letter Elizabeth Marsh had received that seemed to have spurred the attack on her husband.

In just forty-eight hours, this was turning into one of the most frustrating cases the detectives had ever been faced with. Even the gruesome murders committed by the Spring Strangler, at the time, seemed to make more sense. Whoever they were dealing with this time around was playing a very different game. And Ben was determined to keep them from winning at all costs.

Chapter Fifty-Two

Ben led the way down the stairs from the second floor with Tommy close on his heels, his suit jacket casually slung over his shoulder like a model in the J.C. Penney catalogue. The building was quieter than usual for mid-afternoon. A hot summer day tended to have that effect.

"I can't stop thinking about the two coffee cups at the Marsh house," Ben said as they hit the landing. "It's been bothering me ever since I remembered them last night… Or this morning, I guess, depending on how you look at it. But, someone was there with him. The place was tidy. Alfred clearly wasn't the kind of guy to leave an extra mug sitting around for days on end."

Tommy shrugged. "Maybe he was entertaining a ghost. This whole case feels like it's haunted."

Ben sighed. "Is that your next theory? A ghost did it? Seriously, though. Either someone was invited in, or…what, they were comfortable enough to help themselves after stabbing Alfred?"

"Either way," Tommy added, "it doesn't sound like some random nutcase breaking in off the street. It was someone Marsh knew."

"Exactly."

They exited into the first-floor hallway, heading toward the stairs that would take them down to the door that led out to the department parking lot. Ben slowed for a moment as they passed the breakroom, the unmistakable sound of a vending machine slamming shut followed by the crack of a soda can opening catching his ear.

From inside came a familiar voice, thick and gravelly: "I told him, if that kid keeps parking in my spot, I'm gonna key his damn car."

Tommy rolled his eyes so hard it looked like it hurt. "LuCoco," he muttered.

Ben gave him a look. "He was part of the original investigation. We need to talk to him. See if he remembers anything about the case."

Tommy sighed. "Fine. But if he starts talking with his mouth full again, I'm walking out."

They stepped into the breakroom just as Al Shepard was leaving, a fresh cup of coffee in his hand. Inside, Officer Buck LuCoco was hunched over the round table near the fridge, a doughnut in one hand, a can of root beer in the other, and his patrol cap hanging off the back of the chair. He was still in uniform, though his shirt was rumpled and the top button undone.

Tommy wondered how the poor metal chair was able to support a man with such a large and unhealthy frame. He'd wondered for years why LuCoco hadn't been kicked off the force for any number of reasons, but seniority still accounted for something, it seemed. Much to his displeasure.

LuCoco looked up at the detectives. "Well, well. If it ain't the Hardy Boys," he said, a few crumbs landing on the table in front of him as he talked.

"Afternoon, Buck," Ben said politely. "Got a minute?"

"Always got a minute. Or ten. Or an hour." He wiped his fingers on a napkin and gestured to the seats across from him. "What's up?"

Ben sat. Tommy remained standing, arms tightly crossed, his jacket draped over them.

"We're working that case—the attack on Alfred Marsh. Ties back to sixty-five. The Elizabeth Blakely letters," Ben said.

LuCoco gave a low whistle. "Blast from the past."

"You were around then," Ben said. "You remember much?"

Buck leaned back in his chair, causing it to groan under his weight. "Not much. I was only on the investigating team for a short time. I remember the buzz, though. Bunch of women getting creepy letters. Made the front page more than once. The mayor and old Chief Stanley were howling mad, I can tell you."

"Any solid leads?" Ben asked.

LuCoco snorted. "Hell no. Not till Wallenbeck accidentally tripped over that weirdo. Guy gave himself away. What a mook. Wasn't all that right in the head either if you ask me."

Ignoring the commentary, Ben said, more statement than question, "But Kerns wasn't convinced Sanderson was the one stalking Elizabeth."

"No, he wasn't," LuCoco agreed, shaking his head and scratching his fleshy cheek. "He thought Sanderson wrote the bulk of the letters to the other girls, sure. But Elizabeth…that didn't fit the pattern. Breakin' into her apartment and all."

"Then there's the little matter of the fact she got grabbed *after* Sanderson was behind bars," Tommy pointed out dryly.

"Exactly."

Ben nodded slowly. "So, if Sanderson wasn't the guy, do you remember anyone else standing out at the time? Friends? Coworkers?"

LuCoco scratched his chin. "Not really. Bunch of names floated around, but nothing stuck. There was an arrogant prick that worked at Upton's. What was his name? Calahan? Cunningham? Calhoun! That was it. But at one point, I thought it all might have been the Marsh guy tryin' to get her to run into his arms. Which I understand she ended up doin.' But I guess he didn't go and put himself in the hospital. Most people thought he was a saint. Saw him as that pretty little girl's protector."

Ben leaned forward. "What about Joyce Osbourne? You interviewed her, right?"

LuCoco chuckled. "Oh yeah. Joyce. Firecracker. Women's Libber. But I kinda liked her."

"She and Elizabeth were close."

"Roommates, right? She didn't take any crap from anybody. Sharp tongue. Kerns had me ask her some follow-up questions. She answered everything straight. No dodging. Never got the impression she was anything but a loyal friend. Definitely didn't peg her as a suspect…if you're goin' down that track."

Tommy, who had been leaning against the wall, pushed off with a grunt. "Well, thanks, Buck. That was…helpful."

LuCoco raised his soda in salute. "Anytime, boys. Just remember, retirement's in three weeks. After that, you want me, you'll find me fishing down in Florida."

As they stepped back into the hallway, Tommy muttered under his breath, "If that man ever chased a suspect in his life, I'll eat my badge."

Ben smiled. "Still, that was useful. Confirms a few things."

"Yeah. Confirms LuCoco's still as lazy as ever."

Ben clapped his partner on the back as they stepped into the warm June sun. "Let's see what Noble remembers. Maybe we'll finally get lucky."

"Or maybe we'll just add more names to that web on the chalkboard you've drawn," Tommy grumbled. "We should probably stop and at least pick up some more string."

Ben slid into the driver's seat and started the engine. "Can't solve a twenty-year mystery without getting tangled up a little."

With that, they pulled out of the lot, the car rolling into the heat of the afternoon, heading west toward Middleboro and whatever answers the past might still be holding.

Chapter Fifty-Three

1966...

Kerns felt as though his head was spinning as he stepped out of the room following his conversation with Elizabeth Blakely. Standing outside the door, he leaned against the wall for a moment, rubbing the bridge of his nose. A mental list of tasks quickly began forming—each item as important as the next, and all adding to the urgency of the situation.

Elizabeth would need to make a formal statement—he'd have Caruso take care of that. Hopefully, he'd be finished with the McGreeveys. They seemed like a decent couple, so he was very glad they'd been near the park that morning when Elizabeth needed someone.

Wallenbeck—he'd send him out to Upton's to ask some questions. One of the salesclerks might have been looking out the window at the right moment and seen the man or his car. Elizabeth's lack of knowledge about automobiles left them with an extremely vague description. Nothing more than "it was brown." Hopefully, someone might have gotten a better look.

Kerns wanted to visit Jefferson Park to personally look around the area where Elizabeth said she'd been taken. There could be something there that would help identify the man. Not that Kerns was holding his breath.

But there was something he needed to do first—inform the chief about the incident. Kern's shoulders sank. There was no way that conversation would go well. And he realized, once there was an official report filed, the odds were good that the press would get a hold of it. They knew there were those in the PCPD who were close to the sheriff and seemed to be all too willing to pass information on to him, as evidenced by the leaks of the letter and information about the investigation back in December.

It was going to be a nightmare. The press would start asking all manner of questions, which would only serve to whip the city up into a frenzy again. And he knew, he'd be the one Chief Stanley shifted all the blame onto, even though *he'd* been the one reluctant to believe Sanderson was the same person stalking Blakely. But that didn't matter at the moment.

There was a man out there who needed to be caught. He'd escalated from delivering threatening letters to breaking into Blakely's apartment and destroying a dress to kidnapping her right off the street outside her place of work. Kerns didn't know what would happen next if they didn't catch this guy once and for all.

Steeling himself for the conversation with the chief, he started down the hallway so engrossed in his own thoughts that he didn't hear the two uniformed officers coming from the opposite direction greet him. The two gave each other a look because it was so unlike Wallace Kerns to ignore any of the men. But as the lieutenant rounded the corner, he literally ran into Jimmy Stull. Behind him, Joyce Osbourne stood with a look of panic on her face.

"Lieutenant!" Stull said, taking a step back. "Miss Blakely's roommate is—"

Pushing past the young officer, Joyce charged toward Kerns, waving a piece of paper in his face. "I got home this morning and found this letter shoved under our door. I called Elizabeth at work, and no one knew where she was. So I came here, and he said Elizabeth was kidnapped! What the hell is going on!?"

Kerns placed his hands on Joyce's arms and, in his most comforting tone, said, "Elizabeth is here. She's safe." He felt the slightest release of tension in her shoulders, but it was clear she was still in a panic. "You can see her in a minute. But what about a letter?"

She handed him the paper, saying, "I stayed at a friend's last night. When I got home, I saw this pushed under the door. He must have put it there after

Liz left for work. I called the store and talked to one of the other secretaries, Donna, and Alfred…Alfred Marsh. He's beside himself. No one knew where she'd gone. She'd been there earlier, but then just disappeared. I got scared, so I came right here."

Carefully, taking the note from her, he saw the telltale red ink and sharp, slashing letters on the white page. He couldn't help but think it looked as though the message was written in blood.

ELIZABETH, ELIZABETH,
   I'VE BEEN WATCHING YOU.
   THE TIME HAS COME.

He reread the words a second and then a third time.

The time has come.

Was he talking about the abduction? And where had he been for the last four months?

Chapter Fifty-Four

By the time Kerns was finished speaking with Chief Stanley, the entire station house was talking. If they hadn't heard through the usual channels, one person telling another—as news so often spread through the PCPD—it was from the shouting coming from the chief's office. Even with the doors closed, there were officers on the first floor who could hear Stanley's booming voice coming from his corner office upstairs.

In the end, however, Kerns emerged relatively unscathed, but with the order received to find and apprehend the man who'd abducted Elizabeth at all costs. And the sooner, the better, which the lieutenant knew was easier said than done.

He'd finished with the chief in time to see Blakely escorted out of the station by her roommate. Joyce said she'd be taking Elizabeth back to her parents' house for the time being. Kerns promised he would check in with the family as soon as he was able.

As he drove toward Jefferson Park, to the spot where Elizabeth had escaped from her abductor, Kerns was thinking about what she had told him about the man. More specifically, how little she'd told him. After years on the job, he knew not everyone had a good memory. It was even more the case when they found themselves in a stressful situation. So, it stood to reason that Elizabeth might not be able to fully describe her kidnapper. But other than saying he had a mustache, the description she'd given was the most broad, and common he could imagine. It wasn't giving them much—if anything, really—to work with. Nor was her recollection of the car. Though, he couldn't fault her for that because he didn't know many women who could tell the difference between a Ford and Chrysler.

He knew he was just feeling frustrated by the fact they had so little information.

Easing the squad car to the curb, Kerns shut off the engine and stepped out onto the sidewalk. The air was brisk, but at the moment, he found it refreshing. It was beginning to look and feel like they were in for a spring shower that afternoon. The sun had disappeared behind a sheet of gray clouds which had overtaken the sky.

Placing his hat on his head and adjusting the holster on his belt, he looked up and down the street. This was where Elizabeth was found by the McGreeveys. This side of the park was mostly covered by trees—very natural and rustic. Jefferson Park was a thirty-acre plot with lush green grass, sports fields, and walking paths. On the west side, a bandshell had been constructed a few years earlier, where, during the summer, concerts were held for the public. At any given time, the park was filled with people playing, picnicking, just enjoying themselves and their time outdoors. The most unique feature of the park—Kerns's favorite—was an old Civil War battlement. It was a unique piece of the city's distinct history that connected it to a very difficult time in the country's past.

From where he was standing now, across the street to the east of the park, was Saint Joseph's Episcopal Church. Kerns found that interesting. That's where Clifford Blakely said the family attended church. Could that be where the suspect first saw Elizabeth? Was that why he brought her to this side of the park? It could be an avenue to explore.

As questions piled up, Kerns walked into the trees looking for any sign of Elizabeth Blakely's ordeal. Because the afternoon was still cool, and the trees provided so much shade, the ground was still damp from the morning dew. Continuing to scan the ground as he went, nothing was jumping out at him. Until he rounded a large White Oak, where he found a woman's raincoat. It was balled up at the base of the tree with some leaves strewn on top of it. Kerns couldn't tell if the coat was supposed to be hidden or if it had simply been tossed aside.

Looking around, he was trying to find the branch that Elizabeth used to defend herself, but there didn't appear to be anything large enough to use as a weapon. Would the mystery man have taken that and left Elizabeth's jacket behind? That seemed highly unlikely.

"Sonofabitch," Kerns mumbled.

There was a sudden movement off to Kerns's right. His hand automatically moved toward his revolver. For all he knew, Blakely's abductor was still hiding amongst the trees. But when the man responsible for the noise stepped from the shadows, Kerns relaxed.

Ray Noble stood next to the oak tree in his customary brown suit and matching fedora, hands shoved deep in his pockets. A square man all around, he was no longer as firm and muscular as he'd been when he was younger. Once he'd reached forty, he found he wasn't as concerned with his physical appearance and fitness any longer. And that was fifteen years ago, so he knew there was no way he'd be seen jogging down the street now. He left that up to the younger fellas.

The one thing that had unquestionably gotten better with his age was Noble's mind. He was one of the brightest people Kerns knew. He was a puzzle solver. Which is how he'd become the chief of detectives in the Parker County Sheriff's Department, and one of the most respected lawmen around.

"Hi there, Ray. What brings you here?"

"Same thing as you, Wallace. I understand there's been a development in the Elizabeth Blakely case."

"You do, do you? And how'd you hear that?"

"You know the sheriff has eyes and ears everywhere, and he was gunning for the Letters Case last Christmas. Now it looks like Blakely wasn't actually a part of that."

"Yeah. Looks that way." Kerns sighed. "I was all for working together last year, but you know how it is."

"Colsh and Stanley hate each other's guts." Noble smiled.

"Yep. But Stanley's not gonna give this up either. He was pissed to find out Ralph Sanderson wasn't behind all of it, but still…"

"Well, he might not have a choice anymore."

"How's that?" Kerns asked, genuinely interested in how Sheriff Colsh might try and take over the case. "I know Stanley hasn't called you in. So, unless the mayor did in the last twenty minutes. This is still a city matter."

"Actually, and here's the thing, Jefferson Park is *technically* a *county* park. The sheriff says we now have jurisdiction. At least shared jurisdiction. That's why I'm here. He wanted me to personally come over and take a look around." Noble paused. "Hey, I'm not trying to push you out. But it's not my call."

"Stanley's gonna have a fit."

"I'm sure he will. But you and I both know that's not what's important here. Let our bosses duke it out while we try and figure out who's trying to scare this poor girl."

Kerns had always liked Detective Noble. He was a straight shooter and didn't care for the politics of it all. They were men of the same generation who just wanted to do their job.

Looking around, Noble asked, "Find anything?"

"Looks like Elizabeth Blakely's jacket. She said the suspect pulled it off her as she ran away. She also said she hit him with a branch. I haven't found anything large enough."

Kerns was talking to Noble's back. He'd been carefully walking the area around the big oak.

"Did you happen to notice what kind of shoes she was wearing?" Noble asked, stopping and staring down at the damp ground.

The lieutenant thought for a moment. "I don't recall anything special about them. Normal women's shoes."

"Heels?"

Kerns nodded. "She was dressed for work."

"Interesting."

"What's that?" Kerns stepped up next to the detective and followed his eyes to the ground.

Noble pointed to the impression of Elizabeth's high-heeled shoes in the grass. Then he pointed to the prints he'd made walking over. And finally, Kerns's. "Hers, mine, yours. What's missing?"

Lifting his hat with one hand and running the other through his hair, Kerns sighed, *"His* footprints."

Chapter Fifty-Five

Detective Noble sat at the dining table with Lieutenant Kerns to his right and Elizabeth Blakely across from them. Her parents, Clifford and Marian, sat in their usual spots at either end of the table, and next to Elizabeth, holding her trembling hand, was Alfred Marsh. From the moment he'd walked into their home, he could tell the toll that had been taken on the family. There was an overwhelming sense of fear and uncertainty. The tension was palpable.

After their time spent examining the area in Jefferson Park, Noble followed Kerns back to the PCPD, where he'd been brought up to speed on the entire case. The lieutenant, along with Officers Caruso and Wallenbeck, walked him through every step—from the moment the first anonymous letter arrived in the mail right up until that morning when Blakely was brought into the station, shaken and terrified.

Noble was careful to note what actions were taken by Ralph Sanderson and which were now being attributed to Elizabeth Blakely's mysterious stalker. It didn't take a detective of his experience to see that things didn't add up. If the Sheriff's Department had been brought in at the beginning, he would have treated the Blakely portion of the investigation completely separately. It was clear from the start whoever was targeting her was not the same person who'd been sending threatening letters through the mail. Kerns had clearly been right about that, but he let it go when Sanderson was arrested. Noble couldn't blame him. His own boss could be a real hardhead, and when he gave an order, he expected it to be followed without question. And by all accounts, Edgar Stanley was a hundred times worse.

Following the briefing at the station, he decided it was best to meet with Blakely, introduce himself, and let her know he would now be running the case. Plus, he wanted to hear everything from her firsthand. Even if he asked the same questions she'd been asked a dozen times—which he was certain he was going to do—he wanted to give Elizabeth another chance to tell her story. People remembered things differently as time passed and they'd had a chance to think. Details that first seemed insignificant could suddenly become very important.

For the first hour, after Marian Blakely had served coffee all around, the detective walked Elizabeth through everything that had happened, beginning with the first letter she received the week after her sister's wedding. At first, her voice trembled as she spoke, but as the minutes ticked by, she seemed to gain strength, casting her eyes over to Alfred from time to time looking for support.

When they reached the events of earlier that day, he waited until she'd finished before trying to dig a little deeper into the story. From all accounts, she was terribly shaken when she'd arrived at the station, so maybe now—a few hours later and being in the comfort of her childhood home—she may be able to remember something she couldn't when emotions were still so raw.

Referring to the notes he'd taken during the initial briefing with Kerns and his men, Noble said, "You described the man who took you as having worn sunglasses and a dark overcoat."

It was delivered as a statement, not a question. To which Elizabeth nodded in agreement.

"And you saw the man's face but didn't recognize him."

Another statement.

"Well, it was hard to see his face. His mustache was so big. It looked fake, like it was part of a costume. And he had his hat pulled down low the whole time."

Noble looked up from his little leather notebook. "He was wearing a hat?"

"Yes. Didn't I say that?"

"No, you didn't," Lieutenant Kerns said, frowning and flipping back through his own notes.

"Oh. Yes. He was wearing a hat too. Like the man last night. I thought I'd mentioned that."

Elizabeth Blakely looked pale and drawn. Her eyes were red and puffy from crying.

"And you say the mustache looked fake?" Noble cocked his head to the side.

"It looked too big and bushy to be real, and it covered most of his mouth."

"Interesting." Noble exchanged a thoughtful look with his PCPD counterpart.

"With that and the hat," Elizabeth added, her voice growing quieter, "it's why I couldn't really get a good look at his face."

"So…" Kerns began, then paused so he could choose his words carefully, "is it possible the man who abducted you *could* be someone you know, you just couldn't recognize them?"

As her eyes filled with tears, she offered a weak shrug of her shoulders.

"Interesting," Detective Noble said, leaning back in his chair, studying her for a long moment. He wasn't just watching her face, he was watching the entire room—Alfred Marsh's tight jaw, Marian's wringing hands, Clifford's narrowed eyes. Everyone had a stake in this, and everyone was scared.

Noble closed his notebook and, lacing his fingers together and resting his hands on top of it, repeated, "Interesting."

Chapter Fifty-Six

Detective Ray Noble pushed through the heavy wooden doors of the Parker County Courthouse just after eight o'clock the next morning. The courthouse wore its history like a badge of honor, every scuff on the marble floors and nick in the woodwork a testament to the generations that had passed through its halls. From the outside, there was no mistaking the Samuel J. Tildon Courthouse as anything but the heart of Parker County's judicial system. Named after the county's Civil War-era sheriff, the grand structure had been completed shortly after Tildon's death, when the original courthouse could no longer keep pace with the county's growing needs. Set back from the street, its red brick walls and towering white marble columns rose stately behind a carefully manicured garden—a serene patch of green that stood in striking contrast to the courthouse's imposing, almost stern presence.

The Sheriff's Department took up most of the ground floor and half of the basement level. Noble nodded at the handful of clerks and deputies already starting their day as he wound his way through the halls to his office in the Criminal Investigation Bureau with all of the other detectives under his command.

Word had traveled fast around the courthouse that the Sheriff's Department had officially taken over the Blakely case from the Parker City Police. Noble was well aware of the pressure he was now under to solve the damn case, considering how the sheriff had been itching to get his hands on it. Not that Colsh would be the one doing any of the legwork. But the detective knew there was no love lost between Colsh and the PCPD—especially Chief

Edgar Stanley—and now he had a high-profile case dropped neatly into his lap. Colsh would no doubt milk it for everything it was worth.

Noble didn't care about the politics. All he cared about was getting the thing solved before something else happened to Elizabeth Blakely. With the way the suspect seemed to be escalating in his actions, he didn't even want to think about the worst-case scenario.

He made his way down the hallway to his cramped office tucked in the back corner of the CIB, balancing a folded copy of the *Blue Ridge Herald* under his arm while holding a cup of coffee in one hand and a thick stack of paperwork in the other.

Tossing the newspaper down on his battered desk, the headline screamed at him in bold black letters:

WOMAN ABDUCTED OUTSIDE UPTON'S, ESCAPES; SHERIFF'S DEPARTMENT ON THE CASE

Below it was a grainy photo of the department store with a smaller picture halfway down the page of himself a photographer had managed to capture once when he was walking out of the courthouse. Noble quickly read the piece, not expecting to find much in it except speculation and very few facts. When he was finished, however, he was surprised at how many details the reporter had been able to get his hands on. He'd barely had a chance to get through the original case file from Kerns and the PCPD, so this reporter clearly had a source feeding him the most salient—and salacious—details. Most likely at the direction of the sheriff.

The article was a recap of everything that had happened to Blakely, concluding with a paragraph about how the Sheriff's Department's "most respected detective," Ray Noble, was now personally overseeing the case.

He rolled his eyes as he read that, shrugging off his jacket and hanging it on the coat rack in the corner. His hat was placed on the top of one of the filing cabinets behind his desk. The paperwork he'd picked up from his department mailbox was standard stuff—additional information he'd requested from the PCPD, copies of the letters Elizabeth had received, inconclusive fingerprint reports, a couple of memos, and some general mail that seemed to have found its way to his office. He thumbed through the pile absentmindedly, setting things into the appropriate stack on his desk.

The office was quiet except for the soft ticking of the wall clock and murmur of voices coming from the outer office as the other men in the division arrived for the day.

Halfway through the stack, something caught his eye.

It was an envelope. Plain white, no return address, and no postage stamp. His name was handwritten across the front in bright red letters.

His gut tightened.

Carefully holding the envelope by its edges, trying to prevent adding any more of his own fingerprints, he slid a letter opener under the flap. Then, using his handkerchief, he pulled out a single sheet of paper, the same common paper used in the other letters Elizabeth had received.

The same hand had written this one, too. He recognized it easily from the copies he'd been given.

The message was short.

> DETECTIVE NOBLE,
>   YOU'RE TOO LATE.

No signature.

Noble leaned back in his chair and stared at the letter laying on his desk. Whoever had been playing games with Elizabeth Blakely was now taunting him.

Chapter Fifty-Seven

The days immediately following Elizabeth's abduction saw a flurry of activity as Detective Noble and his men went to work. They descended on Upton's Department Store, questioning every person on the payroll—even Old Man Upton himself. Noble wasn't pulling any punches, and the city's newspapers kept a watchful eye on the story. For days, the headlines announced updates, though the articles themselves soon became little more than rehashed details and speculation.

Though Lieutenant Kerns was kept in the loop out of professional courtesy, the case was no longer his to solve. All he could do was hope that with the Sheriff's Department's resources, whoever had been stalking Elizabeth Blakely would soon be found and thrown behind bars alongside Ralph Sanderson. Kerns truly felt for Elizabeth and her family and only wished he could have done more to help.

But with all the hours spent chasing leads, knocking on doors, and interviewing half the city, it wasn't anything the police did that made the biggest difference in Elizabeth's life—it was Alfred Marsh.

In the days after Elizabeth came face-to-face with her tormentor, she stayed at her parents' house, too shaken to return to her own apartment. Alfred spent each evening by her side after work, as a steady and comforting presence. One evening, after dinner, he suggested they take a walk around the neighborhood. The spring air was fresh with the scent of blooming gardens, and as the sun began to dip below the tree line, casting a golden glow over the quiet streets, Alfred stopped, knelt down, and asked Elizabeth to marry him. He promised her a new life, somewhere far from Parker City, where no one would ever be able to hurt her.

Within a few short weeks, Elizabeth and Alfred married and moved to Virginia, putting distance between themselves and the memories that haunted her. They stayed in touch with Elizabeth's family, exchanging letters and holiday cards, but for the most part, they chose to live simply and quietly, far away from the city that had once been home.

Back in Parker City, the investigation eventually dried up. The trail grew cold, the leads—which were already few and far between—slowed to a trickle, and no further letters ever arrived. Whoever had been terrifying Elizabeth seemed to vanish, leaving only unanswered questions in his wake. Detective Noble kept the case file in his office, tucked away but never forgotten—a reminder that some mysteries, no matter how hard you chase them, never truly get solved.

Chapter Fifty-Eight

1985…

Middleboro was the kind of town where time seemed to move a little slower, and the front porches still held rocking chairs that saw regular use. Just outside of Parker City, the main street was lined with beautiful, old Victorian homes, leading to two blocks which were considered "downtown." Maybe two thousand people called the quiet enclave home.

Ben and Tommy pulled up in front of a life-sized dollhouse, complete with a gabled roof, an elaborate balustrade over the wrap-around porch, and a tower turret with a classic witch's cap. A flagstone walkway led from the street to the front steps, lined on either side by rows of perfectly trimmed hedges.

"Nice place," Tommy said as he climbed out of the car, squinting into the sun.

Ben nodded. "This is the kind of house Nat wants to buy. I'm thinking we need to look for something a little smaller. We actually found a listing for one out by the park. Needs a lot of work, but I think we could get it to look like this eventually."

"Ever the optimist," Tommy said, climbing the steps to the porch.

A series of flower boxes hung in the windows. Their brightly blossoming flowers gave the air a hint of sweetness.

The doorbell was a vintage—though probably original to the home—

twist-turn doorbell that rang much louder than expected as Ben turned the decorative key.

"Never seen one of those in real life," Tommy admitted as they stood in front of the heavy wooden door waiting for it to be answered.

After several moments, a small woman with gray hair pulled up in a bun who didn't look like she had the strength to open such a heavy door appeared before them. Wearing a simple housedress with an apron tied around her waist, Ben figured her to be Noble's wife.

Greeting them with a smile, she asked, "Yes? Can I help you, gentlemen?"

"Mrs. Noble?" Ben asked in return.

"Yes. That's right. But you can call me Angie."

"Angie, good afternoon. I'm Detective Sergeant Ben Winters and this is my partner, Tommy Mason. We're with the Parker City Police Department."

"I recognize the names from the newspaper," she said pointing a crooked finger at them. "What can I do for you?"

"Well, we were actually hoping we could speak with your husband if he's home," Ben answered, tucking his badge wallet back into his jacket pocket.

"Of course. No reason two police detectives would show up here to talk to me unless they found out about..." her voice trailed off.

Tommy quickly gave Ben a concerned look, then saw Angela Noble begin to giggle and give him a mischievous wink.

"I'm just kidding. Just an old lady's way of having some fun is all. The worst thing I've ever done is...well, better not to talk about it. Come in. Come in. I'll get Ray for you."

They followed her into a wood-paneled entryway that smelled as if it had been freshly polished, then through to what must have been the formal parlor back when the house was first built. Besides a set of antique armchairs and matching sofa, between which a carved coffee table sat, there was a large rolltop desk against the far wall, flanked on either side by bookcases. Above the desk was a framed map of Parker County from 1901, according to the banner printed at the top.

Angela Noble disappeared through a side door, leaving the detectives to admire the room, feeling as if they'd stepped back in time. Ben couldn't help but examine the map. Parker City was so much smaller back then. And Middleboro was nothing more than a single street with a few roads branching off of it. It was difficult to imagine what it would have been like at the turn of the century. Parker County had been very rural in its beginning. Not that the vast majority of it still wasn't. But some of the largest farms were being turned into residential neighborhood developments at an alarming rate. This, in turn, was causing Parker City, for example, to expand far beyond its original borders.

"That map's been hanging in that spot since it was first printed," a deep, husky voice said behind Ben. "It belonged to Angie's father. This is the house she grew up in. Her grandfather built it for her mother as a wedding present."

Ray Noble stood in the doorway wearing a dark blue camp collar shirt and gray slacks. He looked much more casual than the pictures Ben had seen of him. But those were from his days on the job when he was known for always wearing brown suits. Ben had never met the man but had certainly heard stories about him. Though what hair remained on his head was white and much thinner than it used to be, his shoulders were still broad, and he carried himself like a man who'd never quite stopped being a detective. Behind the wire-rimmed glasses he wore, his eyes were sharp and alert.

At his side sat a yellow Labrador retriever, slowly thumping its tail on the floor, waiting to see if the visitors were friend or foe.

"Ray Noble," he said, stepping into the room. "This is Max. Forgive the dog hair. Angie and I can't keep up with it. He sheds like he's trying to make himself a friend."

Then men all shook hands, and Max, seeing that his master appeared to be in no danger, walked over and settled on the floor next to the roll top.

"Please. Have a seat," he said, motioning to the armchairs while he sat in the middle of the sofa. "Angie says you're the detectives from the PCPD. I figured I'd be hearing from you."

Ben made the introductions. "Ben Winters and Tommy Mason."

"You say you were expecting us?" Tommy asked.

"Not like I figured you boys drove out here to talk about the weather. But when I saw the article in the paper about Alfred Marsh being stabbed…I had a feeling you'd want to talk."

Ben had also seen the article in the *Herald-Dispatch* that morning. Luckily, they hadn't connected Alfred Marsh to what happened back in '65, or it would have been a much bigger story. In fact, Elizabeth's name hadn't even been mentioned. Ben was glad for that. The longer the press kept from connecting all the dots, the better it would be for the investigation. Though, along with Lieutenant Clover's messages that morning, he'd also had one from the reporter who'd written the article about the stabbing, looking for any information he'd be willing to share.

"Call it a hunch," Noble continued. "I'm also guessing something else has happened that didn't make it into the paper."

"You've still got it, Detective," Ben said, laying the case files he'd brought with them on the coffee table. "Two days ago, Elizabeth Marsh received a letter. Whether it was from the same person who was stalking her back in sixty-five or someone who just knew about what she'd gone through, we can't say just yet."

"But then her husband goes and gets stabbed…" Noble trailed off as he looked out the window. "Damn strange case. Stranger now, if someone's come back around after all these years."

Tommy leaned forward. "We've been through the old files, both the city's and the sheriff's, but we're hoping to get your perspective. Anything you remember that didn't make it into the reports? Theories you never shared with anyone."

Just then, Angie Noble walked in carrying a tray with three mugs of steaming coffee, milk, sugar, and a plate of cookies. From the smell, it was obvious they were fresh out of the oven.

"I figured you boys would need something to keep your strength up if you're in here talking about work."

"Thank you, hun," Noble said as his wife quietly retreated through the side door, pulling it closed behind her. "She's wonderful. Either of you married?"

"In a few weeks," Ben said, picking up one of the cups and adding some milk.

"Congratulations. Does she understand what she's getting herself into, marrying a police detective?"

Smiling, Ben was pleased to answer, "Yes. She understands how important the work is to me. But, of course, she wants me to be careful."

"That's good. But make sure you don't take it for granted. Understand. Angie was what kept me from sinking into the bottle like so many other cops I knew."

Ben hadn't been expecting the life lesson when he'd said they needed to talk with the former sheriff's detective, but something about him made him feel like he was on the right track with his life. Ray Noble had been there. He had the experience, and he was willing to share it. Ben should listen.

"But about the case," Noble said after swallowing a gulp of coffee. "The whole thing never sat right with me. First of all, we weren't allowed to get involved in the investigation in the beginning. Chief Stanley and Sheriff Colsh hated each other. And unless Stanley asked for our help, the case stayed with the PCPD since all the letters were being delivered to women who lived in the city. And then they caught the guy. Case closed."

"So they thought," Tommy said, taking a bite of a cookie. "Wow. This is good. What is that? Nutmeg?"

"It's something called cardamom," Noble said with a shrug. "Angie's the baker. But I can grill a steak like no one else. But yes. Everyone thought the case was closed when they arrested that Sanderson fella."

"Then a few months later, Elizabeth Blakely was abducted right off the street in front of Upton's," Ben said.

"I think it was right around Easter when it happened. When the sheriff found out she'd been taken to the east side of Jefferson Park—which was under the county's control at the time—he had every right to put me on the case. At that point, the mayor also thought it best to turn it over to us because we had more resources."

"Do you think if you'd been brought in from the beginning, you'd have seen they were two different cases?" Tommy asked.

"Wallace Kerns was a good cop. He was smart, and he was honest. I think he did what he could under the circumstances. Did you two know Edgar Stanley?"

Both detectives nodded.

"Then you know what he was like. If he forced Wallace to work with one arm tied behind his back, he wasn't the kind of guy who was going to complain. But I saw copies of the city's investigation. There were some things that would have made me think twice about it all being connected."

Ben put his mug down and reached for the case files. "Is there anything at all that you can think of that still bothers you?"

"Other than never having caught the guy?" Noble asked with a half smile.

"Sorry," Ben said, instantly feeling as though he'd put his foot in his mouth. "Something that nags at you. A question you were never able to answer?"

Noble leaned back and thought for a moment. If he was really like the stories he'd heard, Ben knew the former detective still knew every aspect of the case as if he'd been working it just the day before. No one ever understood how he could remember so many details, large and small.

Finally, he said, "There was one thing that both Wallace and I found interesting."

He sat forward and took the old Sheriff's Department file into his lap. Thumbing through the pages, he found an envelope from which he took a series of photographs. Laying them out on the coffee table, he pointed to them.

"These are the photos I had made of the area where Elizabeth Blakely said she'd been taken. See here, there's the jacket she said she'd been wearing but pulled out of to get away. And here…the footprints."

Ben and Tommy leaned over so they could see what he was pointing at.

"These footprints were Elizabeth's. You can see the high-heeled shoe imprints. The ground was damp so they were easy to see. What else do you see?" he asked as if he were a teacher quizzing his students.

Ben studied the images. They showed a wooded area on the outskirts of the park, mostly brush and dirt. Along with Elizabeth's, the photos captured two other sets of footprints.

"You see these?" Noble said, tapping the glossy image. "Those are mine from when I got there. These here are Wallace Kerns, who got there right before I did."

"Something's missing," Tommy said slowly.

"The kidnapper's footprints," Ben answered, picking up one of the photographs and looking more closely.

"Exactly." Noble's eyes lit, glad they saw it as well. Or…didn't see it.

Ben frowned. "Could he have brushed away his tracks after Elizabeth ran away? Before you got there."

Noble shook his head. "Why not get rid of hers, too? And you can see, there's nothing that looks like anything was covered up."

"What about her description of her abductor?" Ben asked. "That was pretty vague."

"I agree." Noble nodded. "I never understood how she couldn't have gotten a better look at him. Even if he was wearing sunglasses and a hat. And if I recall correctly…" he trailed off as he flipped through the file looking for something specific. "Here, it is. She didn't even mention the hat at first. It was an afterthought."

"You remembered that?" Tommy asked, impressed.

"I've thought a lot about this case, Detective Mason. Things just didn't all add up for me."

"And you got a letter from him, just like Lieutenant Kerns," Ben said.

"Right after I took over the case."

Circling back to the missing footprints, Ben asked, "Why didn't anyone question the fact there were no footprints from the kidnapper? Didn't that make anyone suspicious? Other than you?"

"No," Noble admitted. "At least no one wanted to say anything about it. Colsh said it might sound like we were calling her a liar. And after what she'd been through, no one wanted to do that. Plus, we had no proof that the guy didn't brush away his prints somehow."

A silence settled over the room. Ben was thinking through everything Noble was telling them. And not just what he was saying, the feeling he was giving off. It was forcing something to come into focus for Ben which had been alluding him until now. A shadow in the back of his mind that he hadn't quite been able to make out.

After another moment, Ben asked a question he regretted. "Did you believe her?"

Chapter Fifty-Nine

Sitting in the car in front of Ray Noble's home, Ben stared out the window. Tommy, cigarette in hand, looked at his partner. It was obvious the wheels in his head were turning. He could almost see him mentally sifting through all of the facts of the case, arranging them and rearranging them.

"Want a cigarette? It always helps me think better?"

"Have I ever taken you up on your offer?" Ben asked. Raising an eyebrow.

"There is a first time for everything." Then more seriously, he said, "I can tell you're on to something."

"Not yet. Maybe. Just a passing thought."

"Well, that clears that up." Tommy laughed.

"No. It's just…two coffee cups."

"Still on that? Not that I'm not saying it doesn't mean something. But you seem a little fixated on that detail."

"We need to see if CSU found any fingerprints," Ben said, reaching for the radio mic. "Dispatch, this is PC-12."

"Hey, sugar. What can I do for you?" Shirley asked, her southern drawl heavier than usual.

"Can you connect me with Lieutenant Clover at the State Police Barracks?"

"I can certainly try. Just hang on a sec and let me make the call."

Ben tapped the fingers of his free hand on the steering wheel as he waited. Finally, a crackling came over the radio.

"Ben, are you there?" It was Clover.

"I'm here. I just wanted to check in and see if you'd found any prints at the crime scene or on either of the letters?"

"The only definitive prints we have identified match the samples you gave me of Alfred and Elizabeth Marsh. There are a few partials and smudges here and there. But nothing in any place that there wouldn't be. The knife used to stab Marsh only had his prints and hers. But that's expected. It was part of their kitchen set. Same with the letters. Again, if they're the only ones that handled them, it makes sense. Your guy probably wore gloves."

"What about the coffee cups?"

"Same thing. Just their prints. I'm having the initial report put together now. I'll make sure you have it tomorrow morning."

"Thanks," Ben said, clicking off.

"No fingerprints," Tommy said, throwing his cigarette butt out the window. "No real surprise there."

Ben was chewing on his lower lip. "Does that really make any sense? Guy comes over to the house wearing gloves on a hot summer day, and Marsh doesn't question it?"

"He could have put the gloves on after he got there."

"To have coffee? Still might have made Marsh suspicious."

"Okay…then…he wiped his prints off the cup and knife," Tommy suggested, grasping at straws.

"But somehow left Elizabeth and Alfred's prints untouched?"

Tommy ran his finger along his mustache. "I'm starting to see why the two coffee cups are bothering you."

"Are you?" Ben asked, sounding more serious than Tommy liked to hear him.

Starting the engine and throwing the car into gear, Ben pulled his notebook out and handed it to Tommy. "I have the sister's address in there with the notes from the hospital. I think we need to go talk to her next."

Flipping through the pages, Tommy was once again reminded of his partner's immaculate handwriting. Even when he was scribbling notes, his writing still looked better than his own. But it made it easy for Tommy to find Patty Sharpe's address. She lived in Harper Mills on the north side of the city. One of the most upscale parts of Parker, the neighborhood was full of mini-mansions. There'd been a murder a couple months earlier in the area that they'd worked. A very popular philanthropist was found dead in her home. It was a case that surprised him and Ben because it ended up connecting to a crime spree in Baltimore back in the '20s.

Giving Ben the address, he could tell his partner wasn't in the mood for small talk, so he sat back and watched the city go by as Ben guided the Crown Vic through the streets. Judging by how loud Ben was being quiet, Tommy could tell he might be on to something. And if he was starting to think the same thing, he could understand why Ben was so concerned.

Chapter Sixty

Elizabeth Marsh's sister lived in a large Tudor-style home on a tree-lined street alongside other Tudor-style houses. All of them were spacious and just this side of being ostentatious. There was no denying it was a beautiful neighborhood. The kind that whispered wealth without having to shout it, with precisely manicured lawns, sculpted hedgerows, and stone walkways that gleamed in the sunlight.

Ben noticed gardeners working outside three separate homes as he pulled into the driveway beside a dark green BMW.

Stepping out of the car, Tommy cracked his neck. "Any particular piece of information we're looking to get out of the sister?" he asked, stretching his arms.

"Just some background," Ben replied, locking the car. "I want to know more about Elizabeth from the person who might know her best. When I spoke with her, she seemed… unassuming. Kind. Like a woman who just wanted a quiet life. But you said Calhoun claimed she sought attention. Said she flaunted her looks. Which is it? Because the answer could be the key to everything."

Tommy grumbled, "Yeah, well, Calhoun's a jackass, so let's not put too much stock into what he says."

Ben smiled as he rang the doorbell.

When the door opened, Patty Sharpe stood before them. The resemblance to Elizabeth was unmistakable. Same elegant cheekbones and similar frame, but where Elizabeth's eyes were a sharp, penetrating blue, Patty's were emerald green, clear and sparkling. They complimented the BMW out front, Ben thought.

At the sight of the detectives, panic flashed across Patty's face. "Oh, my God! Has something happened to Elizabeth? Is Alfred alright?"

"Mrs. Sharpe," Ben said gently, raising his hands, "nothing's happened. We were just hoping to speak with you, if you have a few minutes."

Her hand pressed against her chest as she exhaled. "Of course. I'm sorry. I just thought… Please, come in."

They followed her through the house and into the kitchen. Spacious and modern, it was filled with sleek appliances and countertops that were almost entirely covered in flower arrangements. On the kitchen table sat an organized mess of insurance papers, bank statements, and what looked like legal documents.

"We didn't know if you'd be with your sister at the hospital," Ben said.

"Oh, well, she's staying here with me since you have her house all locked up. But that's where she is right now. Joyce is with her. I was going over later to make sure she has dinner."

"It's good that she has you for support," Tommy offered.

"You'll have to excuse the clutter," she said, gesturing toward all the paperwork. "With my husband's passing, there's a lot to sort through. I'm still trying to get my head around it all. Kenneth usually handled everything like that. I never imagined he'd…not be here."

"I'm sorry," Ben said softly.

"It's alright. It all happened so fast, really. And then no sooner do we bury Kenneth, than Alfred is attacked and in the hospital. It's almost too impossible to believe."

She began clearing away papers and motioned for them to sit.

"When exactly did your husband pass?" Tommy asked, his tone more sympathetic than usual.

"Last week. The funeral was this past Monday," she said, dabbing at a tear with the edge of her sleeve.

"Just three days ago?" Ben asked.

"Yes. Monday."

"And then the next day Elizabeth found a letter in her mail," Ben murmured, almost to himself. "Did she mention it to you?"

"Not until we were at the hospital." Patty sat, wringing her hands. "How can all of this be happening again?"

"That's what we wanted to speak with you about, Mrs. Sharpe," Ben explained. "From what we read in the old reports, you and your sister were very close."

"Absolutely. We were best friends."

"You're the younger sister, correct?"

"By a couple of years, yes."

Ben flipped open his notebook. "Tell me what Elizabeth was like in 1965. We've read the case files, but we want to know her as a person. From someone who truly knew her."

Patty took a moment, thinking. "She was...*is*...one of the most caring people I know. She's never been the adventurous type. She'd rather stay home with a book than go out to a party. Always a little shy."

"Interesting," Tommy said, raising an eyebrow. "Especially since her best friend Joyce seems like the exact opposite."

Patty laughed. "You have no idea. Joyce was wild. A total free spirit. Burning bras and marching for everything under the sun. But she adores Liz. She was like a third sister. My parents loved her. Even when she was on one of her feminist soapboxes."

"And your parents?" Ben asked.

"Oh, they've both passed."

"I'm sorry."

"They had good lives. Long ones. I always thought Kenneth and I would be the same."

Ben paused respectfully before continuing. "Do you remember when Elizabeth got the first letter?"

"I don't. I didn't even know what happened until I got back from my honeymoon."

Ben raised his eyebrows

"She got that first letter the week after my wedding," Patty explained.

"And then someone broke into her apartment and tore up the bridesmaid dress she wore at your wedding."

"Yes. While Kenneth and I were away. I was angry when I found out later. I said they should have called and told me what was happening, but they said they didn't want to ruin our honeymoon."

Turning to a later page in his notebook, Ben asked, "Do you remember when Elizabeth was abducted from in front of Upton's?"

"Yes. Of course. It was right after Easter."

"Do you remember anything special about that Easter? Or anything that happened in the days leading up to her being taken?"

A smile appeared on Patty's face. "That's when Kenneth and I found out we were going to have a baby. We told the family at Easter dinner. Everyone was so happy and excited. I still remember it like it was yesterday."

Slowly tapping his finger on the table, Ben sat quietly for a moment. A lot of big, emotional events all clustered together. Wedding. Honeymoon. Pregnancy. Then the letters… then the abduction.

Suddenly, Patty jumped up from her chair. "I'm so sorry. I haven't offered you anything to drink. Can I get you some water? Or coffee?"

Seeing that Ben was completely distracted by his own thoughts, Tommy politely declined for the both of them. Then, nudging him with his knee, he quietly asked, "You good?"

Ben blinked. "Yeah. Sorry. Just thinking."

As Patty busied herself at the counter, Tommy leaned closer. "What's going on in that head of yours?"

Ben looked up. "Just a theory. Still forming."

Tommy rolled his eyes. "Here we go…"

Ben stood slowly and closed his notebook. "Mrs. Sharpe, you've been incredibly helpful. Thank you. I think we've got enough for now."

"I hope I was able to help," she said, walking them to the door.

"You have," Ben assured her. "More than you know."

They stepped back into the summer sunlight. As they walked down the stone path to the car, Tommy glanced at Ben.

"Alright. Out with it. You know something."

"I might," Ben said. "It's the timeline. There were things we didn't know."

"And now?"

Ben opened the car door and looked across the roof at his partner.

"Now," he said, "we have to find a way to prove something I really would rather not."

Chapter Sixty-One

By the time Ben pulled the Crown Vic into its parking spot at the station, the sky had become as dark as his mood. A summer storm was rolling in from the west, and though they'd been able to hear rumbles of thunder for the last several minutes, the first drops of rain were yet to fall. Judging by the feeling in the air, however, it was going to be a monster of a storm.

Sitting behind the computer, Tommy was typing up the reports on their recent interviews. A third case file had now been opened with Elizabeth Blakely/Marsh's name on it. As well as one for the attack on her husband.

As Tommy pecked away at the keyboard, Ben sat feverishly scribbling on a legal pad. Every so often, he'd turn to look at the chalkboard or flip through one of the files looking for a specific detail. He hadn't said much since leaving Patty Sharpe's house and Tommy was giving him time to think through his theory.

If Tommy was starting to put the pieces together the way Ben did, he understood why his partner wasn't in the mood to talk. And once again, he was very thankful he wasn't the senior officer on the case. More than enough people had been impacted by this stalker case over the years. If the person behind all of it was who it appeared to be, it would be devastating.

But theorizing and proving who it was were two completely different things.

After Tommy printed off the last of the reports, he looked at the clock on the wall and said, "Do you want to pick all of this up fresh in the morning? Take a night to sleep on everything?"

Looking at his watch, Ben said, "Yeah. I think that might be a good idea."

"Do you and Nat have any plans tonight?" Tommy asked, standing and pulling his jacket off the back of his chair.

"Nothing special. Though she did say if I hadn't solved the case by tonight, she was going to do it for me."

Tommy laughed. "I wouldn't put it past her. Is there anything that woman can't do?"

"If there is, I haven't figured it out yet."

Taking a more serious tone, Tommy looked at Ben and said, "Clear your head when you get home. Let Nat take your mind off things, if you know what I mean. A little time away might help make everything make sense. Then we can talk it all through in the morning. And if it shakes out the way I think you're thinking it's going to, then that's just the way it is. We don't get to decide who the bad guys are. We just follow the clues to find them."

"See. I told you you were going to make a good detective one day." Ben smiled.

"Shut up," Tommy said over his shoulder as he walked out the door.

Collecting all the files, Ben put them in his briefcase. After dinner, he would look through everything one more time. If he still felt like he'd uncovered the identity of Elizabeth's stalker, then he'd start thinking about ways to prove it. Because right now, all he had was circumstantial evidence. And that was using the term "evidence" loosely.

Opening the door out to the parking lot, Ben was struck by a deluge of water. Without an umbrella, he used his briefcase to shield himself as best he could from the downpour. But by the time he'd pulled the car door closed behind him, he was soaked.

He'd found himself in the same situation once he arrived home. Parking in his usual spot, he ran through the parking lot heading for the cover of the building. He told himself he was going to remember to put an umbrella in the car for the next surprise storm.

Opening the door to the apartment building, the sky lit up as a lightning bolt streaked overhead. A couple of seconds later, the earth shook with a rumble of thunder that sounded like a bomb went off just down the road.

Shaking himself off as he climbed the stairs to his floor, Ben peeled his suit jacket off and held it away from him, watching the water drip from the edges of the fabric. He couldn't wait to get inside and change his clothes. The worst part was the rain wasn't cooling things off. It was still hot, making it that much more uncomfortable.

Unlocking the door to the apartment, Ben sloshed inside and immediately kicked his shoes off.

Natalie, standing in the kitchen, looked over and said, "Oh, you look damp."

Ben raised an eyebrow and shook his head as she burst out laughing.

"Come in and get dried off," she said, tossing him a dish towel, which he used to dab at the water dripping from his hair.

"I think I'm going to need something bigger."

"Go change. Dinner's almost ready. We're having lasagna."

He'd almost forgotten about the club sandwich Tommy had brought him for lunch the way his stomach began growling when he smelled the delicious aroma coming from the oven. For an Irish girl, Natalie could make some incredible Italian dishes.

As always, the dinner was beyond filling and helped to turn Ben's mood around. By the time they pushed themselves away from the table, he wasn't even sure he wanted to work on the case that evening.

But after cleaning up and walking into the living room, he found a stack of papers sitting on the coffee table. They were copies of newspaper articles all about the mysterious letters, along with some about Elizabeth Blakely and her abduction.

"I went to the library today," Nat said, joining him with two cups of coffee. "I thought reading about the case through a contemporary lens might give you a new perspective. Though, going through everything, I can't see how the guy they arrested was the one who kidnapped her. He was in jail. And," she paused, sorting through the pages, pulling out an obituary, "he died six years ago. So, he can't be your guy."

Quickly reading the obituary for Ralph Sanderson, he saw that he did die back in 1979. If he hadn't already ruled him out, that would have done it.

CHAPTER SIXTY-ONE

Death is a pretty solid alibi. Any cop would tell you that.

Sitting down on the sofa and pulling her legs up under her, Nat said, "Now that I've read all of the newspaper articles and have familiarized myself with the case, I thought I could take a look at your files."

"You did?" Ben sat down next to her. "You know I really shouldn't be showing you official police documents, right? Besides, we're getting married in a few weeks. Isn't there some sort of wedding thing you should be worrying about?"

"Ben, I've had the wedding planned since I was thirteen years old. All I needed to do was replace Davy Jones's name with yours on the invitations. And it's not like we haven't talked about your cases before."

"But I've never let you look at the actual files," he pointed out.

"Who's going to know?" she protested. "Besides, won't it all be made public at trial anyway? Just consider this a pre-trial review."

Ben huffed and took a sip of his coffee to prolong having to respond. After a moment, he finally said, "Let me go through and pull some things out first. Not everything will be made public. Trial or not."

"Fine. I'll wait," she said, then sat there staring at him as he went through and removed several items from the case files.

When he was finished, Natalie dug into them. Devouring page after page of information. As she went, he skimmed the news articles she'd collected. Every once in a while, she'd reach over and take an article from him to compare what it said with details she was reading. By the time she was finished, he was beginning to nod off.

"Um…did you look at the timing here?" she asked, holding up the copy of the article from the *Blue Ridge Herald* with Ray Noble's photo.

Through groggy eyes, Ben looked at what she was pointing out to him. "What? What about it?"

"This was the announcement that Sheriff Colsh had put this Detective Noble in charge of the investigation."

"Right. They took over after the abduction. The sheriff had more resources."

"Yes…but…" Natalie was becoming animated. "Look here. According to what was filed by Lieutenant Wallace Kerns," she said, shuffling around looking for the police report, "Elizabeth Blakely was abducted on Tuesday, April twelfth. Both he and Detective Noble have notes saying they went and examined the area of Jefferson Park where she'd been taken and then went and spoke with her at her parents' house that evening."

"I've seen all that." The cobwebs in Ben's head were beginning to clear. Nat thought she was on to something, so he wanted to hear her out.

"Presumably, the sheriff would have put out a statement letting everyone know he was now running the case. No doubt he did it pretty fast, considering how you said he'd been dying to get his hands on the case from the beginning."

"Makes sense," Ben agreed, taking the *Blue Ridge Herald* article from her, "considering the story ran in the paper the next day. Wednesday, April thirteenth."

"Okay." There was a twinkle in her eye. She pulled another page out of the sheriff's folder. "Here is the report Noble filed, saying he received a letter from the stalker when he arrived at the courthouse."

"Kerns got one, too, when he was on the case. After he met with Elizabeth."

"Ben!" she snapped. "Think about the timing."

Rubbing his eyes with the palms of his hands, he focused on what she'd said. Elizabeth Blakely was abducted the Tuesday after Easter. The investigators spoke with her, while at some time during that day, Sheriff Colsh let the press know his department—specifically, Ray Noble—was now on the case. The next morning, the papers ran the story, and Noble got a letter at the courthouse.

Ben sat up straight and leaned forward.

"I think he got it," Nat said, the excitement building in her voice.

"How did the stalker know Ray Noble was on the case? Unless they'd seen a really early printing of the paper and rushed over to the courthouse."

"But what are the odds of that?" Natalie asked.

"It was someone that already knew he was on the case from the day before. Which means, out of everyone, it could only be one person."

Ben shook his head. He'd been right. Even though he didn't want to be.

He knew who'd written all the letters. And thereby, who'd stabbed Alfred Marsh. It was the two coffee cups that had told him. But this was the first piece of evidence he could use to back up his theory. And then something Lieutenant Clover said that afternoon about the fingerprints popped into his head. He had the answer. But now it was time to test it out.

Turning to Natalie, he began at the beginning and methodically walked her through everything he'd been thinking. Laying out the entire case, connecting all the dots using information from twenty years ago and everything that had happened in just the last few days. Slowly but surely, the tangled web began to unwind. When he was finished, the look on Natalie's face told him she was as shocked as he'd first been, but that it all made sense now.

"I think you've got your perp," she said with an uneasy smile, using a term she'd heard on television.

Chapter Sixty-Two

The next morning, Ben was out of the apartment early. He'd barely slept, spending most of the night tossing and turning. At some point, he gave up and moved to the living room, flipping through TV channels until something mindless finally lulled him into a couple hours of restless sleep, only to jolt awake shortly before six, just ahead of his alarm.

Skipping breakfast at home, he grabbed a couple Egg McMuffins and a coffee from McDonald's on the drive to the State Police Barracks. He needed to see the letter CSU had recovered from under the Marshes' refrigerator. If his hunch was right, that letter could be the final piece of evidence he needed to confirm everything. And with any luck, Alfred Marsh would soon wake up and tell them exactly what happened that morning.

Before leaving the apartment, he'd called Tommy and told him to meet at the station early. He explained he was picking up the letter registered as evidence, and that they'd need to make a stop before confronting the person he now believed had written all the letters to Elizabeth Blakely—later, Elizabeth Marsh. When Tommy started peppering him with questions, Ben stopped him.

"I'll explain everything in person," he said. "I want to walk you through the case the same way I did with Nat last night."

"So…Natalie did solve the case?" Tommy asked. "I thought she was just kidding."

"She helped confirm what I was already thinking. We were all looking too closely at the story. Too focused on the narrative instead of the details. I think that's what happened to Wallace Kerns and Ray Noble back in the day. That's why no one ever really solved the case."

Ben kept replaying it in his mind as he drove to meet Lieutenant Clover. If he was wrong—if he'd somehow misread all the signs—he could only imagine the consequences. But nothing anyone else could say or do would punish him more than he would punish himself. He'd never forgive such a mistake.

But deep down, he knew he wasn't wrong. He just needed something solid to back it up.

At the station, once he'd taken Tommy through everything—starting from 1965 and ending with the stabbing of Alfred Marsh and the letter found by CSU—Tommy leaned back in his chair and exhaled hard.

"Sonofabitch."

"I know," Ben said, standing in front of the chalkboard, where all the pieces finally clicked into place.

"When we left last night," Tommy said, standing to study the board, "I was starting to think the same thing. I just couldn't explain why. It was more of a gut feeling. You kept saying it was someone no one would ever expect. Well…here we are."

He pulled the photo of their suspect off the board and stared at it before handing it to Ben.

"Now what?"

"We go back to the Marshes' house."

"You think CSU missed something?"

"Not exactly. They just might not have known what they were looking for."

"Do we?"

"We will… When we see it."

As they headed for the stairs, Tommy asked, "Have you told the chief or Nelson?"

"Not yet."

"The papers are going to have a field day with this, you know?"

"Yeah. I don't think there's any way around it."

"I just thought you'd want to give Brent a heads up."

"I will. Once we're certain."

"You're the boss," Tommy said as he slid into the cruiser and instinctively pulled out his pack of cigarettes. "Want one? Clear your head?"

Ben smirked and shook his head.

The Marsh house looked the same as it had a few days earlier…except this time, there was a crisscross of yellow police tape over the front door. Captain Nelson hadn't approved a patrol to guard the place, said the budget wouldn't allow it, especially with the department's budget under review ahead of the implementation of the chief's reorganization plan.

Ben peeled the tape from the doorframe and rolled it up, handing it to Tommy, who looked at it a moment before stuffing it into his jacket pocket.

Pushing inside, they were immediately hit by a wave of stifling heat and humidity. The house had been sealed for two days, and if it had an air conditioning system, it wasn't on. Worse still was the lingering smell. Until a crime scene was officially released, the cleanup process couldn't begin. And that meant anything biological—blood, tissue, who knew what else— just sat there, festering.

"Let's get some fresh air in here," Ben said, motioning for Tommy to open a window in the living room. He went to the kitchen window over the sink.

They weren't too worried about leaving fingerprints at this point. CSU had already processed the scene, but they'd still be careful. Anything they found would be handled with a handkerchief and bagged immediately. Ben had brought a small supply of plastic evidence bags from CSU earlier that morning.

"Where should we start?" Tommy asked, stepping into the kitchen and carefully navigating around the dark stains spoiling the otherwise pristine white tile.

"It won't be out in the open," Ben said, scanning the room.

"Even if it is, would anyone realize what they were looking at?"

"Probably not."

Ben began opening drawers, searching for what every home inevitably had—the junk drawer. The kitchen was immaculate. Everything had a place. Silverware perfectly aligned. Dish towels folded and stacked. Cooking utensils arranged by size. Finally, at the far end of the kitchen, he found it: the catch-all drawer. Scissors, rubber bands, notecards, a ruler, and a plastic tray holding pens and pencils.

Nothing jumped out at him. At least not what *he* was looking for.

Leaving the kitchen, he moved down the hall. The first door opened into a small home office. It looked like where Alfred did his work on the days he stayed home. A pair of bulky adding machines sat on one side of the desk. On the other, a computer—similar to the one at the station.

"See? I told you computers were going to be popular," Ben said.

"So far, I haven't seen how it's made our job easier," Tommy replied. "Besides, you won't let me play video games on it."

Ben rolled his eyes and opened the desk drawers. Tax tables, accounting ledgers, notebooks, and client folders filled the drawers. A ream of graph paper sat neatly stacked beside a ruler. Nothing out of place. Everything looked like what a tax man would keep on hand.

On the credenza behind the desk sat a framed photo of Elizabeth and Alfred standing in front of Niagara Falls. They looked so happy. Ben stared at it for a moment. He couldn't imagine someone doing to Natalie what had been done to Elizabeth.

He left Tommy to search the credenza and filing cabinets and walked farther down the hallway to the master bedroom. The pale pink carpet matched the bedspread and the delicate rose pattern on the cream and gold wallpaper. It was clearly Elizabeth's design. Based on what little Ben knew of Alfred, and the heavy mahogany and dark blue wallpaper in his office, this room had Elizabeth's fingerprints all over it.

Ben didn't like digging through people's things. Literally. He hated going through people's personal items. But it was his job. So he carefully started going through the dresser drawers. He tried to make sure he put everything back the way he'd found it.

As he pushed the final drawer closed, Ben began to wonder if maybe he was wrong. Or, if there'd be no way to prove his theory.

After finishing in Alfred's office, Tommy had followed Ben into the bedroom and started going through the couple's closet. And just as Ben was having serious doubts, Tommy poked his head out and said, "Um, Ben…I think we've got it."

Quickly crossing the room, Ben joined his partner, who was standing in the doorway to the walk-in closet. In his hands was an old shoebox from Upton's Department Store. Looking into the box, Ben's emotions were mixed. He was excited that his theory had been correct and they'd be able to close the case once and for all. But he was heartbroken at the way it was going to end.

Chapter Sixty-Three

The next couple of hours were spent back at the station putting everything in place for them to make an arrest. Ben spent most of that time on the telephone with an assistant state's attorney, working through the charges and how to handle what was going to cause a stir when the press got a hold of it. Tommy was tasked with logging the evidence they found at the Marshes' and briefing Captain Nelson. Normally, Ben would have preferred to fill him in on what they'd uncovered, but speaking with the State's Attorney's Office was more pressing, and if the chief was, in fact, going to expand the Detective Squad and he was going to remain its commanding officer, he needed to practice the art of delegating. And knowing they were at the end game and it wasn't any time for his wisecracking tomfoolery, Tommy turned into the serious investigator Ben knew he truly was and handled his assignments with the cool composure he showed when the cards were on the table.

Once everything was in place for the arrest, the detectives began making calls to determine where their suspect was. They didn't want to be randomly driving around town with no idea where they were going.

Learning that Patty and Joyce were with Elizabeth at the hospital, Ben called Tasker Valley Memorial and asked that the three women be put in a private waiting room so he could speak with them.

When they entered the same room where they'd first spoken with the women after Alfred's attacked, they found Elizabeth sitting on the uncomfortable sofa staring at the painting of the generic landscape on the wall. She looked exhausted. Her sister Patty sat beside her, flipping through a magazine with a nervous thumb. Joyce Osbourne stood by the window, arms crossed. Her face betrayed no emotion.

As Ben took a seat opposite Elizabeth, all three women looked to him.

"How is Alfred doing?" he asked.

"Dr. Baxter says he's doing well," Elizabeth answered. "They've taken him off the sedatives and are starting to see signs he may be waking up soon."

Ben smiled. "That's good to hear."

"We were told you had an update," Elizabeth said. Her voice trembled slightly.

Ben nodded. "We do. We know who wrote all the letters."

Elizabeth's hand shot to her mouth. Tears welled in her eyes. "Oh…oh, thank God."

Patty placed a steadying hand on her sister's arm. Joyce didn't react, just kept her arms crossed, gaze fixed on Ben.

"We wanted to tell you in person," Ben said. "But we also wanted to go over some things. Some pieces that finally started to make sense."

Elizabeth sniffed and looked up at him, blinking through tears. "Of course."

Ben leaned forward, glancing at Tommy. Then he looked back at the three women.

"We've been looking closely at the timeline of events. Not just recently. All the way back."

Joyce raised an eyebrow. Patty looked confused.

Ben continued. "There was a pattern. One we didn't see until we laid everything out. It wasn't about the stalker or the random threats. It was about the connection to *you*, Elizabeth."

She frowned.

"Every time something significant happened in Patty's life," Ben explained, looking to her, then back to Elizabeth, "something happened to you. After her wedding, you got your first letter. Then the dress incident. Torn up in your apartment. But when the police investigated at the time, they found no signs of forced entry and couldn't figure out how the person got in. No broken lock. No broken windows."

Elizabeth opened her mouth, but Ben held up a hand.

"Then there was the letter left at Upton's when Patty came back from her honeymoon. The letters stopped for a while after that. The timing seemed to work because that's when Ralph Sanderson was arrested. He confessed to sending all the letters but denied ever having anything to do with what happened to you.

"Then the next year, right after Easter, when Patty announced her pregnancy, you were abducted. You said someone pulled you off the sidewalk, took you to Jefferson Park."

"Because they did," Elizabeth said, voice cracking.

"No," Ben said gently. "They didn't."

The room went quiet. Only the soft beeping from a heart monitor down the hall and the hum of the hospital ventilation system filled the silence.

Ben turned to Tommy, who handed him the Sheriff's Department photos. Ben opened the folder and laid one on the small coffee table between him and Elizabeth.

"This is from Jefferson Park. Right where you said you'd been taken. See your coat there? But there's something missing."

Elizabeth blinked, not understanding.

"Your abductor's footprints," Ben explained.

"What are you talking about, Detective?" Patty snapped. "I see footprints all over that picture."

"Yes. Only three sets of footprints," Ben said. "Elizabeth's. Ray Noble's. And Wallace Kerns's. That's it. There was never any trace of the man you said kidnapped you. Nothing to show anyone else was ever there except you."

Elizabeth's face went pale.

"Elizabeth," Ben said carefully, "this isn't just about the past. Last week, your brother-in-law died. And the day after his funeral, you received a letter for the first time in twenty years."

Patty looked up, startled. She was now beginning to see it.

After a moment, Ben continued, "It's also about what happened to Alfred. We kept asking who would he have let into the house that morning? He wouldn't have let in a stranger. He was home, waiting for Todd Kimble, but Todd canceled that morning. So the only person who could've been sitting at that table across from Alfred, drinking from that second cup we found, was someone he trusted."

Ben's voice softened.

"It was you."

Elizabeth was frozen. "No," she whispered.

"We checked the prints. The second cup had only two sets. Yours and Alfred's. CSU confirmed it. There was no stalker in the house. No intruder. Just you and your husband."

Joyce straightened. "Detective! What are you talking about?"

"There's more," he said. He pulled a plastic evidence sleeve from the folder and held it out. Inside was the red-lettered note recovered from beneath the refrigerator at the Marsh house.

"We found this at the scene. It apparently slid beneath the fridge. It reads, *Did you miss me?* Look familiar?"

Elizabeth didn't answer. Then she shook her head.

"No. I never saw that."

"That proves Elizabeth's stalker is the one who stabbed Alfred. And he left that note behind," Joyce argued, her voice raised to a fevered pitch.

"That is true…to an extent," Ben agreed. "The problem is, Elizabeth's fingerprints are on it. If you'd never seen it, how'd they get there?"

Elizabeth swayed in her seat.

"Just like your prints were on *all* of the letters. It made perfect sense that they would be. Everyone assumed whoever wrote them wore gloves or was somehow extremely careful. No one ever thought there was a simpler answer to why only your fingerprints were on the letter."

"Detective…please." Elizabeth was beginning to shake.

"We also found a box with some interesting items in your bedroom closet."

"No!" she snapped. "I know I should have never kept those articles or the copy of that letter, but I couldn't bring myself to throw them away."

Ben began to shake his head. "I'm not talking about the wooden box. I'm talking about the one from Upton's that you had buried under all the other shoe boxes."

"No. What box?" Elizabeth was breathing heavily, shaking her head violently.

"Inside were red pens. The same kind used to write the letters you received. Along with other notes written to you but never shown anyone."

Elizabeth's lips parted slightly. Her eyes were glassy.

"I don't understand," she whispered. "I didn't...I wouldn't..."

Patty stared at her sister, horrified. Joyce turned away, one hand pressed against the wall for support.

"I don't..." Elizabeth's voice broke. "I remember...flashes. Writing...being afraid... But I thought those were just dreams. At night I was... I thought I was just having nightmares. I didn't... The headaches... I never meant... I can't..." She couldn't finish. She slumped forward, sobbing.

Ben slowly stood. "I think a part of you believed it was real. That the stalker existed. I'm not a psychiatrist, so I can't explain it. But all I have is the evidence. I truly am sorry."

A long, dreadful silence fell over them. The revelation weighing on each person in the room.

"I'm sorry," Ben said again. "I believe you didn't know what you were doing. But Alfred was stabbed. This has to go through the proper channels."

Tears ran down Elizabeth's face. Patty held her hand but looked lost. Joyce just closed her eyes.

Ben turned to Tommy, who was pulling out his handcuffs. Quickly shaking his head, Ben silently told his partner to put them away. Reaching a hand out, he helped Elizabeth to her feet, then gently guided her out of the room.

The case was over.

Chapter Sixty-Four

Alfred Marsh woke up two days later.

It had been a small moment in the grand scheme of things—his eyelids fluttering, then opening, his fingers twitching against the edge of the sheet—but for those waiting, it had meant everything. And now, two days after that, Detectives Ben Winters and Tommy Mason sat in the small Detective Squad office with Chief Brent perched on the corner of Ben's desk, wrapping up one of the longest open cases in the department's history.

Ben leaned forward, elbows on his desk, thumbing through a worn copy of the *Diagnostic and Statistical Manual of Mental Disorders*, the one he kept in the bottom drawer under the Yellow Pages.

"Factitious Disorder," Ben said, holding up the book like a preacher quoting from the *Bible*. "It's Munchausen syndrome by proxy's quieter cousin. Except instead of hurting someone else to get attention, the person does it to themselves. In this case…psychologically.

"I went to the library to see what I could find on this stuff. The couple of articles I read were a little more detailed than I was ready for. A lot of it went over my head, but what I could understand sounds like it's pretty serious."

Chief Brent raised an eyebrow, arms folded across his chest. "And you think that's what Elizabeth Marsh has?"

"No," Ben said. "I *know* that's what she has. Or something very close to it. She's already been seen by two different psychiatrists at Tasker Valley Memorial. Both of them say she's suffering from a dissociative break. She convinced herself it was all real. She needed the attention. But she didn't remember doing any of it. She was in a…fugue state," Ben said, referring to a note he'd made after speaking with one of the psychiatrists. "In layman's terms, that's when someone does something they don't know they're doing and then don't remember."

"Is there any chance it's all an act?" Brent questioned, not wanting to believe someone would purposely put themselves through what apparently Elizabeth had caused herself to suffer.

"She's not faking," Tommy answered rather definitively, leaning back in his chair. "If she were, she would've folded the second Ben confronted her. But what she did? That was a slow-motion collapse. I don't think she knew until the moment it all came out."

Brent exhaled heavily and rubbed the back of his neck. "The press is going to town."

"Out for blood," Ben said. "They're all over it. 'Local Woman Behind Twisted 20-Year Stalking Mystery.' 'Beauty Turned Bogeyman.' They're treating it like some Gothic novel. Meanwhile, Elizabeth's in the psychiatric wing under observation, and the state's attorney's already discussing a plea deal with her lawyer. They're being cautious."

Brent grimaced. "What about the husband? Marsh?"

"Physically, he's lucky. Mentally? That's going to take time," Tommy said.

"When we spoke with him," Ben said, "he was still a little hazy, but he remembered everything. After breakfast, he'd gone into his office to make a phone call. He then went into the bedroom to get something and found her sitting on the bed writing the last letter—the one that ended up under the refrigerator. He took it from her and asked what she was doing?

"She ran out of the room into the kitchen. He followed her, but said it was like she was in a trance. That was the fugue state the doctors talked about. He couldn't get through to her. Said she wasn't being herself. He remembers yelling, then her grabbing a knife. Then nothing else."

Brent let out a whistle.

Ben closed the *DSM* and set it on his desk. "We've explained everything to him. Patty and Joyce were with him. He didn't say much after that."

The chief nodded slowly, taking it in. "You two did good work."

Tommy smiled. "So we're not fired?"

Brent gave a dry laugh. "Not yet."

There was a knock at the door. Officer Bronson stuck his head in. "Lieutenant Clover sent over the CSU supplementals, Detective."

"Thanks," Ben said, taking the thick envelope.

Once the door shut again, Brent looked from one man to the other. "You're sure this all adds up?"

Ben nodded. "It all came down to the timeline. Once we figured that out, it was almost impossible not to see it. But I understand why they couldn't figure it out in sixty-five. They had all the letters being sent by Sanderson muddying the water and the political pressure from the chief and the sheriff."

"And honestly," Tommy added, "who'd want to blame the victim?"

Brent leaned back in his chair. "What about the sister?"

"She's standing by Elizabeth," Ben said. "So is Joyce. That hasn't changed. They're shaken, of course. Who wouldn't be? But they're with her."

"She's lucky," Brent said quietly. "Damn lucky."

Tommy looked over at Ben. "You want to tell him the last part?"

Ben nodded, tapping his finger on the desk. "After everyone had some time to digest all of this, Joyce remembered something. From one of the nights back when she and Elizabeth were staying with the Blakelys. She remembers hearing voices in Elizabeth's room. Like she was talking to someone. When Joyce brought it up the next day, Elizabeth had no idea what she was talking about. She could have been having an episode. But at the time, no one would have ever suspected Elizabeth. Joyce certainly didn't, so never brought it up again. And after twenty years, forgot about it."

"She's getting help now," Tommy said. "That's what matters."

Chief Brent stood and nodded. "You did good work. Shame this is how it turned out, though."

"Yeah. The bad guy isn't always a bad guy," Ben said thoughtfully.

As the chief walked out, Ben picked up the *DSM* again and looked at the cover.

"So, you just keep a copy of that in your desk?" Tommy asked.

"Yep. I'm still trying to figure out what's wrong with you," he answered with a smile.

Tommy sighed, stood up, and grabbed his jacket. "Ha…ha…ha."

Ben laughed, though he still felt a heaviness in his chest. He wondered how long it would last.

They both headed out of the office, the door clicking shut behind them. The headlines would scream for weeks, the questions would keep coming. But for the first time in twenty years, the case was closed.

Outside the station, the summer sun was beginning to set, casting long shadows over the city. Ben stepped out into the parking lot, the evening air warm against his skin. The familiar rhythm of the city settled over him. Closing his eyes, he took a deep breath, trying to clear his head, to let all the thoughts of the case disappear before going home. But there was something different about this case. Something he knew would stick with him. Sometimes the hardest cases to close were the ones where no one meant to do anything wrong.

About the Author

Justin is a theatre producer, director, and mystery writer. More often than not, he can usually be found sitting in his library devising new and clever ways to kill people (*for his mysteries*). One of the former owners of The Way Off Broadway Dinner Theatre outside of Washington, DC, during his time as the company's President & Managing Director, he produced over one hundred productions. In addition to writing the Parker City Mysteries Series, which includes *Now & Then* (Finalist for the 2022 Silver Falchion Award for Best Investigator), *Vice & Virtue*, *Fact & Fiction* (Killer Nashville Top Pick and Finalist for the Chanticleer CLUE Award), *Black & White* (Finalist for the 2025 Silver Falchion Award for Best Investigator), and *Cops & Robbers*, he is also the mastermind behind Marquee Mysteries, a series of interactive mystery events he has been writing and producing for nearly twenty years. Justin and his wife, Jessica, live along Lake Linganore outside of Frederick, Maryland, with their pups Brownie and Cocoa.

AUTHOR WEBSITE:
   www.JustinKiska.com

SOCIAL MEDIA HANDLES:
  Facebook: @JMKiska
  Instagram: @JMKiska
  Goodreads: @JustinKiska
  BookBub: @JMKiska

Also by Justin M. Kiska

Parker City Mysteries
> *Now & Then*
> *Vice & Virtue*
> *Fact & Fiction*
> *Black & White*
> *Cops & Robbers*